GRIEVANCE

ALSO BY CHRISTINE BELL

Saint

The Perez Family

The Seven-Year Atomic Make-Over Guide

GRIEVANCE

CHRISTINE BELL

LAKE UNION
PUBLISHING

Text copyright © 2017 by Christine Bell
All rights reserved.

Published by Lake Union Publishing, Seattle

www.apub.com

Amazon, the Amazon logo, and Lake Union Publishing are trademarks of Amazon.com, Inc., or its affiliates.

ISBN-13: 9781477848487
ISBN-10: 1477848487

Cover design by Rex Bonomelli

Printed in the United States of America

For Maeve

———

And in memoriam: Franko and M.L.

—the angels who wait for us to pause
During the most ordinary of days

And sing our praise to forgetfulness
Before they slap our souls with their cold wings.

Those angels burden and unbalance us.
Those fucking angels ride us piggyback.

Those angels, forever falling, snare us
And haul us, prey and praying, into dust.

—Sherman Alexie

PART I

Make me happy, and I shall again be virtuous.

—*Mary Shelley*

Chapter 1: Nashville

Lily had known her grief would be a constant companion but hadn't known how greedy it would be, how fierce when not attended to. Its shape-shifting discomposed her. It shuffled after her in the house. It sprang at her from car radio songs: "Take Me in Your Arms (Rock Me a Little While)." Grief distorted time and bent memory around every ordinary thing. The music played from the radio, and she fell back to the present. *Pay attention!*

A fox crossed the road, caught in the car's headlights.

You brake the car, save all the lives that remain, wait, continue the drive home.

Her boys, her fatherless boys, continued their conversation in the backseat.

Sam, kindergarten: "If we bring valentines tomorrow, we have to bring them for everybody, but I don't want to give one to Amanda."

Finn, seventh grade: "Why? 'Cause you like her?"

Sam: "No, 'cause I don't like her. At all. Mom, could you please turn down the radio?"

Finn: "So don't sign it."

The radio softer: "Rock me a little while . . ."

Sam: "What if she finds out anyway?"

Finn: "Then you're screwed. But if you don't hand out any valentines, you'll look snotty, so you're screwed then, too."

"Easy," Lily said. "And it's snooty, not snotty." She turned off the radio, pulled in to the driveway.

Embrace your pain, she'd been told. *Offer your grief compassion.* Was this what the song on the radio meant? Motown admonishing her to hold her sadness in her arms tomorrow, the first Valentine's Day since her husband's death? But grief had grown too menacing for tenderness. Tomorrow already felt unmanageable. A hallway to walk through unnoticed. It wasn't as if Valentine's Day had been a petal-strewn, find-a-babysitter night in their marriage. It had been noted, though. A rose from Des to Lily, a cupcake from Lily to Des. A bright-red day in the middle of dull February.

Finn wheeled the garbage bin out to the curb for tomorrow's pickup. He looked so much like his father that it was painful some days to look at him. A young phantom of his father long before Lily knew the man. Finn had gotten tall in the past year, but his face was still boy and his body still skinny. She'd see him come around a corner or appear on the front steps of school, and she'd do a double take. That tall-boy roll when he walked. The ghost of Desmond past.

Sam looked more like her side of the family, solid like his uncle Owen and with the compact gracefulness of his great-grandfather Samuel. Samuel, dead now. But Sam had Des's big voice and sweeping gestures. Finn had her Appalachian wariness. She didn't need to do this, she reminded herself, trying to bring the dead forward in her boys. They were their own, and for all their differences they looked like brothers.

Sam got the mail from the box. There was a pink envelope addressed to Lily in curly script. No time now to read it. There was the dog to be walked and fed, dinner, homework, showers, laundry. The ordeal of Sam so carefully addressing his Valentine's cards according to the list his teacher had sent home. After deliberation, Sam signed his name on a card for Amanda.

Lily cleaned the kitchen sink. Dried the cast-iron skillet too heavy for Sam when it was his turn to dry the pots. She had learned to govern with care the things she had control over. She swept the kitchen floor. Folded warm laundry. She didn't sit with the mail till almost eleven. Bills, flyers, and the pink envelope. Inside was a Valentine's Day card. An imprinted pink heart held the words: "The best thing to hold in life is each other." An enclosed typed letter read: "Dear Lillian—"

Well, it isn't from someone close, Lily thought. She'd been born on Easter and baptized Lily. She checked the postmark and return address: Chicago. Maybe somebody Des grew up with.

Dear Lillian,

Please excuse the Valentine's card. I went to three different stores, but I could not find a sympathy card that I liked. I have been out of the country and only just returned to see Desmond's obituary in the University of Chicago alumni magazine. I am shocked! Not only by Desmond's untimely death but also that he died ten months ago and I didn't somehow know. My heart should've stopped beating. An angel should've appeared in a dream. Or did signs appear and I didn't know how to interpret them? The alumni notice said multiple myeloma. That kind of cancer has a high survival rate in someone as young as Desmond—so what happened? His death seems as absurd as my not knowing!

I offer my very deepest sympathy for the loss of your husband and father of your children. Finn—I read the name in the notice. How Desmond loved Mark Twain and told me he always wanted to raft down the Mississippi. The first grand adventure he'd ever imagined as a child. And Sam—of course it would have to be either Mark or Clem or Sam! Do they sing? Do they have big voices like Desmond? They must be very handsome boys if they take after their dad!

I love my spouse, Lillian, so I can understand the pain you are going through. I am so sorry for you.

Please allow me to share this memory:

Desmond had a wonderful sense of humor and used to make us all hoot. He wasn't an opera singer back then in college, and I remember the laughter of him trying to cram his large voice into radio songs. Elton John's "I Guess That's Why They Call It the Blues" (he loved the oldies station). Stone Temple Pilots' "Plush." Sooo funny.

I hope you are able to open your heart to me at this point (as I said, this devastation is fresh and new for me. I envy you your year of grief. I've had no time passing).

I have a thousand other memories I'd love to share with you. We were quite the soul mates back then, as I'm sure he told you. Know that you have a place to share your memories with someone who understands your loss. It's important for us to correspond. If your sorrow has passed, I envy you that, too, but at least do me the courtesy of letting me know you have received my letter and my deepest sympathy.

Jaz Elwin

(it's short for Jasmine—we share a flower name)

Wait—your heart should've stopped beating? You should've known? You want to know what happened? Who the fuck are you? Des would've mentioned a soul mate. And his family overshared everything.

She and Des had been inseparable since Lily was twenty-two and Des two years older. Lily had adored being swept into Des's world: every Chicago visit crammed with the dense sidewalks and crowded parish of his boyhood. Classmates and relatives at every Chicago holiday and at every neighborhood landmark, and they'd welcomed her.

The signature was handwritten in large, flowery script, the capital *J* like two joined paisleys and the *E* like three loosely coiled spirals. *How could you understand my loss?*

Exhaustion overtook Lily's anger. She went to bed. She dreamed she hadn't braked on time on the ride home, and she'd hit the fox. The car spun into the night and woke her. Lily got up, her footfalls soft in the hallway to stand outside the boys' bedroom and make sure there was no eyeshine of wild animal in the darkness. Still she couldn't get back to sleep, restless with the feeling that the dead fox had come for the children.

Chapter 2:
The Black Crow and Doritos

The veil between life and death was very thin some mornings and she'd forget, just forget, that Des was dead. This morning when she half woke to let the dog out back and passed the pink envelope on the kitchen table, she thought: *Sweet of Des to leave a card for Valentine's Day.*

Then she remembered the disquieting words of condolence from the woman who envied her year of hell. No, not a card from Des; he was dead, and the card held the well-meaning arrogance of people who are so certain they know what you're going through. A woman at the funeral, a coloratura who used to sing with Des, had patted Lily's arm and told her she knew how she felt because she'd just gone through a divorce. Gert—Lily remembered her name—had a British accent, and she'd leaned in close to convey her *knowing*. Yeah, sure, divorce is just like death. Except for the body.

Lily put the pink envelope in a kitchen drawer, put coffee on, fed the dog.

Something else Gert'd said about the comfort of knowing where your husband was. A reference to Des in heaven? Des in a better place? Lily's hearing had been jammed with tears at the funeral, the murmurings, the din of consolations.

She went to get the paper from the driveway. It was cold out. She wore Des's thick terry robe over his worn flannel pajama shirt. She hadn't washed the robe in the ten months since he died, but the woody smell of him had faded just the same.

Across the street, Des's hair gleamed black and bright in the pale light. So low to the ground. Was he lying dead at the edge of the neighbor's lawn? Then the glossy hair moved, a dark eye turned toward her. A crow's eye. He puffed his chest, looked her straight in the face, and spoke. Brash. Loud. Unintelligible.

Grief hallucinations, the counselor at the Circle of Compassion called them. They were a normal part of mourning. They simply appeared when perception lagged behind reality. She'd said not to be frightened, and Lily wasn't, but she'd expected Des to appear as a ghost, not a bird.

The crow cawed. Maybe it was just a crow. Lily walked into the street to get a better look. Of course it was Des—he was pecking at a bag of Doritos chips. Des loved Doritos. "Happy Valentine's Day, darling," Lily said.

She wondered if Des had left a message for her. Had left a Valentine's kiss for her. All the while knowing the absurdity of wondering this and wondering anyway. Knew she had to lick the bag in case he'd left a kiss for her. She crossed the street. It was the most beautiful single moment she'd had since he died: the black iridescent wings and the red shiny bag against the milky morning light. If this was a hallucination, then so be it.

The crow flew away as she came closer. Bold breaths of dark wing above her. "Bye Bye Blackbird." Des used to whistle that sometimes, even after he was sick, like he hadn't a care in the world. She knelt to examine the foil surface, smelled what was left of crow and corn, searched for evidence of another world.

A car honked. Lily bolted upright, caught herself from falling.

"Are you okay, Lily?" asked Beth from up the street. The car window rolled down.

Lily smiled, waved, acted as if she were okay. Acted as if she were just looking at a piece of litter from the neighbor's yard while dressed in her nightclothes. She went back into the house. Best to ignore these lapses. The apophenia of grief is brutal: pennies from heaven, carrion crows from the grave.

Chapter 3: Big and Little Des

"Why are you calling so early? Is everything all right?" Lily's mother-in-law said.

"Yes, Kaye, everything's fine. Did I wake you?" Lily said.

"No. I don't sleep much since my son died. Now with Kevin's wedding, it's more stress. You know Kevin is getting married?"

"Yes, ma'am, of course," Lily replied into the phone. She knew her mother-in-law didn't like to be addressed as "ma'am." Sounded like a shop clerk, she said. Sometimes Lily forgot. Sometimes she didn't.

Lily knew what was coming. They'd had this conversation before:

"I want to give Kevin's new bride something from the family to welcome her into the clan. Kevin and Des were very close. They always stuck together."

"I know. Kevin was so good coming here when Des was sick."

"How about that silver tea set from my aunt Dana? It's not like you need a formal tea set."

So far, her mother-in-law had asked for the return of dessert plates, childhood books, a needlepoint pillow, a watercolor painting. She'd also asked for the return of monogrammed family silverware that Lily didn't have. Des's parents had downsized five years ago, moving from a cramped four-bedroom stand-alone in a not-so-nice section of Chicago to a cramped two-bedroom duplex in a less not-so-nice section. Kaye had agonized over what to give each of her children. For people so proud of their potato-famine heritage, they seemed to have a lot of good china and silver sets.

"I'm sorry, I haven't had time to go through all of Des's things yet. A friend of Des's sent a condolence letter. The name was Jaz, short for Jasmine, Jasmine Elwin. Do you know her?"

"Never heard of her."

"Maybe Elwin is her married name. She said she knew Des in college."

"I don't recall, but all my boys were popular. When Des had that growth spurt in high school, the girls started noticing him in a hurry. And Craig had girls knocking down the door before Deidre snagged him. Is Jasmine an Indian name? I don't remember him having a girlfriend from India."

"She just said friend."

"Well, he married you, Little Des, and that's the end of it."

Her mother-in-law was the only one who called her Little Des. Lily would have to ask her not to anymore. It was strange to be called the little version of a dead man, even one she loved.

Big Des and Little Des, Lily's mother-in-law had called them. They looked alike the way some couples do after long years, long years they'd never have. Hair: curly, bordering on black. Skin: pale, almost luminous. Eyes: long and dark beneath unruly lashes. Body: wide-shouldered with a smooth gait. Here the resemblance ended. Desmond was six five, stage ready, rugged. Lily was small, supernumerary. Her family had come down from the mountains of east Tennessee in the thirties. Her father was a retired high school music teacher. Her mother worked at Michaels craft store near their home in Maryville.

Lily's master's degree was the first in her family. Her BA in American folk studies at UT Knoxville led to her graduate certificate in Archives and Records Management from Middle Tennessee State. Lily now worked on staff for a private music collector, a lawyer who'd started a nonprofit foundation to preserve Tennessee music history. She classified and entered minutiae into computer databases, organizing word counts from regional folk sayings and songs. She documented old recordings, radio shows, verifying dates and transcriptions.

Des sang onstage, first bass in the Nashville Opera Chorus. The Chicago Declans were cops, firemen, nurses, teachers. For all their silver tea sets, they were suspicious of opera as occupation.

The first time Lily Moore and Desmond Declan met was backstage during a sound check. Lily was still a grad student then, interning at the State Library Archives a few blocks from the Tennessee Performing Arts Center. Des was at TPAC to sing, along with the rest of the opera company, at Nashville's Celebration of Music, a well-intentioned showpiece to introduce school children to music they might not have access to: opera, Broadway, folk. Lily wandered backstage, looking for the director to give the large envelope of song charts she'd been sent to deliver. Onstage, a Wagnerian soprano had been badly matched to the tinny yearning of "Dink's Song":

> If I had wings like Noah's dove
> I'd fly up the river to the man I love
> Fare thee well, O honey, fare thee well

It was beyond bad. "Holy crap," Lily said. She turned away from the stage and straight into a large man muffling laughter with his large hand.

"Amen to that," Des said.

He sang *Carmen*'s "Flower Aria" to Lily the night he asked her to marry him. Not easy to fit the low vocal strings of his *dramatic basso profondo* into those high notes. Even with a lowered register, he had to climb a precarious falsetto. He had to whisper. She could barely breathe.

You can barely breathe since he's dead. But you breathe. She had to remember to eat, take a shower, wash her hair, wear clothes that matched, put gas in the car. An algorithm for living. Hold on to her job. Pay the bills. Bring the boys to school. Pick up the boys from after-school care. Feed them. Go through their backpacks for notes that needed to be signed. Feed the dog. Let the dog out. Let the dog in.

She slept soundly. There was no sleep deprivation—more an awake deprivation, clawing through the cold ruche of morning bedcovers to reach for the warmth of Des on his side of the bed. An apnea of awareness when she would forget, just forget, that Des was dead and have to suck in reality like a fresh punch.

Chapter 4: Eddie Money

The pink envelope didn't stay long in the kitchen drawer. She reread it several times. The assumed intimacy from Jaz grappled at Lily's skin. She went through an online alumni website for the University of Chicago and found no corresponding Jasmines or Jazes or Elwins. She brought the letter to work and read it to her office-mate.

"It was a reach-out, Lily," Iris said in her lovely Bahamian singsong. "That's all. Poorly worded, yes, but a reach-out just the same. You don't know her, do you?"

"No. Never heard Des mention her, either."

"So you don't respond." Iris, Bahamas-born, forty, and gay, was an ally at work and a friend. She made sense when Lily couldn't, so Lily listened to her. Yes, of course there was no reason to respond to a stranger. Iris had brought groceries to the house when Des was sick, picked the boys up from school when Lily was at the hospital. She'd loved Des, too, said he made her think being straight might not be all that bad.

On Friday morning when Lily dropped off Sam for school at Lockeland Elementary, he asked for ten dollars for a field trip to the Adventure Science Center. He'd asked her for it the night before, he claimed.

"You remember, Mom. I handed you the permission sheet from Ms. Greene while you were eating dessert. You signed it and said you had a ten in your purse." Sam was small for his age. He made up for it with a little-man voice. Little Man Sam, Des used to call him when that voice entered a conversation.

She didn't remember, but Sam might very well have asked. She didn't remember eating dessert. A Jell-O pudding cup? A cookie? Homemade fudge from her neighbor? In the side compartment of her purse was a hundred-dollar bill. A gulp of air. She didn't remember putting it there. It was a week since she'd been at the ATM at the grocery, and the ATMs spouted twenties, not hundreds. Why would she have a hundred-dollar bill? She found a ten in her wallet and gave it to Sam.

A hundred-dollar bill—you'd remember that.

Watkins Park Magnet Middle School was a traffic-jammed seven miles across town from the elementary school.

"What'd we have for dessert last night, Finn?"

"I don't know. I had another glass of milk and left the table to finish my math homework so I could watch basketball."

He'd become obsessed with his father's sports teams since Des had died. Aside from a nominal interest in the Tennessee Titans, whose stadium they drove by every school day, he'd been an indifferent fan before. Now he read the sports pages for news of the Bulls and the Cubs, in season, off season. He negotiated extra chores and A's on his report cards to watch games on TV on school nights.

Finn got out at the school drop-off. Lily turned on the car radio. The first words of a song each time she turned on the radio were from Des. She'd established that months before, when she was less grounded than she was now. Des had programmed all the radio buttons to college alternative stations, oldies, classic rock. The songs could only come from him. Heartland rock whispered from the dashboard. Bob Seger? No, definitely not. She turned the volume high. "Two Tickets to Paradise" blared through the car. Why would Des send this song to her? Did he want her to pack her bags for eternity? Did he want her to die to be with him tonight? It would happen soon enough in the grand scheme of things, but for now she needed to take care of the boys. She felt warm, opened the windows to the cold morning.

Eddie Money. Eddie *Money* was the singer, Lily remembered. That was the message from The Other Side. Des had put the money in her bag.

She turned off the radio. Telling herself: *You know you are crazy. Death is common. Des might've been uncommon, but somebody dies first and somebody is left behind. You know that. So why are you out of your mind?*

Chapter 5:

Theme from *Love Story*

Saturday morning, Lily drove Finn to the Mullens' in Ashland City. Sam played on his Game Boy during the ride, still in his pajamas. Somehow Gogo ended up in the car.

"Who brought the dog? Did anyone ask permission to bring the dog? Did anyone remember the dog's leash?"

There was no answer, but Finn's eye roll in the rearview mirror silenced her. It wasn't important, really it wasn't important.

"She just *came* with us," Sam said. "We didn't *bring* her."

Lily hadn't been so nervous about the dog when Des was alive, but now the dog looked to her for alpha direction, and she was clueless.

Gogo weighed 113 pounds. Des had told Lily that female German shepherds don't get over seventy pounds, but this dog was huge. Lily had grown up with purse dogs, yappy mixed breeds from the shelter. Iago, Des had named the puppy after his favorite Verdi role. Had it been a joke—a mezzo-soprano dog with a baritone name?—Lily couldn't remember as Sam had changed Iago to Gogo on her first day at home. The dog would rest on the floor by Lily's feet, sometimes on top of Lily's feet, at night after the boys went to bed. Gogo would go to her dog bed in the kitchen to sleep when Lily commanded. But she snarled if Lily came too close to her food bowl. She would heel for the boys, but she tugged on the leash for Lily. She'd come or not when Lily called her.

The boys had met the Mullens at the children's grief group at Gilda's Club. Josh Mullen was the same age as Finn. The family had lost their youngest daughter to brain cancer the year before. Lily couldn't imagine their pain and didn't try to. There was a hierarchy of grief, and theirs was at the top.

The ride to Ashland City held promise of spring. Wide fields glowed with early grass. Redbud trees were hazed in pink.

Alice Mullen leaned toward the driver's window; her gold chain and filigree cross dangled in front of Lily's eyes. She asked Lily in for a coffee and pastry. Lily declined the offer. The Mullens had a full day planned with Finn: the children's group at Gilda's Club, lunch at Pancake Pantry, an afternoon baseball game at Vanderbilt. Finn wore the Chicago Cubs track jacket he'd asked for at Christmas.

"Finn told you we're planting this morning?" Alice said.

"No," Lily said. "I don't know what that means."

"The boys picked out places up on the hill a few weeks ago. We're planting two dogwoods: one for Joella and one for Des. They didn't know each other in this life, but now Josh and Finn have brought them together."

"You guys are great. Thanks for doing this."

"Thanks for loaning us Finn. He's been a good friend to Josh."

Lily drove away. She turned on the radio. Turned off the radio. She opened the front windows. The air smelled of new earth and green pushing through the dull patina of winter. Here she was, looking for messages from the dead on the radio, and the Mullens were out in nature planting memorial trees. She didn't doubt their faith. They looked at poor Jesus on the cross and saw salvation. Lily looked and saw another victim. She wondered if she could learn faith, learn like an alcoholic learns to drink until one day you find you are under the influence all the time. From the backseat, Sam declared with a sleepy voice: "I wish I was dead."

Your heart screams. You cram it back down your throat, the scream, the heart; you swallow. You say calmly, "Why, sweetie?"

"'Cause I'd come back as a horse. Amanda at school said that grass tastes like chocolate to horses, so I could eat chocolate grass all day long."

"Hmmm. That would be yummy."

Good. Wanting chocolate-flavored grass did not presage suicidal tendencies in her five-year-old. Sam's chocolate death wish pulled Lily back from her musings on faith and planting memorial trees. Looking through the windshield and realizing she didn't know why she was on River Road Pike and not on Route 12. Realizing she didn't know why she was returning home on this road and not the usual way.

She fingered the pink envelope in her purse and wondered why she'd kept it in her purse and not returned it to the kitchen drawer or thrown it in the trash. *So what happened?* She felt an unexpected sympathy for the writer, learning of an old love's death from an alumni magazine.

That first year after the diagnosis, they thought Des had a chronic, manageable disease. The year after that had been the unmanageable, the unimaginable. Clinical trials and out-of-town consultations had yielded nothing more than the word *comfortable*—he would be made comfortable.

Sitting in the comfortable armchair in the den, his breathing labored, wide shoulders pushed back, Des had turned to Lily and said, "You know, your voice sounds like an old scratchy record. I'll miss your voice." He spoke slowly. He was due back at the hospital for more palliative chemo. "You can't sing for shit, and your accent isn't kind to the ear, but I love to hear you talk. You always sound like you're getting ready to dance to your own 45." He stuck a twang into *dance*, day-ance, in imitation of her east Tennessee accent.

"Are you okay?" she'd asked. *Are you okay?*—it'd sounded right then, ridiculous to remember now.

"I'm okay, Lil. Most of the time, the pain management works. If dying is okay then I'm okay."

That's what happened, Jaz Elwin. The suddenness of one breath here and (turning the glossy alumni magazine page) no breath there.

———

The house was always cold when she first entered. The air thin with abandonment. The smell of mice in empty kitchen cabinets. Chairs without cushions. Lily knew this emptiness was Des gone. But understanding did not trump her need to turn the heat up, drink her coffee when it was too hot, pile comforters on the beds. The kitchen cabinets were not empty. There were no mice. There were cushions on the chairs. It was just how the house felt with Des dead.

Sam put on a Winnie-the-Pooh video in the living room. It was too young for him; he wouldn't watch it in front of his brother. There was something comforting, watching life in the Hundred Acre Wood. Something textural, too: the shiny cartoon screen, the soft butter-suede chair, the worn cotton blanket, the Power Rangers pj's that had been Finn's.

Lily put on a pot of coffee and phoned her mother from the kitchen. She read the Jaz Elwin letter into the phone.

"Reminds me of that Tate woman at Des's funeral," Ella Moore said. Her voice was mountain thick. She had a fine-boned, timid face until she smiled or laughed, and the world opened. "Remember she told you her husband had left her, so she knew just how you felt."

"The British accent? I thought of her the other day, too. Was her name Tate? I thought it was Gert."

"Don't remember. I thought she meant he'd died, but then she talked about her divorce and said at least you knew where your husband was."

"I thought she meant heaven."

"Not hardly. I was right next to you on the receiving line. I took her arm and nudged her forward to the next person, Uncle Dan I think."

"I get your point, Mom; people say strange things. But what the hell business of Jasmine's is it about the boys? And I look at that last part about having the courtesy to answer her letter and want to write back: fuck you, bitch."

"Your French is pardoned. Okay, though. Let's agree that it doesn't deserve an answer."

"Except maybe I should answer. She asked what happened. She sounded hurt."

"She sounded demanding."

Yes, she sounded demanding. Lily poured herself more coffee. Demanding about the boys. Demanding about Des's diagnosis. Lily cradled the phone in the crook of her neck and wrapped her cold hands around the warm mug.

"Really, Lil," Ella said. "It's nothing more than an earworm. I had 'Who Let the Dogs Out' running through my head all last weekend. Your dad told me that when you get an earworm, you should replace it with a different song to confuse your brain."

"Mom, this isn't a self-help exercise."

"Yeah, it is. The more time you spend getting angry at some idiot, the less time you spend on the more important things. Burn the letter. And if it comes to mind when you don't want it, start singing 'Who Let the Dogs Out' or the theme from *Love Story*."

"I'll try." She didn't know the theme from *Love Story*. "What does it mean when a fox crosses your path?" Her mother knew mountain lore, knew the signs the old people thought significant.

"Is this a why-did-the-chicken-cross-the-road thing?"

"No. The other night driving, there was a red fox in the road, and I had to screech brake to miss it."

"It means to pay attention while you're driving, and you did."

"Funny, Mom. I mean what's the folk translation?"

"To pay attention, like I told you. You sure it wasn't a coyote? They're all over River Run, and up by Bethel Church they killed a dachshund that was on the back porch of his own house. Thank goodness Gogo is big enough to take care of herself. I also need to tell you your father put a hundred-dollar bill into your purse two weekends ago when you were here and didn't want to tell you. He thought you wouldn't take it if he plain and simple handed it to you. So I'm telling you so you don't think you're insane. His retirement is driving *me* insane, Lily. I keep asking for extra hours at work."

Lily cried afterward. Because her father was so kind. Because the hundred dollars wasn't from Des. Because "Who Let the Dogs Out" reminded her of the Stone Temple Pilots song Jaz Elwin had mentioned in her letter. The lead singer of Stone Temple Pilots was dead now, too. Des had sung those lyrics to her once, the part about the dogs tracking by scent. Des on his knees, laughing, his face in her crotch as he peeled off her jeans.

Chapter 6:
Circle of Compassion

Lily's brother, Owen Moore Jr., came to Nashville for a construction job two years before Lily graduated from college in Knoxville. Owen was compact and strong with a perennial Tennessee Titans bandanna triangled over his dark curls. It seemed fated that the master's program Lily wanted was located at Middle Tennessee University, so close to where her brother had moved. Fated that Desmond Declan would move from Chicago to sign a training contract with the Nashville Opera Company that same year. Fated that Owen would marry Anne-Claire, Lily's graduate-school suite-mate. Never mind the other million and a half people in Nashville's environs.

She dropped the boys at her brother's, which was on the way to the Agape Fellowship Church in Old Hickory. On Tuesday evenings the grief group met in a room with marbled Kmart linoleum and cast-off living room chairs. After it rained, there was a damp barroom smell of long-ago cigarettes. A single fluorescent in the back corner flickered a pale hissing light.

Bereavement counselor Miriam wore a cream-colored linen dress, seams askew like a slipcover on a favorite couch. There were shopworn exercises at the Circle of Compassion: letters to the dead, poems, memory boxes, picture collages. Lily had tried two other groups before arriving here. The arts-and-crafts of grief was a small price to pay for the earth mother of Miriam. The first time Lily looked at the seated Miriam, she'd thought how wonderful it would be to climb into her lap. To be protected by the largess of her empathy.

Tonight they wrote free-form haikus. Lily wrote:

> Holding breath same as
> being dead—a moment—
> then the dead exhale

She liked best the poem by Carly, sitting beside her.

> Fuck you living
> Fuck you dead
> Fuck me

Carly had perfect nails. Lily noted how perfectly put together Carly was, a sophisticated grunge look. *I used to have style,* Lily thought, unable to remember why style had been important. She waited until all had shared their poems. Three lines didn't take long with a half dozen mourners. Then with little preamble ("I received this in the mail last week"), Lily read aloud the letter from Jaz Elwin.

"That's very sweet," Mrs. Henrietta said. They used only first names in group, but Henrietta insisted on the "Mrs." She sat always with her purse in her lap, as if ready at any moment to flee the league of grief. Her husband had died eight years before.

"Your husband sounds like a funny guy," Leon said.

"I love when I get a sympathy letter, and they tell me something nice about Meghan," Olivia said. "Something I didn't know or a cute story like that one about your husband singing." They were Anglophiles,

Olivia had told them. She and her partner liked wallpaper with flowers and had collected delicate mismatched china.

"Don't you get it?" Lily said. She wasn't going to mention the Stone Temple Pilots song and Des's use of the lyrics. That was nobody else's business. Maybe that's what bothered her: the lyrics were hers, not an old girlfriend's. "Why should an angel appear to her? Why should *she* see signs?"

"Well, signs didn't appear to her, did they?" Miriam said.

"Yes, but she thinks they should've. She says she has a thousand other memories of Des. She demands I write back. And that 'I envy you your year of grief.'"

"That *was* awkwardly phrased," Mrs. Henrietta said.

"I'll take the letter," Miriam said. She walked behind Lily. "Looking at the sheet of paper, you've read it far too many times. This needs to stop. I'll keep it safe if you ever need it back."

There was a slight tug-of-war as Lily hesitated to give the letter to Miriam. Miriam moved back to her chair, the paper going with her. She stuffed it under the sheets on her clipboard.

"You're allowed your anger," Miriam said. "Her demand for a reply. Her request for details of your husband's illness. Her request that you open your heart to her. You don't know this woman, right?"

"Never heard of her. Called my mother-in-law and she never heard of her, either."

"The person who wrote this letter is unable to recognize boundaries. You would've heard of her if there were something to hear. If you thought your husband was carrying on with her while he was with you, you'd be wrong. She'd have contacted you long ago if there'd been something. You understand that?" Miriam said.

"Yes. Maybe. It went through my mind, but I decided no. The sheer gall, I guess, is what made me mad."

"I'd hunt the bitch down," Carly said.

"Why would you give her the time of day? Don't clutter your mind," Miriam said.

"My mother pretty much said the same thing," Lily said. "At first the letter just sounded clumsy. Then it felt rude. Then I felt bad for her. Then it felt demanding, and I got mad all over again. When I called my mother-in-law about it, she called me 'Little Des' and I got mad about that again, too."

"You said you were going to ask her not to call you that anymore," Mrs. Henrietta said. "Not appropriate."

"Lily, remember that story you told once about that woman at your husband's funeral who told you she was getting a divorce so she knew how you felt?" Miriam said.

Blythe, Lily remembered finally. That was her name, not Gert, not Tate. "She said her husband had left her, but at least I knew where my husband was."

"Yes. You were stuck on that a while back. I bring it up because death is so far removed from our culture that some people haven't a clue what to say."

"My cousin told me to get a dog," Leon said. "It was good advice but out of place at my wife's funeral."

"Yes, out of place, Leon," Miriam said. "The operative word being *place.* Lily, when something comes *into* your house, like a piece of mail, it can seem like an encroachment, but it's not really, not against your person or your boys. It was a breach of etiquette. Now I have the letter, so it's no longer in your house."

"I'm afraid of getting a letter like Lily's," Carly blurted. "I mean a real one, not a crazy-lady one. A letter that says I knew him better, I loved him better. And with Gabe it wouldn't have been about fun times with Elton John songs. Gabe's been dead nine months, and I still track him on the Internet. I found his password for his e-mail and I never shut down his Facebook. I check it a few times a week."

"You find anything?" Lily asked.

"A high school classmate requested friend status on Facebook. I wanted to string her along and see what she really wanted, but I was mature and sent her a fuck-you back. One woman sent him a request on LinkedIn—but it was a business associate. Gabe was a landscaper. There's a demo on YouTube of him showing how to repair a garden hose. Almost tore my heart out."

Chapter 7:
Kindergarten and Death

Now that the letter had been ripped from her hands, Lily felt lonely for it. It felt good to be angry at a person with a name rather than a clinical diagnosis that had made Des suffer and die at age thirty-eight.

As the days wore on, something better materialized: since she didn't have the whole letter to read at once, there was more time to focus on smaller aspects she could remember. And Lily's crosstown commute gave her plenty of time to think about Jasmine's words. The Linden Foundation was a massive antebellum manor located between Belle Meade Country Club and Cheekwood Botanical Garden, a good twenty minutes away from school drop-off. The naming of Finn and Sam became more intrusive than the have-the-courtesy-to-respond command. It felt as if Des had discussed the naming of their children with a stranger. That this had happened long before Lily knew Des existed gave it a time-travel feel, a cosmic breach.

"It wasn't admiration; I wanted to *be* Huckleberry Finn," Des had told her in the long, lazy Sunday mornings of new love. They discovered they were both lactose intolerant, both preferred peanut M&M's, both couldn't understand why people liked apples so much—holy shit, they *were* meant to be together. Was we-share-a-flower-name Jasmine also lactose intolerant? Was she also not an apple fan? Had the two of them had the same conversation, fed each other peanut M&M's tangled in morning sheets? Had he told Jaz he wanted to name *their* first child Finn?

As for Sam—yes, the world knew the Mark Twain/Samuel Clemens connection. Their Sam, however, had been named for her grandfather, who had died the year before Sam was born. Right?

At work, Lily felt like a dry drunk, white-knuckling her runaway thoughts into efficiency. The Linden song collection was the largest private music library outside a university system. Founder Henry Linden had been a music industry lawyer for thirty years before he gave in to his song-collector passion. Lily had a good ear, and what had started out as a part-time assignment cataloging the song library had morphed into a listening job, where she checked old radio shows and recordings against their transcripts. She compiled the findings into academic databases.

Iris would be in and out of the office most of the month working on the program for the upcoming fund-raiser: the annual black-tie gala for the rich and musically inclined. There were days Lily liked being alone at work. She wore headphones connected to her computer, and she kept the volume high. She checked the transcription of an old radio tape from the thirties. Static ran wild through the Texas accents. When she substituted *Cain-tuck* for *coon dog*, the stage patter finally started to make sense. More likely to introduce a singer as a Kentuckian than a coon dog. But what was a mott of trees?

She took off the headphones at five and listened to a message on her cell phone.

"Mrs. Declan. This is Ms. Greene, Sam's kindergarten teacher. Your son is fine. Everybody's fine. I'm wondering if you could stop by my room before you pick up Sam from aftercare. I'm here till six today. Or we can make an appointment for the morning."

Lily called the number back. With no answer, she left a message that she was on her way. Leaving an hour early, leaving enough mess on her desk to suggest she hadn't left for the day. Grateful at one red light that Ms. Greene mentioned that everything was all right. Knowing at the next light that people don't mention that everything is all right when everything *is* all right.

———

The kindergarten room was empty. Lily found Sam's photo on the bulletin board in the middle of a daisy atop a long stem in the eighteen-kid bouquet belonging to Ms. Greene's class. Of course everything was all right. It wasn't a call from an emergency room. She found his desk neat, like Sam was neat at home.

"Mrs. Declan, thanks for coming." Ms. Greene closed the door behind her. She was calm, unhurried. Lily smiled and continued her search for classroom evidence of Sam. She found a clothespin with Sam's name on it clipped to a cutout of a red traffic light.

"Please sit down, Lily. May I call you Lily? Please call me Willa."

They'd met at open house and a parent-teacher meeting. Ms. Greene was middle-aged and enthusiastic with a profusion of gray hair she kept high on her head in a messy bun. She produced an adult-size chair from the back of the classroom and moved it by her desk. "I'm concerned about Sam. There was an incident today."

Lily sat.

"I watch out for him, you know that," Ms. Greene said.

"Go on."

"Several of the boys were on top of the wooden box train on the playground taunting him. I quote: 'Na na-na na-na, you've got a dead dad.' It's a kids' song, you know: 'nanner nanner booboo, you can't catch me.' We barely pay attention. Sam pulled the chief taunter off the top of the train and pummeled him. The train's three feet high; he yanked him off by his ankles. And I mean pummeled. He threw him to the ground, kicked him, then sat on him and punched the back and side of his face. Sam was yelling *hell* or *hellie*. The other boy was bigger, but Sam had anger on his side."

Willa Greene gently bent her head down as she spoke. She was used to speaking to children. Administration usually handled the angry parents, their blazing eyes.

"Here's where I came in," Ms. Greene continued. "I pulled him off, and Sam started screaming at the boy: 'You're a dead man. You're a dead man walking.' A peculiar choice of words, no? The usual kiddie curse is 'You're a meanie' or 'a spaghetti head,' although in the past few years I've heard nastier. I'm not condoning what the boys were saying to Sam, but the anger in Sam's little body was frightening, and what he said could be considered a threat."

"How many boys were taunting him? And I have to ask, Willa, where were the adults during this?" *This woman is on Sam's side*, Lily reminded herself, chastised herself.

"Well, I'll tell you where we were. There were two kindergarten classes out there. The teaching assistant for Mrs. Hardin's class was retrieving one of the boys' shoes that the girls threw over the fence. I was returning from bringing a vomiting child, and I mean vomiting, to the principal's office. The vice principal was out on the playground also and heard the singsong but not the words and thought they were playing tag. Mrs. Hardin was disentangling a girl's very long hair caught in the swings."

"Sounds like a dangerous place," Lily said.

"It's not. Or at least no more dangerous than childhood."

"I do not want my son bullied."

"Neither do I."

"I'm not here to protect him. You are."

"Principal Roxwell will meet with all the boys separately and, if she sees fit, together. The parents of the beat-up boy are extremely angry. They've threatened a lawsuit. Ms. Roxwell is doing her best to settle them down."

"A lawsuit? They're in kindergarten! And their son was the one after my boy."

"I don't know how kindergarten lawsuits work. I got the impression that the lawsuit was against the school, not Sam, but I may be speaking out of turn. I do know that technically, Sam could be suspended for hitting the boy and for the you're-a-dead-man threat. Ms. Roxwell may want to see you, but I asked to speak to you first. I wanted to explain personally because I watch him so closely, and I failed him."

Hard to stay angry at her words, her head dipping toward Lily. Willa had Lily sign a form to send Sam to a counselor at school. If the beat-up boy's parents took the issue to the school board, Sam probably would be suspended.

"To answer your other question: there were five, maybe six boys taunting him. He probably felt like he was fighting an army. My heart is with him, but that's not the way the world works. Talk to your son, Lily. Tell him he's not to seek retribution on his own. That he's to come and get a teacher if he's being antagonized."

———

Lily was quiet on the ride home. Sam barely had a scratch on him. She thought about Ms. Greene's vocabulary: being antagonized, taunted, seeking retribution, pummeling. Maybe the kids just didn't understand her.

"Don't pummel your antagonistic friends, little kindergartner."

"I'm not, Ms. Greene, I'm just hitting him."

Sam stayed by Lily in the kitchen while she cooked. She listened to him. She talked to him. She surrounded him with her love, her hands, a Tofutti Cutie from the freezer. She had him promise that he'd get a teacher if any of the kids were mean. This weekend, she told him, they'd play-act, like one of Dad's operas, and work out scenes to practice what to do if somebody bullied him. He liked that idea. They'd practice confusing the enemy, say, *En garde!* or *What's your point?* or start singing

"Who Let the Dogs Out." Or walk away. They would practice walking away.

"Where'd you hear that expression, 'dead man walking,' honey?" she asked.

He shrugged. Finn came from the hallway. "Dad told Granny Kaye that," Finn said. "Granny Kaye said, 'Baby, you look better, you look great,' and Dad said, 'Mom, I'm a dead man walking and I'm enjoying every single step.' It sounded pretty cool, like vampire stuff."

Yes, Lily remembered Des saying that.

"Is that where you heard it, Sam?"

"I don't remember Dad saying it, but Finn used to say it. You know I used the code word today on the playground, Mom."

"What code word?"

"*Helley* for Helley's Comet. Remember Dad taught us that if we're in trouble we should say *Helley*."

"I don't remember this, baby."

"You got it wrong, Sam. It's Halley, not Helley, and that's the code if someone was picking us up, so we won't go with strangers," Finn said. Finn turned to Lily: "We went over it again when Dad was in the hospital. In case something happened to him, and you couldn't leave, and somebody had to come get us like if he was dying or something. He said we could go with them if they said the code *Halley's Comet*."

"What's the word if you're supposed to run away from someone?" Sam asked.

"I don't think we had a word for that," Lily said.

"Yeah, we did," Finn said. "If somebody was creeping us out or if he wanted us to run away, we could say Gogo's name. Like 'Let's go visit Gogo' or 'Gogo's coming.'"

"I don't remember that," Lily said. "But I think a code word should be something we don't say every day, in case Gogo is with us."

"We could say *Amanda*," Finn said, "'cause that's the girl Sam likes and is always running away from."

"I do not like her," Sam said, his voice resolute.

"Okay," Lily said. "We'll use the word *Amanda* if we need to run away, and we'll keep the code *Halley's Comet* for an emergency pickup. We can ride on a comet, but we'll run from Amanda. It's time to get ready for bed."

The world wasn't safe anymore. She'd known this since Des got sick, but it had seemed confined to illness and doctors reading lab charts. Lily eased herself onto the kitchen floor, thought of burying her face in Gogo's soft neck but opted to run her hand through the fur on her curled back. *You were gulping down hope while Des and Finn were setting up safe words in case of death. While Sam is defending himself from vicious taunts in the real world, you are stuck on a stranger's clumsy letter.*

Pay attention!

Chapter 8: Landline

The landline in the hallway rang past midnight. Lily didn't get up to answer, and the ringing stopped. *Thank God,* she thought through the dark brume of her sleep, because if it'd been the hospital about Des, they would've kept ringing or called back. The next sound she woke to was Finn, outlined in the doorway by the hall night-light. He was scruffy with sleep, looked young, a tall boy and not a near teen. He held the phone by his side, one hand over the mouthpiece.

"Mom, wake up. Someone wants to talk to Dad."

A robocall, of course. Des had the number on a no-call list, but they got through anyway. The computer scramble of numbers to wake you in the middle of the night, to call into the kitchen while you fixed dinner. That pause before the taped message came on.

"Mom!"

Lily's anger poked through her half-sleeping brain into the dark room: "Don't tell me—Mr. Declan's won a free vacation? Just hang up, Finn. It's a computer message."

"What're you talking about, Mom? It's some lady crying who wants to speak to Des then asked if I was Little Des."

Lily sat up and turned on her bedside lamp. She took the phone from Finn's outstretched hand and held it against her angry ear.

"Hello," she said. She heard a sharp intake of breath. Then a click. The line went dead.

Chapter 9: Graphics

Not yet sunup. Lily unplugged the upstairs extension in the hallway and went to the kitchen to make coffee and phone calls. She could hear Des's voice in her head giving her instructions on how to reenter the home phone number in the government do-not-call-list website.

Except it wasn't a robocall, so Des could just take his instructional-guy voice out of her head and let her make the coffee and feed the dog and make her calls. She was tired. She'd never gotten back to sleep after she'd heard the breath, the click of the phone, the dead line.

Angry and wired, Lily waited till seven to put out calls to Chicago relatives. She left messages with Des's parents and Des's older sister, Briana; his older brother, Craig; and his baby brother, Kevin.

It was Kevin on the first callback. She explained the phone call.

"Was it your cell or the landline?" Kevin asked.

"Landline. Hardly ever use it and it doesn't have caller ID."

"It was probably Mom," he said. "I've heard her call you Little Des before, and I've gotten a few funny phone calls from her myself. I'm tense about both of them right now. Dad's gotten even quieter since Des died. Mom will latch on to some detail, real or imagined, about Des and worry it to hell. Lately, she's been getting together with one of her gal pals from the old neighborhood, and they lift a glass in Des's honor. She calls it 'girlfriend therapy.' I don't remember her drinking much when I was growing up, although I can't say the same for my father. *Maybe* Mom would have a beer at home watching a Cubs game or *maybe* a Tom Collins at a wedding."

"Finn said first the woman asked for Des and then asked if he were Little Des."

"Maybe she got embarrassed. I can't tell you how often I think I have to tell Des something and almost hit his number on my cell. And I'm sober. She's the only one who calls you Little Des."

"Is she all right? Is there something I can do, Kevin?"

"You should say something to Briana. Mom listens to her. A few months ago, Mom decided I hadn't told her how sick Des was and that's why she wasn't there when he died. She was angry at you, too, for not telling her."

"I told her. I told her beforehand. I told her then."

"I know. I heard you. I told her, too. I had to get Briana to tell her to lay off. Here we should be consoling each other, and I'm having to tell my sister to tell my mother to lay off."

Kevin had been there. The alarm sounding every time the IV bags needed to be replaced. There hadn't been time for hospice. Death had been sooner rather than later after the stem-cell transplant. That awful cardiac monitor: the graphics of death, showing the heartbeats growing wide and slow. Owen turned the monitor toward the window when the nurses left the room. Craig and Deidre had been less than an hour away, driving down from Chicago. Briana had been at work. Kevin called her several times, but she'd said she couldn't come until her shift was cleared. She was a trauma nurse at Chicago's Children's Hospital. Kevin had been more upset about Briana's absence than Lily was.

It was out of place in the conversation. Lily knew it was out of place, but she asked anyway: "You know anybody named Jaz or Jasmine who was an old girlfriend of Des's?"

"Nope. Name's not familiar. Why?"

"I think she's from U Chicago. Got a condolence letter from her. Jaz Elwin? Just wondered."

"Didn't really know his college friends. Sorry."

Chapter 10: Who Loved Me?

The dinginess of the upstairs room of the Circle of Compassion comforted Lily again this Tuesday. New people tonight. A woman in a baggy jean skirt handed Miriam her clipboard, then made herself coffee. Another woman, in a fitted black shirtwaist, hesitated in the doorway. *So much death,* Lily thought. Miriam wore a pale gray dress that seemed to function as camouflage in the faded room. Carly spoke with her by the coffee urn. Carly wore a red plaid mini with knee socks and heels. Lily had the impression Miriam was a nun and Carly a Catholic-school dropout. Carly got coffee and sat by Lily.

Miriam waved over the woman in black to sit in the circle and introduced her as Yvonne. Her husband had died three weeks ago, and her minister thought she should come here.

"I respect what you're doing," Yvonne said. "But I'm only trying it out because my pastor recommended me. My husband is in the arms of Jesus, and I'm happy for him."

Yvonne was blonde and slender with a PTA-smooth voice. "I'm actually rejoicing. My husband was a true believer."

"Oh Jesus," Carly said softly, leaning in to Lily. "Going to be one of those nights."

"Jesus wept," Leon said. He knew his Bible. Leon was the only man and the only African American in the group. Lily wondered what he did in the daytime. He had a teacher's voice. For all Lily knew, he could be the minister of the Agape Fellowship Church. They didn't introduce themselves by profession.

"That was before he died and guaranteed our salvation," Yvonne said.

"That was after his friend Lazarus died," Leon said.

"I have faith," Yvonne said and closed her eyes.

Miriam waited, then said: "Before we continue, I want to introduce our new assistant counselor, Renée. Renée is a licensed clinical social worker who is getting her doctorate at TSU. And just to let you know: I'm going on sabbatical for two months next fall, and I'll be traveling out of the country. Renée will hopefully be able to arrange her schedule to fill in for me then. I think a certain continuity is best." Renée darted her arm up as if answering roll call and sat by Miriam outside the circle.

It was strange for Lily to think of Miriam leaving them, of Miriam having a life away from them. She knew Miriam had a clinical practice up north in Clarksville, but *sabbatical* sounded academic. Was it context travel or fun travel? Did she travel alone, with family or friends?

Renée was pleasant looking, a hint of overbite and sympathetic brown eyes. And there was something eczemic going on. She scratched at a patch of livid red scales on the back of her hand, stopped, then scratched her scalp beneath honey waves.

"You're allowed to be sad when your husband dies," Mrs. Henrietta said, abruptly turning to Yvonne.

"I try to stay positive. I'm *allowed* to be positive," Yvonne said.

With communion solemnity, Olivia passed around a plate of fresh Rice Krispies Treats. She often baked. Tonight's warm marshmallow fragrance wafted like a counterpunch to the dingy room.

"I'm envious," Lily said. It came out in a shrill peep. She made her voice bigger: "I envy you." She turned to Yvonne, who stuck more hair behind her ear. *Envy* wasn't a word Lily used often. Yet it'd been on her mind from the sympathy note—*I envy you.* What had Jaz envied?

Lily's devastation? Her time to mourn? She couldn't remember the exact words, since Miriam had taken the letter.

"You don't *have* to be pessimistic," Yvonne said. "You can *choose* to be optimistic."

"That's not what I mean. It's how you skip over the pain. Tomorrow is my wedding anniversary. I want to skip over the whole day."

"I don't skip over the pain. I give it to Jesus. It's part of my faith." Yvonne pulled back more hair, played with a small stud earring in her delicate ear. "I can't tell if you're being sarcastic."

"I'm not being sarcastic. I'm not envious as in I hope you come crashing down. I'm envious that you know how to give away the pain. You know how to offer it up."

"A time to mourn, a time to dance," Leon said in his preacher voice.

"We'd all rather be dancing," Carly said.

The plate of Rice Krispies Treats came round again. It was a small group tonight, small enough for everyone to have seconds. Lily chewed the sweetness till it enclosed her, once removed from the present.

"Tonight we will do what is called the empty-chair exercise," Miriam said. "You sit across from an empty chair and tell the deceased how you feel. If you prefer to do this at home, that's fine. Find a place where you're alone or where no one will judge, like here, and talk to your loved one aloud. You can say how you feel. For example: Lily, you said that tomorrow would've been your wedding anniversary. You could talk about that."

"Not *would've been*. Is. Tomorrow *is* our wedding anniversary." No anger in Lily's voice, only correction of misinformation. "Someone called the house in the middle of the night last week, didn't say who it was, asked for Little Des, then hung up when I answered."

"Does this have to do with your wedding anniversary?" Mrs. Henrietta said.

"I have no idea."

"You go first tonight, Lily," Miriam said. "Tell your husband about your anniversary if you'd like. Or the phone call. Be as general or as personal as you need."

Renée clanged open a folding chair leaning against the wall and carried it into the center of the circle. Turned it to face Lily, empty.

Lily wished she wasn't the first in the group to go. It felt theatrical, forced. She preferred the poem writing, the memory boxes.

"Her husband wouldn't even fit in that chair," Carly said. "He was a big guy."

"He lost about seventy pounds by the end," Lily said. "He told me he was so drugged up sometimes he felt like he was watching somebody else die."

"I've heard critically ill people talk of out-of-body experiences," Miriam said.

"As in dying?" Carly said, her tone flat.

"How'd you know he was big?" Lily asked Carly.

"Looked him up online. You talked about him singing opera. He was a good-looking guy."

"Don't do that," Lily said.

"Do what?"

"Look him up online."

"Jesus, what's the big deal? I look everybody up online when I'm bored at work. More fun, since we don't do last names. Leon teaches constitutional law over at NSL. I'd guessed he was a minister."

"I would've been happy to tell you what I do, Carly," Leon said. "You only had to ask."

Renée clanged closed the folding chair and moved it back outside the circle. She took one of the empty circle chairs, a large patched leather, and pushed it into the center, facing Lily. "That better?" Renée said to Carly, who nodded.

Yes, one of those nights.

Des had told her, near the end, that death was all mixed up. That he'd always thought you lived and then you died. But now he wasn't sure if he was dying or she was dying or the boys were dying, and he was the only one who understood this and didn't know how to make them live. She'd taken his hands and kissed them. They'd smelled of dry bones, hospital antiseptic.

Lily stared at the chair. Even the void of him was cavernous. She wished they'd left the folding chair because Des *wouldn't* have fit in it. It would've been less real.

Please be the man and I will speak for you

Lily sang in a whisper. Crying and singing in that scratchy 45-rpm voice that couldn't sing for shit. That Des loved and would know wherever he was.

Flames and lakes and mountains I will be
Who loved me?

Chapter 11: Fall to Pieces

Windy, almost balmy the whole day. Lily left work early to pick up Sam at aftercare and drive to see the tail end of Finn's soccer game: the bluster of children up and down the field and voices cheering and the river behind the bleachers through the barely leafed trees. The field lights were on at Shelby Park, and their glare drained color from the faces of people she'd known for years, and she could not fill in the blanks of their names. Watkins Park lost four to three, but Finn scored a goal and was happy.

They drove to All Seasons Sports because Finn reported that the coach told him he needed new cleats and that secondhand wasn't an option at this level of play and did we need help.

"What does that mean, Finn—*do we need help?*"

He shrugged. "I forget how Coach said it—does your mom need help, or maybe it was does your family need help. Don't remember."

Sam moved euphorically through the racks of Tennessee Titans official wear. The shoe clerk leaned over Finn to fit him with the new cleats. Lily leaned over to look also. She smelled Des on the back of the clerk's neck, his hair. He looked nothing like her dead husband; the clerk was twenty years old, Hispanic, skinny, and slight like a distance runner. She moved her hand to touch his hair, moved her head to smell the back of his neck.

The back of his head conked into Lily's face when he straightened up. "Oops, sorry," the clerk said. "I need a reverse beep. Are you all right?"

No, you are not all right. You are dizzy. You smell your dead husband on a stranger's neck.

"I'm good. Sorry about that," she said.

In the parking lot, Finn spoke: "What were you doing, Mom? That was wack."

His anger was unexpected. What was she doing? She was putting the package in the trunk of the car. "What're you talking about?"

"You were sniffing at that guy. You were bending over him. You were kinda smiling. That was beyond embarrassing."

They got in the car, buckled.

"Did he have perfume on or something, Mom?" Sam asked.

"Yeah," Lily said. "Some kind of perfume or something."

"Like popcorn," Sam said. "I thought I smelled popcorn."

———

It was late when they got home. A large package from Nordstrom waited on the front stoop. Lily hadn't ordered anything. She opened it at the kitchen table. Inside the mailing box were wads of packing paper and a suit box wrapped in silver with a satin bow. Sam crowded round with Christmas-morning anticipation. "Save the paper for birthdays," he said.

"No, rip it off," Finn said. He'd come out of his sulk and wore his new cleats to break them in. She ripped the paper, opened the box. The white tissue paper unfolded to reveal an elaborate white nightgown. The translucent bodice had an overlay of silk flowers. The skirt was cascading layers of thin chiffon.

"Is that a wedding dress, Mom?" Sam asked.

"Almost looks like it, but I think it's a nightgown," she said. "Must be a wrong address."

She had Finn check the address label. Her name and her address. She felt around the box for a card and found a tiny gift envelope beneath the tissue paper.

"Happy anniversary, Little Des," Finn read aloud over his mother's shoulder.

"That's what Granny Kaye calls Mom," Sam explained in his little-man voice.

Lily stuffed the gown and the tissue paper back into the box and closed the lid.

"Weird," Finn said. "Why would Granny Kaye give you stuff this fancy?"

"Don't know," she said. She heard the wind at the kitchen window above the sink. Heard the leaves tremble against the windowpane.

Finn: "Is it your wedding anniversary?"

"Yes," she answered.

Sam: "Were we supposed to get you presents, too?"

Finn: "No. This is like a sad day for Mom. So it's out-there that Granny sent this."

"It is out-there. I'll need to call and make sure Granny is okay. Your dad's death has been hard on her."

Sam: "It's hard on me, too."

Finn: "It's not a competition, duh."

"No, it's not a competition. Granny seems a little confused lately. Do me a favor, Finn, honey. There's Boar's Head turkey in the fridge, and if you would make yourself a sandwich and help Sam make one, too. There are Terra Chips in the cabinet. I'll eat later. I have to make some phone calls. Don't say duh to your brother."

"Why are you yelling, Mom?" Finn said.

Chapter 12:
Not a Wedding Gown

Lily's anger innerved her. It didn't matter if the gift was meant with misplaced good intentions, don't *not* sign a card. Like the phone call in the middle of the night for "Little Des"—don't *not* identify yourself. *Don't* hang up.

In the den with the door shut, she emptied the box. Shook the gown out. Shook the box and the tissue paper out. Searched the wrapping for a credit card receipt, packing slips, shipping labels, anything with more information. Where she came from, in the folklore of the mountains, to dream of yourself in your wedding gown was to augur your death. Back in the day, women wore their wedding dresses twice. One time for their wedding. One time, for all time, in their coffin. Hair fixed, hands folded, the lid closing.

She began to dial her mother-in-law. Her fingers jumbled the numbers and dialed her mother instead. Her father answered. Even better. Sometimes she just forgot to talk to him. His thirty-five years as a high school teacher had given him patience and practice in dealing with the difficult. He listened to his daughter, her irate questions: *Am I supposed to wear this like the* Corpse Bride? Heard the angry vibrato of her tone.

"The *Corpse Bride* is a movie?" he said.

"Yes but not the point."

"What's the action here?"

"My mother-in-law called in the middle of the night last week and hung up. She sent me a white gown and did not sign the card." Lily tried to keep her voice under scream volume.

"No. What is *your* action? She sent you a wedding gown, which is not appropriate, so what is *your* next step?"

"It's not a wedding gown."

"It's not an appropriate gown. Would it help for you to talk with her? Or call Kevin or Briana or Craig. Does their mother need to be evaluated by a professional? Could this be dementia?"

Lily heard her mother in the background: "Ask her if maybe Kaye just called the store and asked the salesperson to pick out a nightgown to send?"

Then why not sign the card? Lily got off the phone, forced herself calm. Reminded herself that she wasn't the only one grieving. Reminded herself that her mother-in-law had done loads of things right, had raised Des. Called her mother-in-law, who said she did not send anything.

"Why would I send you an anniversary present?" Kaye said. "I didn't even know it was your anniversary, and my son is dead. Half the time I don't remember my own anniversary. Why would you think I sent you something?"

"The card was addressed to Little Des. You're the only one who calls me that."

"Wasn't me. Call the store. I didn't send it."

"Did you call in the middle of the night last week?"

"No. Like I told you when you asked me. No. Like I told Kevin when he asked. No."

"Please don't call me Little Des anymore. It's upsetting."

"No problem. I won't call you that. And by the by, it was a term of affection, not an affront to your identity."

She sounds so reasonable, Lily thought, and realized how crazy she must sound to her mother-in-law. If she hadn't sent it.

A taped voice at Nordstrom advised her to call back during business hours. She left voice messages with Briana and Kevin. Lily's sister-in-law Deidre, Craig's wife, said it sounded monstrous and would see if they could come up with an answer.

All the time, Lily realized, all the time pacing the room and all the time sitting in the chair with the cell phone to her ear, she'd been holding the gown slung across her forearm as if she were deciding whether to keep it. Fingering the silk flowers, the tiny beads on the chiffon. She let it fall to the floor. What to do with it? Throw it out? Burn it? It lay dead on the rug. She put it in the big armchair, arranged the chiffon as if she had brought it to life. Take a picture on her cell to show Iris? Show Miriam the insolent anniversary gown sitting in Des's chair?

Chapter 13:
The Best-Kept Secret

High winds brought days of rain. Poor visibility abolished roads and created all-day dusk. Earth felt ancient and murky. As if the dark and light hadn't yet been separated.

So drippy wet Lily almost didn't go to her grief group, but she'd missed the week before because Sam had been home from school with pink eye. It mattered when she didn't go. Everything got too big and too loud when she couldn't contain her sorrow in the Circle of Compassion. In the end, she was late, the traffic backed up with fender benders and hydroplanes to the side of the road. She took off her raincoat in the doorway before she took a seat.

"I got a puppy a few months after my wife died," Leon said. "Sometimes I think my wife sent him to watch over me. To make sure I get out of bed in the morning. To make sure I get out of the house to exercise him. I calculated the puppy's date of birth to a week after my wife died, and that seemed to open the possibility of reincarnation. Does that count?"

Miriam nodded. Miriam always nodded after their shares. She wore a botanic print dress, bold and unnatural in the rainy light. Coming late, Lily didn't know what the topic was this evening. Reincarnation?

Emma was next. She'd had a late miscarriage six months prior. She was still hormonal and raw. Her breasts leaked milk, as if they were weeping, she'd said.

"I hear my baby crying. It's his real voice. I sing to him, and he stops. It's disconcerting, but it's a gift in a way, that I can comfort him," she said.

"Sometimes when I sit in the garden and look through old photo albums, I feel Meghan's hand on my shoulder," Olivia said. "If I'm still, her hand stays. When I turn to her, it fades. It's not a hallucination. Her hand is warm and weighted and real."

No, not reincarnation. How we connect to the dead?

Carly moved over two seats to sit by Lily. She grabbed Lily's hand and turned to her. "He danced with me," Carly said. "I looked up, and there he was. Must've been a hundred people on the dance floor, and there he was in front of me." Carly's eyes were bright and love-as-drug dilated.

Yvonne was back. "You must test the spirits," she said. She tucked a piece of bone-straight hair behind her delicate ear.

"How do you test a spirit?" Leon said.

"Your wife in the form of a dog might be an unclean spirit or a demon," Yvonne said.

"You look so freakin' normal," Carly said to Yvonne.

"What about Jesus appearing to his disciples after the resurrection?" Leon said. "How would you test his spirit?"

"So freakin' normal," Carly whispered to Lily.

"I know that for some of you we've talked about this before," Miriam said. "But it is worth repeating. Seeing, hearing, feeling the dead doesn't mean you're having some sort of breakdown. This can be a normal part of the separation process."

Renée darted her hand up, sitting in back beside Miriam. Was she asking permission to speak? She cleared her throat several times, the sound bouncing off the sharp corners of the damp room.

"Do you need water?" Leon asked.

"No," Renée said. "I just wanted to add, with Miriam's consent, that these spiritual feelings are not a sign of a breakdown *unless* your dead one, your beloved I mean, asks you to do something out of character, to join them or hurt yourself or others. Then it *could* indicate a psychotic break."

"He was just dancing, for God sakes," Carly said. "We loved to dance."

"I was speaking in general," Renée said.

"Maybe I'll go back to the club next week," Carly said. "I wore an amazingly hot dress Gabe loved. I'll wear it again. I keep trying to remember exactly what I had to drink and how much. We'd smoked some pot earlier. I have to find the exact combination again."

"So this was a drug experience?" Yvonne said.

"Carly, I don't think alcohol or drugs are an appropriate conduit for your connection with Gabe," Miriam said. "We need to talk afterward, please."

"Prayer, on the other hand," Yvonne said. "Not liquor or marijuana, but prayer is the way to connect to God, who can connect you with your loved one."

Carly's angry hands alternated between fist and splay. Lily leaned in and whispered, "I'm glad you got to dance with him. I wish Des would come to dance with me."

Miriam got up for coffee. It was what she did when she wanted to change the topic of conversation.

"Now, Lily, you have two sad anniversaries so close in time, with your wedding anniversary a couple of weeks ago," Miriam said, still standing in back at the coffee table. "How will you mark the anniversary of your husband's death next week?"

Miriam always remembered the death anniversaries, always asked that people plan them out ahead of time.

"I booked a room at the state park. The boys want to write letters to their dad and make them into paper boats to release into the lake. I'm going to rent a boat like we used to when Des was alive. I want it to be the start of a yearly ritual, at dawn, as the sun comes up. A new beginning."

"Lily, this is all sweet," Mrs. Henrietta said. Lily suspected Mrs. H., with the Chanel jacket over her jeans and the Kors handbag in her lap, came from a better part of town. "But I do need to tell you the best-kept secret of widowdom: the second year is worse than the first."

Miriam, unmoving, stood by the coffee urn. They waited for her soothing voice to interrupt, to correct Mrs. H., but she said nothing.

"That was so unnecessary, Mrs. H.," Carly said.

"Go ahead, Mrs. H., finish what you have to say," Lily said. She tilted her head back; she was aware of the water stains on the acoustic tile ceiling. Lily listened. She didn't listen. She was aware for the first time, just as if someone had walked in the door and handed her a note: these people here knew about her wedding anniversary. They knew about her wedding anniversary and the upcoming anniversary of her husband's death and knew that she didn't like her mother-in-law calling her Little Des. She'd wanted to talk about the anniversary gown, but now she was guarded.

"For me, at least, that first year held a tragic heroism," Mrs. H. said. "You hold your head up. Your friends bring flowers, casseroles. Their husbands mow your lawn. You're 'the widow.' You're admired for your bravery."

Lily didn't have to look around at the faces, and she didn't have to connect each face with a reason; there was no reason any of them would call her in the middle of the night and ask for Little Des. No reason for any of them to send her a gown for her wedding anniversary. It was simply awareness.

Mrs. H. continued: "Then the one-year anniversary comes, and your friends have run out of casserole recipes. After a year, people think the names of the dead shouldn't wander off their tombstones, shouldn't come up in casual conversation. And things do change after a year: your own shock wears off, and you get left with real life. You want the shock back because it insulated you. You think, wait—is this real life?"

"You're such a bitch," Carly said.

"You know what, Carly?" Mrs. Henrietta said. "You are mourning a boyfriend, a dance partner. I was married for thirty-four years to my husband. We had four children. You think I don't know what real life is?"

"You," Carly accused. "You have no idea how I loved him. You think this is a grief competition? Fresh young love versus years on the job? You have no idea what our love was."

"Sometimes I wish you'd both be quiet," Emma said. Her crying baby, her breasts still leaking milk. What song was it, Lily wondered, that Emma sang to comfort the dead?

Chapter 14: Lavender

Lily didn't get up from the pink upholstered chair after the circle broke up. She fingered a long-ago cigarette burn in the armrest.

"Was it the rain? Is that why things went the way they did tonight?" Miriam said. "Our topic was how nature can offer a spiritual connection, and suddenly we were under the influence at the disco and testing the spirits of dogs." She sat down in the chair next to Lily. Renée put away the rolling table with the coffee urn; her footsteps to the kitchenette reverberated in the hall. Carly hadn't stayed as requested. "I don't ever remember such a contentious evening here," Miriam said. "Not just the words, the tone. Are you all right, Lily?"

"No worse than when I got here," she said.

"Sorry no better. This may be a night to forget. We respect all religious backgrounds here, but that talk about demons and testing spirits. That's never come up before. And Mrs. H.'s pronouncement about the second year—that's not true for everyone."

"Don't forget her dance partner comment to Carly."

"Wish I could forget it."

"Is there a phone list here?" Lily said. "Or a list of addresses?"

"Why?"

"On my wedding anniversary, someone sent me an expensive night-gown with an unsigned card. I called my relatives, and no one knew anything about it. I was furious. I called the 800 number from the store.

Two days of phone calls, and they said it'd been a cash transaction, and they have no record of the sender. It was sent from a Nordstrom in Roseville, California, and I called them. They said that's just computer routing. If you order a certain size and style and the store you're in doesn't have it, the order jumps to another store that does."

"Why does a nightgown upset you? Where are you going with this?"

"It was a honeymoon nightgown. White lace and chiffon. Almost looked like a sheer wedding gown. Who sends a honeymoon gown to a widow? It wasn't signed, but there was a gift card that said 'Happy Anniversary to Little Des.'"

"Which your mother-in-law calls you."

"She denies sending it. I think I believe her."

"And your other relatives?"

"They don't seem to know anything, either."

"We have no lists here. The church board has asked me to get names and numbers and emergency contacts. They said insurance requires it, but I put them off. I don't even know your last name. Not like this is a Twelve-Step program, but we do respect your anonymity. It's how I've always done these groups in the eleven years I've been conducting them. Surely you don't think anyone in the group sent it."

"I have no idea. I can't think why anyone would. The week before that, I had a phone call in the middle of the night asking for my husband. It was the house phone, unlisted. My son who'd answered said they also asked him if he was Little Des."

"You mentioned that last meeting. Have you given your family name or phone number or address to anyone in the group? Some people do."

"No, ma'am. I remembered tonight that we'd talked about my wedding anniversary a few weeks ago, and Mrs. H. mentioned that I'd talked about not being happy to be called Little Des. And Carly had looked up Des on an opera website, so she knows our family name."

Lily scrolled through the photos on her phone. Found the one of the gown draped over the floral chair in the den. She had to show Miriam that it was real. That this hadn't been some figment of her sorrow. Three photos she showed Miriam. On the third photo she handed Miriam her phone, bent over double in the chair, and started crying.

"You took pictures? Lily, where is the gown now?"

There was no composing herself. Lily hadn't cried in a while. And now there were a hundred tears, a million.

"Is it still in your house?"

Lily nodded. She'd reboxed the gown the next morning and put it in the cellar between cartons of Christmas decorations. She had the idea that she needed to keep it as proof, proof of *something*.

Miriam handed Lily a box of tissues.

"I can't imagine how that made you feel, receiving a nightgown with an unsigned card. I can't imagine anyone in the group sending it. And that unfortunate condolence card you got on Valentine's Day. But that was signed. She wanted you to know who she was."

"I didn't feel good when Carly said she'd looked up my husband on the opera website," Lily sobbed.

"And she looked up Leon's profession. You've talked about your husband singing. I don't think I've ever heard Leon mention in group that he was a lawyer or that he taught."

Miriam kept talking. Slow and soothing as Lily's weeping receded from her body into her face, tears streaming, eyes swollen, nose running. "I guess we're all traceable nowadays. Work websites, newspaper obituaries, professional networks, Facebook, blogs. Here, take your phone. Do you and Carly see each other socially out of group?"

No, they'd never approached each other. And children and lifestyle before their losses put them in different social circles. Lily blew her nose. "I was surprised when she said she'd looked up Des. I like Carly. Her humor, her style. I didn't really see her as sneaky," Lily said.

"I might add that, as a professional, I don't see her doing anything sneaky. She looked people up out of boredom. And she was up-front about it."

And Lily couldn't think of reasons for Carly or any of the others to call her in the middle of the night, or to send a gown.

"Which brings me back to my in-laws, I guess. I really believed my mother-in-law when she said she didn't call and didn't send any packages."

"Do you think your mother-in-law has some kind of memory loss? Bereavement can induce temporary or episodic memory loss."

"I don't know. One of her sons says she's drinking, or at least drinking more. She sounded sober when I spoke with her."

"I can recommend some counselors for private therapy."

"In Chicago? For her?"

"No, for you. One-on-one."

Lily was surprised, a little indignant. She was no crazier than the others in the group. "I tried that with a therapist from the hospital right after Des died. This felt better, coming here. Less lonely."

"Some people do both. You have my card with my number and name if you change your mind. I hope you aren't going to let the unfortunate nightgown interfere with your plans for your weekend remembrance. The person might not admit sending it. Or might not remember. You may never find out who sent it."

Miriam rose and leaned in for a hug. Lily inhaled her lavender smell, wanting to feel comforted, but she only felt singled out. Crazier than the rest.

Chapter 15: The Deer

Lily had learned that if she woke early, it was better to move, not wait around in bed for daylight or salvation. She went rapidly: bathroom, hallway, stairs, hallway at the bottom of the stairs to the kitchen. If she stopped anywhere en route, there was that pre-morning ghosty feel: *This is how the house feels when Des is dead.*

In the kitchen, Gogo dashed herself against the sides of her crate. Lily let the dog out back. Pushed the Mr. Coffee button. Heard the thud of the paper in the driveway, went out to retrieve it. She took a breath and lifted her head to the faded darkness speckled with pale stars. No people on the sidewalk. No one else out on the block. Peace. She gathered it in for the day.

Gogo was not at the back door to the yard, nor did she come to Lily's whistle. Lily scanned from the patio, calling Gogo's name.

Then movement in the flat light and one too many creatures in the yard.

No bark from Gogo, no growl, no threat. It was a fawn prancing by the side fence. Spindly legs, graceful body. Gogo joined in the dance, circling, hopping, whining.

"Come," Lily commanded. Whistled again.

Gogo turned to Lily's whistle, then turned back and encircled her jaws around the fawn's neck.

"Drop it! Shit! Sit! Oh God!" Lily ran toward Gogo. Gogo let go of the deer, and Lily grabbed the dog's collar. Gogo was gleeful. Almost smiling. Maybe she hadn't meant any harm.

The fawn was round-eyed and gently spotted. She didn't appear frightened. They were five minutes from downtown Nashville, yet a world away with Shelby Park and the walking trails by the river. They'd seen the occasional deer in the park but not in the fenced backyard. Lily tugged the dog toward the house. The sweet gum dropped hard, round sticker balls that turned walking in her flip-flops into a balancing act with the straining dog.

Lily heard a snort and turned, saw the mother deer jump the fence and stomp toward them. Gogo tore from Lily's grip. The doe stood on hind legs and kicked down. Lily screamed and ran toward the patio. Gogo fought against the tawny blur of anger and more anger. She turned belly up, trapped in the cage of the deer's pounding hooves.

Then Sam was in the yard, crying in his pajamas. Finn, a shovel in his hands, running at the doe. The twentysomething couple a block over—they'd only just moved in—opened the side gate, yelled instructions that Lily couldn't make out. But they'd provided an escape route: the two deer fled through the gate with the twenty-somethings chasing them down the street.

Gogo yelped in circles before crawling under the laurel bushes by the side fence. An adrenaline of sadness pumped through Lily's veins. There was blood on Gogo's face, and one of her beautiful shepherd ears hung loose by her eye. Lily stuck her hand under the bush. "Please please please," she prayed to Gogo. Gogo snarled and snapped air. Des would know what to do here. Would know how to do it. Lily slammed her hand into Gogo's snout and clamped her fingers around the long jaw. The growling was muffled and insistent. The dog's back pushed against the fence and the bushes.

"Sam, get a blanket. Finn, get a roll of gauze from the bathroom closet. Now!"

No, this is not what Des would've done. He wouldn't have put his hand over the powerful jaw of an injured dog at an awkward angle under the thorns of the laurel bush.

"Ease up, Mom," Finn said. "She's afraid. Let her back away." He stood away from the bushes, by Gogo's tail end, and called her firmly. She wiggled backward as Lily loosed her grip, and Finn clicked the lead on Gogo's collar. They covered the backseat with the blanket. Gogo was far too quiet on the ride to the animal clinic.

Chapter 16:
Geography of the Dead

Seven messages on Lily's cell. She hadn't even checked her phone until she got to work. She'd driven the boys to school at noon and signed them each in late, printing "family emergency" in the reason column.

They'd waited at the vet's until Gogo was out of surgery. The still body. The lolling tongue. Forty stitches: eighteen to close a gash over her shoulder, ten to stitch her ear, a dozen to close the cut below it. The clinic would keep her until they were certain there was no internal bleeding beneath her bruised ribs.

Lily checked the settings and found she'd had her phone on vibrate for she didn't know how long. One message from the Mullens to see if Finn could spend the weekend soon. Two from Tiffany, the receptionist at the Foundation, asking if she was coming in to work. One from Iris. Three calls from the Maywood Fertility Center.

She called the fertility clinic from her desk, but the office was closed for lunch, and she didn't leave a message. She remembered the day they'd gone to sign contracts and leave samples. They'd been given the option to freeze sperm when Des's body refused to respond to standard treatment. The new chemo, the possibility of radiation, could leave infertility in its wake. Lily had been only thirty-four then. Sam just three. They hadn't ruled out another child.

The day at the clinic had seemed like a lark. The sweet nurse, Elaine, and the manager, Gina. They signed papers and insurance forms and read all the options, agreeing that in the event of Des's death, the clinic would have the sperm destroyed after a year. Des's death had seemed so out-there back then, so never-going-to-happen. A cakewalk on the moon, she remembered him saying, but didn't remember if that had to do with how easy it would be for him to give a sperm sample or how remote his death. At any rate, Des was unable to get the specimen in the bathroom with the magazines. *I'm more auditory than visual,* he'd said.

"Well, I'm sorry," Nurse Elaine replied, "I'm not allowed to let anyone personal in there to moan for you." She winked at Lily. Des went out to the car for his iPod and headphones and headed back to the sample room for a successful donation. The clinic was happy with the sperm count and motility. He'd never told her what music had guaranteed his success. She'd like to know that now. Puccini? Muscle Shoals?

She called the fertility clinic again from the break room and waited on hold, easy-listening jazz. Lily remembered Gina Blanton's voice, Atlanta sweet but all business.

"This is always a phone call I dread but is sometimes a necessity, Mrs. Declan, which is why I didn't e-mail you. I hope this year hasn't been too excruciating."

"Thank you," Lily said. *Strange wording,* she thought. *How excruciating should it've been?*

"As you may remember, you both signed a statement that it was your wish that the sperm be destroyed a year from the date of your husband's death. Have you thought about your decision?"

Months before, she'd had to write in that date on the annual contact letter.

"What's to decide, then? We already made the decision."

"It's not legally binding. I'm obliged to tell you that. Some people change their minds. The sperm is legally yours after your husband's death."

"I didn't know that. Do I have to think about it right now?"

"No, we can renew its storage temporarily while you decide. A lot of people renew another year. The cost is low on a renewal."

"It seems weird to use Des's body parts now that he's dead. Though I don't know if I could destroy anything of his right now."

"I'll scan you over the renewal form. It'll give you some time. It might feel better to contribute the specimen to the donation pool; this way you won't be destroying anything. You both signed a form for donation, which you can activate."

"I don't remember that," Lily said. It'd been such an out-of-body time. Out of time. Out of their minds.

"Yes, I'm looking at the check mark right here with both your initials."

"Wouldn't his disease pull him from the healthy gene pool?"

"He didn't have a hereditary cancer. We don't do designer babies, but couples are allowed to say in general what their preferences are. Like college grad, general ethnicity, musically inclined."

"Has someone asked for that?"

"Couples ask for that kind of thing all the time."

Her boys having a half brother or sister out there? How would she be sure the parents were kind? Lily going to an opera twenty-five years later and someone sounding like Des onstage?

"Just keep it in mind. Check your e-mail. I'll send the papers as an attachment. I'll put my cell phone number in there, too. You can call anytime with your questions. These are never easy decisions, and you don't have to decide anything right now. I'll put a month renewal down with your verbal consent."

The geography of the dead confused Lily. Was Des at this moment residing in happy little sperm they'd frozen more than two years before? Or was he at the Berry Hill Animal Hospital, where, this morning, Sam had begged his father's spirit to watch over Gogo? Or was he traveling the bend in the river where his ashes had been scattered? The funeral procession had been to the banks of the Cumberland ten miles north of downtown Nashville. Des had told them that's where he wanted his ashes thrown, to eventually make his way to the Mississippi and Huck Finn territory. But the river's bend was too wide and too wild, and the water had swallowed the ashes too quickly into its greedy maw.

Lily went back to her office, put on headphones, and continued transcribing the voices of the dead from 1930s radio.

Chapter 17: Upgrade

"You've been upgraded to the honeymoon suite," the desk clerk said at the Shawnee Lodge.

"What?"

"Are you Lily Declan?"

"Yes."

"You called about an anniversary celebration, it says in the computer."

"Finn, take your brother to the bathroom."

"He goes by himself."

"I don't have to go, Mom," Sam said.

Lily sent mama-laser eyes. Finn took his brother.

"This is really adorable, bringing your kids," the clerk said. Her name tag read JAYLEEN.

"Jayleen, I'd prefer not to have the honeymoon suite."

"It's got a foldout couch for the boys separate from the bedroom and a king size for you and your husband."

"My husband's not here."

Jayleen shrugged. "Okay, when he comes."

"My husband's dead."

Lily tried to pull the words back as soon as she said them. To pull the words back, to take the upgraded suite, to transform her face into a face befitting the generic lobby of a state park inn.

"Jesus. I'm sorry. Did this just happen? The booking agent said you were here for your anniversary."

"*Of his death.* The woman on the phone said you were booked up and asked me if this was a special occasion and I said yes, the anniversary of my husband's death."

"She's right, we are booked up except for the honeymoon suite, but I'll see if I can switch you to a regular room. Maybe trade with another reservation."

"No. I'll take the upgrade. It's very kind."

And why couldn't she accept kindness, even accidental? She'd gone back to check on the groggy Gogo at the vet's. They'd found no internal bleeding, and that was a kindness. The clinic would board her for the weekend. Her new neighbors on the next block had found an opening in the backyard fence by the overgrown back alley where the baby deer had probably gotten into the yard. They'd patched it with chicken wire and left a little note in Lily's mailbox. It looked as if the old lilac tree had just gnarled its way through. The patch job was thorough, and they'd even trimmed the lilac. The note was signed Ken and Kendra Fleming—sweet, a couple's name.

The sixth-floor suite was grand. A complimentary basket of fruit with two white balloons also contained a congratulatory card, free coupons for the dinner buffet, and sparkling wine for two. The balcony brushed the tops of trees. Beyond the wrought-iron balustrade, through the new-leafed forest, the lake dazzled blue in the distance.

"I remember coming here with Dad," Finn said.

"Of course you do, baby. The last time wasn't so long ago, three years maybe."

"No, I remember being little here with him. Real little. You, me, and Dad. Can Sam and I sleep out here on the balcony?"

The balcony was railed, with just enough room for couch cushions and blankets to accommodate the boys. Heights weren't something Lily feared; she wasn't one to go bungee jumping, but she liked a view. Yet she vetoed the idea quickly. The balcony might be a hazardous place for the boys to sleep, heads getting caught between the bars or the railing giving way. She didn't remember the world so dangerous when Des was alive. Deer attacks in the backyard, Gogo's stitched wounds, Des dead; these weren't linked events, she had to remind herself.

They rode bikes through the remaining hours of daylight and the miles of paved bike trails. Sitting around didn't seem like the way to make the world less dangerous.

After dinner, the evening was crowded with crafts. Lily was glad now for the upgrade. The kitchenette had a decent-size table. She'd brought a shopping bag of supplies: paper, crayons, glue sticks, and copies of photos she'd run through the scanner at work.

Sam labored with a tightly held pencil and invented spelling on a letter to his father. Every sentence, every sentence revision, he read aloud to his shushing brother. Finn had already written his letter during study period at school this week and announced that he wasn't sharing it. Lily wrote a honeyed letter praising Des for the time they'd had and the wonderful boys he'd left her. Sam told her in his little-man voice that it was the finest letter he'd ever heard.

They made collages overglued with the scanned photos of Des and drawings of leaves and flowers. They made paper boats; at dawn on Sunday they'd release them to the lake.

They hiked Saturday morning. In fields of neon buttercups, they ate the fruit from the complimentary honeymoon basket. The boys were coltish with energy. Sam twirled till he fell, over and over in the yellow flowers. Lily stopped herself from telling him to calm down, that he'd get too muddy from the still-wet ground, that he'd get nauseous or dizzy. They all seemed nature starved, and Lily promised herself to replace Saturday morning Nickelodeon with the outdoors. This was different from soccer and organized sports, this sweet wilding.

After lunch she set them up with cane poles on the dock. She should've paid more attention to the casting rods Des used to rig for them, but she didn't know then that he wouldn't be around to untangle and bait and demonstrate tie knots and wrist flicks. All the instructions for real life that her boys should've gotten.

———

At the boathouse, Lily requested a small boat with a trolling motor to be ready before dawn the next morning and handed her credit card for the reservation. The reservationist, late teens with a Stones T-shirt and a military haircut, explained that 9:00 a.m. was the earliest she could have it.

"Why?" Lily asked.

"Government cutbacks. We'll be open earlier after Memorial Day, but we're still technically off season: less personnel, less hours."

"Listen, we need to go out early tomorrow morning. How about if I rent it this afternoon and then return it tomorrow late morning?"

"Even if you paid for two days, can't leave the boat unattended overnight, ma'am."

"I was up early this morning, and I saw boats on the water."

"Saturday morning, we open earlier even off-season. More people on Saturday than Sunday with people going to church."

"How can I get a boat early tomorrow? How can we remedy this?"

"There isn't a way. Like I told you."

It was uncomfortable now. Lily knew she was being unreasonable, but she couldn't stop. They were to release their letters and candles into the dark. They were to witness the dawn and the hope of future dawns. This was to be the first of yearly pilgrimages. The queue grew behind her.

"Let them go ahead," Lily said. She waved other groups forward, a man with two teen boys, two elderly men, a woman by herself. *Widowed?* Lily wondered.

When her turn came again, she asked Robbie (she'd overheard his name) to call Jayleen at the front desk so she could explain the situation. This *was* a special occasion.

"My husband died at dawn," Lily said.

Robbie twisted his open hands to her. "Sorry?"

Too much information, she berated herself. She walked over to the dock and stood by the boys. Blue jeans and T-shirts, cane poles cast in the water. She didn't disturb them. She went back to the boat rental hut and Robbie.

"All taken care of, ma'am," he said. "Sunup is around six thirty; the boat will be ready at six."

Lily smiled and handed over her credit card.

"Nope. All taken care of. Already paid."

This was where she was supposed to say thank you. But she was disconcerted, and there were several people waiting behind her. Who was "taking care" of this? Had she told the Circle of Compassion exactly what park they were going to? No, of course not. The management had screwed up on her reservation at the inn, and they were trying to make things right. Or she had blurted out too much info on the death anniversary of her husband, and they were being kind.

Or maybe the Shawnee Lodge was a hospitable place to stay.

Their dinner waitress was an exuberant grandmother named Tina. They knew she was a grandmother, eight times over, because she wore a grandma brooch on her apron with eight different birthstones that she explained in detail to Sam's question. Tina brought extra cherries for Sam's ginger ale and admired Finn's choice of tater tots and fried chicken from the buffet. She substituted Lily's champagne coupons for sparkling apple juice, not on the menu.

They sat by the side windows. Lily was certain they had been seated at the same table the last time they'd been here with Des. That they watched the same light ease through the tops of trees into darkness. It wasn't comforting; it just was. The word *gloaming* came to mind, that

Des had said the word *gloaming* that last time they'd sat at this same table. And that word, which had felt dusky and romantic then, now felt gloomy.

Tina placed a can of aerosol whipped cream on the table after the boys returned from the buffet with blackberry cobbler piled high in dessert bowls. Even Finn was charmed. Tina tousled Sam's hair, and the boys squirted every last crumb with whipped-cream rosettes. They were full and laughing and tired. Lily pulled herself from the gloaming outside the windows and tipped the cheery waitress generously.

Chapter 18: Glad It's Over

She had everything laid out: clothes, snacks, flashlights. In a brown grocery bag: tea candles, waterproof matches, the fleet of paper-boat letters.

It had been a relief when Des died. How strange to remember that now. How she'd stood by the bed while the nurse detached the IV and the oxygen and Lily said to her, "I'm so glad it's over and we can all go home." The nurse nodded. It never entered Lily's mind that Des wasn't coming home with them.

Finn woke and turned on the light. He was awake and ready for their adventure. Sam woke cranky and crying. The overhead light hurt his eyes, but he insisted on reading his letter once more to them: *Dear Daddy, I miss you very much. I hope you are happy in heaven. I made the Y soccer team. I love you, Sam.*

"That's very nice, honey. What're you crying about?"

"I forgot a part. Now I have to start all over again."

"No, you don't. You can just tell him in your heart."

"It's called a P.S., Mr. Crying Kindergartner," Finn said. "You just write it on the bottom with *P.S.*, and it gets added on automatically."

"That's a good idea, Finn. And if you use disrespectful language talking to your brother again, you'll stay here, and we'll go without you."

Finn mumbled an apology. Sam added his P.S., a cheerful "I hear it's fun in heaven."

Five forty-five, walking on the pine-needle earth to the lake with flash-lights. The boat was there, tied to the dock. There were flowers across the front seat, long-stemmed flower-shop roses tied with a ribbon. Whatever human hand had left them—Robbie's, Jayleen's, hotel management's—didn't matter; in Lily's heart the flowers were from Des.

The battery-powered eco motor on the boat hummed a Gregorian chant. Lily maneuvered through the night's vestige to a placid cove near the sluice below an old wooden bridge. She anchored the boat, and they placed their offerings in the gentle current. Tea candles burned in a half dozen of the paper boats; the rest held letters and pictures. They waited till every paper boat was gone, drowned or burned or washed over the sluice edge. A regatta of vanishing. The sun rose.

Coming back, they felt invisible, wondered why people smiled, offered hellos.

The pale brightness of hospital light by day. The pale brightness of hospital light by night. There had been no day. There had been no night. Time had been measured by the changing of IV bags and the nurses' twelve-hour shifts. They'd stayed awake to counter Des's inability to wake up. Death was the only cure.

But the hours later, and the next day, and after everyone finally slept, and the next week, and now—he remained thoughtlessly dead.

Chapter 19: Necromancy

Still quiet, still tired, Lily loaded the boys in the car. Sam fell asleep the minute his seat belt was buckled. Finn played on his Game Boy. They waited in the car while Lily got coffee to go from the lobby urn and fruit from the bowl. She was steps back into the parking lot when last night's waitress called and hurried over.

"I can't accept this," Tina said, and pressed a tightly folded bill into Lily's palm and cupped her hand.

"I don't know what you mean," Lily said. Was it the twenty she'd left with the check?

"Your little boy left it under the whipped-cream canister by his place. Maybe he thought it was a five-dollar bill, but whether he thought it was a five or a fifty, you already left a nice tip and, well, I can't accept it."

Lily unfolded the bill from her hand. It was a fifty.

"This is a mistake, ma'am. We didn't leave this. My boy doesn't have a fifty-dollar bill to leave you. It must be from another diner, and it must be yours."

"I know where it's from, and I can't accept it." Tina turned and left. Could Lily's father be giving the boys money? He'd sneaked a hundred-dollar bill into her purse. She texted her mother. There was no reply; Ella was probably at work.

Lily let Sam sleep on. She whispered to Finn, asking if he knew anything about a tip Sam might've left the nice waitress last night. He didn't know. Had he left money? she asked. No. Did he or Sam have a fifty-dollar bill? Finn thought about this. Thought he might've had one once from Great-Grandpa Sam when he'd come to Finn's preschool graduation, but he wasn't sure. It could've been a twenty, and they'd deposited it, but he couldn't really remember.

On Route 64, maybe five miles from Shawnee State Park, Lily saw Des's picture on a roadside memorial. She'd driven by doing the speed limit, and she'd been thinking of her grandpa Sam, who'd died when she was pregnant with her Sam, so she hadn't gotten a good look. She still breathed, but she couldn't catch her breath. This was more disturbing than the Valentine's Day crow. If she were to have grief hallucinations, she wanted phantoms moonlit and ethereal, not a passing glance at Des's face superimposed on somebody else's laminated photo. The whole dusty experience stapled to a cross going by at fifty miles per hour.

Soon you'll see Des's face next to Mother Teresa's in croissant sandwiches. In babies born with leftover sperm. She got off the next exit and ordered Egg McMuffins and coffee at the McDonald's drive-through.

"Sam, did you leave a tip for the waitress last night?" Lily asked as they waited for their order.

"Was I supposed to?" he said.

"No. The waitress thought you'd left a tip."

Lily turned to see him shrug, shake his head. He was still half-asleep.

"Did anyone give you money? Did Uncle Owen? Or did you find money somewhere?"

"Like for my last birthday? Nana gave me twenty dollars in a card."

Lily let it drop. He seemed confused by the questions.

They retrieved Gogo from the vet. She wore a plastic cone collar that was hard not to smile at. Walked into walls. Three tries to get into the car. "Is it like an invisible force field to her?" Sam asked.

Back at the house, Friday's and Saturday's mail bounded from the mailbox. Someone had been kind enough to throw the Saturday and Sunday papers in the corner of the porch.

Lily disliked Sunday afternoons. Sunday mornings had a little of the weekend left in them. Sunday nights had an inevitability. But the great expanse of Sunday afternoon was a no-man's-land. Des had made up names for her uneasiness: placidodomingophobia, sundangst. He'd take the boys most Sunday afternoons and let her wander off to a movie or a hike.

Lily made a fresh pot of coffee, wondered if she should mail the fifty-dollar bill back to Tina, in care of the restaurant. She put it in the kitchen junk drawer for the time being and settled in with the messages on her cell. She could see the boys in the backyard from where she sat in the kitchen, playing some sort of complicated hide-and-seek with Gogo. Gogo was easy to spot with her collar jamming on trees and bushes.

The first message was from her mother, who wanted her to know that her heart was with her on this sad day but no, her father hadn't been giving the boys money. Friends had left messages, too: her childhood friend Tanya, Iris from work, the Mullens. All remembering, offering sympathy. She opened cards from one of Des's friends and one from his cousin. Her grandmother's card: "You've survived a year with grace and dignity; I'm proud of you."

There was an envelope postmarked from Chicago decorated in the large, round cursive from the crazy lady. She slit open the envelope with a knife. It would feel good to be angry. It would be better to be angry than sad.

It was an art card, like you'd buy in a museum shop, of a bird singing in a bare tree. Inside, a typed note read:

Dear Lillian,

I'm sad that you didn't answer my correspondence (if this is in error and you didn't receive my letter, please excuse me—I'll be happy to send on a copy). I can only offer you and the boys peace on this sad day of memory. I hope they are getting extra attention! Please remember this is new to me. It feels more like a month anniversary than a year, and I feel I'm losing even more time not hearing from you. I didn't have the wake or the funeral to process my grievance. I could have helped you, and this would have gone a long way in assuaging our sorrow. I know you know what a wonderful man Desmond was, but please allow me to add these memories to Desmond's honor:

Desmond was the first love of my life. My first desire and fulfillment. My first entry into what is true and real, and now eternal.

I remember a roaring fireplace in the season's first snowstorm.

I remember his car breaking down on Route 50 and the two of us having to hitchhike to my mom's birthday party.

I remember being the only barefoot dancer in a sea of disco high heels. Desmond in Converse high-tops.

By honoring our memories—we can lift our sorrow. Please acknowledge my deepest condolences. I feel I am crying in the wilderness.

Your servant,

Jaz Elwin

The hand-scripted signature was even larger than on the last letter. Lily had the feeling a child learning cursive had signed it, but that didn't diminish her anger. *Our* sorrow? *Our* memories? *Hoping the boys got extra attention—like what, an extra ice-cream scoop? These are the affronts you concentrate on so you don't have to face someone else's memory of a roaring fireplace and Des in high-tops. You think of the car ride home a year ago with your brother driving your car. Who owns the dead? Who owns their memory? You concentrate on the plastic bag in your lap holding your dead husband's clothes. These are the things you bring home: a pair of jeans, a button-down shirt in a solid color, black or white or denim—you can't remember—a white V-neck undershirt, plaid-ish boxer shorts. You put them in the washer when you get home, then move them to the dryer, in case he rises from the dead and wants to wear them.*

Chapter 20: Bing Crosby

"Kevin," Lily said on the phone, "I need you to please check out an address for me. Do you have a pen?"

She read Jaz's second letter to him. Kevin told her to write the woman back and tell her to go fuck herself. *Can you go to the address,* she begged, *tell her in person to leave me alone?* Tell her to get a life and leave their lives alone.

He said he'd check on the address. He asked her to call his mom, word to the wise that his mom was taking names on who'd tendered condolences and who hadn't. Lily was planning to anyway, or had been planning to before she'd read the card.

Last week her mother-in-law had sounded upset, but today's call was something different. Kaye smoked three cigarettes a day, or owned up to three, but she sounded as if she'd been smoking them all at once. The deep inhales. The long smoky exhalations that Lily could almost smell across the telephone line and into her kitchen.

"Are you all right? You sound hoarse," Lily said.

"That's the sound of tears. Have you called Briana yet?"

Lily didn't know Briana well; older by fifteen years, she'd seemed more aunt to Des and Kevin, the two youngest. When Lily had called Briana about the white nightgown and left a message, Briana had texted back a terse reply.

"No, I haven't spoken to Briana. Is there something wrong, Kaye?"

"Do you know that no one called her today?"

"I'm not sure where this is coming from."

"It's coming from pain, Lily. I've had to take antianxiety medication the doctor told me to take. Ordered me to take. My own religion offers no comfort. The doctor said *take them*."

"Are they helping?"

In the past year, Kaye's soft, dark hair had gone white and wiry in thick visual bedlam.

"Like a Band-Aid on a hemophiliac. You weren't very nice to Briana. She had to cancel work to come to the funeral last year. She's well thought of at the hospital, you know. She's the *charge* nurse in the emergency room. Not like Kevin teaching junior high or Des singing. Or even Craig with his financial services company when we all know it's Deidre who came with the money. We agreed to your having the service in the Episcopal church even though Desmond was raised a good Catholic like all my children."

"Kaye, it was Des who went to the Episcopal church."

"You know we had to sacrifice to send all the boys to Catholic school?"

"Yes, of course you did."

"Pops went to Mass with me this morning and then brunch. Briana would've come, but she had a long shift yesterday."

"That was nice you went to church."

"No, you weren't very nice to her. Briana asked for a Celebration of Life instead of your funeral service. So glum. Briana wanted a slide presentation of her brother's life. We could've remembered what he looked like before he was skin and bones. You know he had a life before you. He had a good life growing up."

"He had a good life with me, too."

"I'm just thinking of his memory. We wanted to remember him happy."

"What medication are you on, Kaye?"

"Xanax or something. I asked for Valium, but he gave me this. Just sometimes I take it, when I get stuck on the pain. God forbid you lose a child, Lily."

"Yes, God forbid."

"So call Briana. Desmond's death affected her more deeply than it did his brothers. Briana is more sensitive. Always was. In some ways the strongest, too. For the slide show, she had Bing Crosby singing the 'Our Father.'"

"I felt it was a time to be sad."

"We were sad, Lily. You didn't have to make it worse."

"Kaye, you don't sound like yourself. I just called to say thank you. You brought up a wonderful son, and he was a good father and a good husband to me."

"A good son, too."

"I got some cards in the mail. A friend of Des's from high school named Billy Harrington. That college friend, Jasmine. She also goes by Jaz."

"Never heard of any of them. I told you already that he never had an Indian girlfriend that I know of." (More cigarette inhalation, exhalation.) "They came last night, Craig and Deidre, and took us out to dinner. It was so thoughtful. Pops wore a tie. My friend Kitty sent a beautiful card and flowers. They're huge. I'm looking at them right now on the kitchen table. She called on the phone early this morning. Had me laughing about Des wanting to name his dog Halley when he was little but then deciding he wanted to save the name in case he had a girl baby when he got big. I think he ended up naming that dog Spike. Kevin and his fiancée were here earlier. They were headed out to some field or park or meadow to think about Des."

"Halley? Des wanted to name the dog Halley?"

"You know, for the comet, Mark Twain's comet."

"Kaye, you know we named Sam for my grandfather, who died while I was pregnant."

"Sure. There are no Sams on our side of the family."

Lily had never heard her mother-in-law this way. She wasn't the cuddly type, as Des put it, but she wasn't nasty. She'd been a stay-at-home mom who brought up four kids in a small house with shag carpet and harvest-gold appliances. Des's father was a pipe layer who came home each night with a six-pack and the need for quiet. Pops was, even now, not so much drunk or unpleasant as immobile. There had been a certain remove to their marriage, still was, without bitterness, without affection.

"Just give Briana a call when you get a chance today, Lily. She doesn't get the support she needs. Her husband has that computer repair thing, but she's the one married to the mortgage. Her kids didn't even call her today. You know Briana has had her eye on that watercolor of Lake Michigan that I gave Des. Do you even have it up on the wall? It definitely would look better in a Chicago house than in Nashville. Des and Briana were very close."

Ah, the watercolor again. A painting that Kaye Declan had never liked because she thought it looked more like ocean than lake.

"Maybe Des died because he worked construction with your brother," Kaye said. "I'd forgotten about his other job with your family, but Briana reminded me. I read an article, and I think he might have inhaled construction chemicals that caused his cancer. He should've sung. He could still be singing today."

Kaye had known for years that Des did woodwork for Owen when chorus jobs were slow. Kaye'd been happy her son had finally gotten a real job, as she put it. It was Des who'd asked Owen for work. Des had been in one of the last years of shop class given in high school, and he was skilled at small, intricate woodwork: turnings for balustrades, gingerbread bracketing for kitchens and porches. There weren't chemicals involved.

"Cancer doesn't run in my family," Kaye said.

"It wasn't a running kind of cancer," Lily said.

God, wait'll you tell Des this conversation with his mother.

You say good-bye.

You remember.

Chapter 21: Trader Joe's

The boys begged off grocery shopping. She left them in front of the television with the doors locked and Gogo in charge. Lily didn't like leaving them by themselves even with strict instructions, but Finn would be thirteen this summer. He knew not to open the door. Knew the emergency numbers, the neighbors' numbers.

She drove across town to Trader Joe's. Aside from a health-food market, there wasn't a clean-enough grocery in the newly gentrified East Nashville. She took the city streets, Main to downtown and over to Broadway. The downtown catered to tourists on the weekends, happy and cowboy-hatted.

Lily got bread and cheese and yogurt cups for the boys' lunches. She got veggies and chicken for the Crock-Pot. Turned into the aisle for juice boxes and there she was—Gert? Tate? Blythe?—Blythe Tate, that was the name. Blythe was halfway down the aisle looking like she'd just crawled out of bed. Gray sweatpants, oversize brown cardigan, pink flip-flops, skewed red hair with dark roots, oven mitts on her hands. Lily walked closer. No, not oven mitts, winter gloves. Blythe squinted at the coconut-water display, pulling liter boxes into her cart.

"How are you?" Lily asked.

"How do I look? Do I know you?"

"You were at my husband's funeral last year."

The hum of supermarket surrounding them became distant to Lily. Their words became isolated.

"I'm sorry I don't remember your name." Still the same perky Brit accent.

"You said being divorced was like being widowed."

"You are?"

"Lily."

"Desmond Declan's wife?"

Lily nodded. "Did you send a condolence card to me?"

"I don't remember. I'm sorry about the divorce comment. That was insensitive."

"No, I mean this week."

"No. Should I have? Please excuse me, Mrs. Declan, but I've got the flu. But it's too late in the season for flu, right? So it must be some other vile disease. I grabbed the gloves so I wouldn't spread contagion."

"Today is the anniversary of my husband's death. What're you doing here?"

"I don't understand your segue. I'm here getting something I can swallow without upchucking. I'm here avoiding death by dehydration. I should get some Vitamin Water, too."

"You said your husband walked out, and at least I had the comfort of knowing where my husband was."

"I was having a very hard time last year. I'm sorry." She wiped the gloves over her feverish brow. "I'm sure I did say something absolutely horrid. But I wouldn't have said that, since I walked out on my husband. Our marriage had been over for years. That's what everyone says when they get caught, I suppose. At least the women. The men say, 'It just happened.' I apologize for what I said. Do you want to talk about this another time, perhaps with a professional? I can't drive, Benadryl, cough medicine—maybe that's what's giving me a yakkity mouth—and I have a taxi outside, so I must hurry."

"Did you send a present to my house?"

"Do you have me mixed up with someone else? Was I supposed to send a present?"

"Do you know anyone named Jaz or Jasmine who my husband may have known?"

Lily's head buzzed. She was sure, since she'd walked down the aisle and saw Blythe Tate, that this was someone like Jaz Elwin, someone shape-shifting before her: the brown hair growing into bright orange spikes, the thick winter gloves on a warm April evening. She could hear music from the Trader Joe's speakers: "Turning Japanese." The Vapors—was that the name of the band? She couldn't remember. Remembered she'd danced to this song with Des at a club in Chicago.

"Did you ever live in Chicago?"

"I live in Hillsboro Village, ten minutes from here. No, I've never lived in Chicago."

"How close were you and Des?"

Had he worn high-tops? Lily would've been wearing heels because it was after Des's cousin's wedding. Was there a message from Des in this song: people turning into strangers?

"This whole conversation is peculiar, Mrs. Declan. Your husband was kind to me when I kept forgetting my lyrics because my husband and I were having problems. Your husband was a bass, adorable and kind, but a bass. I tend toward leading men, tenors. I never knew Desmond to do anything untoward. He was affable, not flirty. I wish you peace in whatever quest you're on."

Blythe Tate walked away, leaning on her cart. Lily continued shopping, the hum moving with her through the crowded store. She got kiwifruit for Des and the uncured pastrami that he liked. She got butter and milk, cornflakes for herself and the kids, and mini shredded wheat for Des.

She got to the checkout line and watched the clerk unload the cart. He was halfway through the order before Lily looked at the groceries and realized what she'd done.

"I'm sorry," she said. "You'll have to cancel the order. I don't feel well."

She sat in the car in the parking lot and watched people come and go. She was proud of herself that she hadn't told the clerk that she'd been buying groceries for her dead husband. Her dead husband on the one-year anniversary of his death. She'd also confronted one of Des's coworkers, who was wearing thick gloves on a warm evening.

Kevin called back while she sat in the car.

"It's a mailbox rental, Lily," he said. "Not a real address. We're here right now. Kind of a sketch neighborhood. A month's rental is $9.99. I don't know if that makes you feel better or worse."

"It looked like an apartment building when I Google Mapped it," Lily said.

"Yeah, well, the address is a storefront below the apartments. Not a great-looking apartment building, either. The 'suites' are aluminum mailboxes. Hold on, Jessie wants to talk to you."

Jessie's voice was childlike, sweet, like everyone's favorite grade-school teacher. They'd be married next month. "Lily? It's Jessie. This place is real sad. If this person was a girlfriend of Des's in college, she's fallen on some hard times. There's an old Burger King bag on the floor, cigarette butts. Some of the mailboxes are falling apart, keyed—no slots. But I have Post-its in my handbag. I could leave a note on her so-called suite number, tell her we're watching and to leave our family alone."

"I don't know, Jessie. I appreciate it, but I need to step up and write her back and tell her we're not pen pals."

Kevin got back on the phone: "You know, Lily, I think Jessie has a good idea here. I might be able to wedge the note into the box. You got family, we're backing you up."

"Okay. Yes, that is a good idea. I appreciate this, Kevin. Tell Jessie thanks, too."

They ordered pizza for dinner. Lily wondered if she should be taking antianxiety medication like her mother-in-law. But she felt perfectly calm, now at least. Just misplaced, even here in the house. Death *was* all mixed up.

Chapter 22:
Can't Stand the Rain

Working in an old mansion gave advantage to sorrow. The long hallways smelled, not unpleasantly, of decomposing lace. The stone foundation had decades ago joined with earth to scent the air with geosmin ghosts. People had lived long in this house; they'd given birth, gotten sick, died. They'd been slaves; they'd been masters. During the Civil War, the first floor had been conscripted as a military hospital. The grounds were maintained in the English-wild style. With the right moon, one wouldn't have been surprised to see a woman in a long black veil roaming the grounds.

"How was your weekend?" ricocheted off her ears Monday morning. Perhaps the one-year anniversary would return Lily to her old fun, pre-widowed self. She poured cream into her coffee in the break room.

"Very touching. The weather was great, the boys were wonderful," she answered her boss.

"Good, good. Iris reminded us of the date," Mr. Linden said. He gave her a side hug. "We worry for you." His attempt at daytime casual was a cashmere sport coat over well-creased jeans.

"Ceremonial, sweet, the boys wrote their dad letters," Lily replied to Amelia, head grant writer.

"I prayed for all of you," Amelia said. "Glad you got a rain break."

"I hope it gets better for you now," Ralph in maintenance said. "You deserve to be happy."

"Thanks, I'm sure it'll get better," Lily said, thinking, *Deserve to be happy*, like Des deserved to be alive.

"Really sucked, eh?" Iris said at her desk. She was barely in the office while she was prepping for the upcoming fund-raiser, and Lily was glad to see her.

"Yeah, it did. They gave us the honeymoon suite at the lodge by accident. On the way home yesterday, I saw one of those roadside memorials with Des's picture nailed to a cross."

"He died in the hospital, end-stage cancer. You know this, Lily. He didn't die on the road."

"I know. I lost it. Just lost it. He doesn't eat anymore, either, but last night in Trader Joe's I bought food for him. That was right after I met a woman Des used to sing with and asked her exactly how friendly she was with Des and if she'd sent a present to my house."

"A present? As in that nightgown last month? You said you thought your mother-in-law sent it."

"I kept it general. No specifics. She had no idea what I was talking about. Just another wigged-out person in the grocery store."

"Whoa, Lily. Time to get a grip."

"I also got another condolence letter from that crazy woman, Jaz, who shared some fun romantic memories and now claims Des deflowered her in college."

"Her first explosion," Iris said. "Sweet of the bitch to share."

"Kevin and his fiancée went to the return address. A down-and-dirty mailbox rental. They left a cease-and-desist Post-it for her."

"Fingers crossed."

"I know a year has passed, but it's still everywhere," Lily said.

"*It* being Des?" Iris said.

"*It* being Des dead."

"You're young, and you got two beautiful baby boys. We're all dancing on our graves, Lily."

Ah, the ol' dancing-on-our-graves bravado, she thought, remembering Des vomiting his guts out after chemo. Remembering him convulsing with fever in the ICU. These knowing little sayings from those who didn't know. This was why Lily went to grief group, to learn to take things with kindness.

"Yes," Lily said. "We're all mortal."

———

Lily picked up Sam from after-school care. He reported that he'd used his words instead of his fists when he got picked on. "It was the same thing, Mom. The same kids. But we had recess in the gym 'cause it started raining. Zeke Byron kept doing that song: *You've got a dead dad.* So I called him a fuckhead and went and got Ms. Greene."

"Do you know what *fuck* means, Sam?" Lily peered at her son in the rearview mirror.

"Well, a fuckhead is like a stupidhead but worse."

"Yes, it's worse. What did Ms. Greene do?"

"She gave Zeke a time-out through all of recess, and she thanked me for getting her. Zeke said I was a tattletale, but Ms. Greene said I was a whistle-blower."

"Did you tell her you said *fuckhead*?"

"Yep. She told me not to waste my words."

Chapter 23: Every Little Bit

Soft fuzz covered the healed incision on Gogo's shoulder. The scar around her ear was almost invisible now that the stitches were out, the cone gone. Gogo seemed unconcerned by the two-week-old trauma.

Finn and Sam went to Saturday soccer practice. Finn could never run fast enough from the car to his buds, never looked back toward Lily. Several fields away in the younger age group, Sam dawdled, making sure his mother had packed his protein bar, his Gatorade in his gear pack, waited for her to wish him luck. She loved watching each of her boys from a distance, loved seeing them in the soccer field, in a group, and knowing they belonged. Knowing she wasn't in charge of every single moment. She turned and went back home.

Lily swept the house, made beds, searched for spring and summer clothes to freshen, went through old boxes of Finn's outgrown clothes that might fit Sam. The large den closet was not so daunting since she'd gotten rid of Des's winter coats. A thick Tennessee Titans parka, a cashmere dress coat, a Lands' End canvas coat, all had gone into the fall clothing drive at Finn's school. But she hadn't been able to part with the jean jacket or the navy hoodie. She took out the hoodie—the plush comfort of sweatshirt fabric—and smelled the back of the neck. Yes, he still roamed the house in these mundane mementos—the navy hoodie, a newly found shopping list for Cumberland Hardware where his handwriting remembered Rust-Oleum and lightbulbs.

She pulled a bulge from the hoodie's front kangaroo pocket, dropped it so fast it came alive. It lay on the floor encased in a dull caul. A dead animal? An animal alive but as afraid to move as she was? She nudged it with her foot. It didn't respond. She turned it over with her foot. That's when she knew what it was. Of course it would be in the front hoodie pocket; he'd been wearing it that day. She'd heard him buzzing off his hair in the hall bathroom. She remembered:

"Where should I put the hair, Lil?"

"In the garbage."

"No, the nurse said if you cut it off early enough before it gets patchy, you can save it for a wig."

"As in *toupee*?"

"If you prefer the French pronunciation, yes, a toupee."

Then there'd been the sound of the shower running. He'd grown a soul patch the week before; the chemo eventually took that, too.

It'd been an autumn morning, hideously exquisite the way days are so close to death. Every leaf overbright. The sky wide with eternity.

She'd tried to be nonchalant when Des came into the den, looking at him from the ground up: running shoes, jeans, T-shirt, too-loose blue hoodie—he'd already lost thirty pounds—soul patch, smile, eyes—oh, those dark-gray eyes—scalp. His shaved pate was the color of bleached bone.

"Not too bad," Lily said.

"Yeah it is, but thanks." Des planted a kiss on the top of her thick hair. Walked to the kitchen and out to the backyard where the boys were.

The caul was only a thin plastic baggie. She picked it off the floor, opened it, and found it strangely devoid of Des and filled with a minty shampoo scent.

What were the guidelines for disposing of the hair of the dead? Was there a religious ceremony? Buried in the yard at midnight or left out for the birds to add to their nests? Was it good luck or bad to keep it, have it crafted into keepsakes the way the Victorians did? It felt like a small living thing in her hand, alive, abandoned, lonely.

She put the bag of hair in the bottom drawer of the desk beneath tax returns and old checkbooks and went to get the boys from soccer practice.

The one-year anniversary had come and gone, and nothing had changed except that a year was a long time. Before, she was only days and weeks and months away from Des. A year was thousands of miles between them. *You couldn't breathe, but you breathed.*

PART II

I shall be with you on your wedding-night.

—*Mary Shelley*

PART II

Chapter 24:
Stop in the Name of Love

The night was slow. A distant road sounded windy and misshapen. It was dark, and Lily didn't know where she was. She knew they'd driven to her parents' for Easter weekend and her birthday. She knew the boys were with her parents and that she'd gone out with friends. She'd ended up here in this field. The scent of grass hung in the air. She tried to focus. She put her hands out and felt earth. She realized she was lying facedown and sat herself up. The stars were spinning.

"You're pasty white," Tanya said. "Please tell me you're not going to throw up again. We'll go back to my house, and I'll make coffee. I can't take you home to your mom's like this."

"Am I okay?" Lily asked. She had to hold on to Tanya to walk, a marathon two blocks back to the parking lot. Lily was as exhausted as she was still under the influence. Her friend Tanya drove a minivan, and Lily balanced her head on her arm in the open window. The spring air rushed through her bones.

"Jesus. I had no idea you were fucked like that," Tanya said. "You'd been dancing just fine. We did 'Stop in the Name of Love' on karaoke, you remember?"

"Everybody does 'Stop in the Name of Love' on karaoke. What do you mean: *fucked like that?*"

"Drunk. Blotto. Maybe you shouldn't have switched from margaritas to piña coladas."

"How long was I gone?"

"I don't know. I thought you'd gone to the bathroom. I called on your cell after ten, fifteen minutes, and when you didn't answer, I went looking for you. Why St. Joseph's churchyard?"

"Beats me." She looked out the window. But she'd gone there to find Des. She'd lain against the earth to feel him. And it felt good.

———

She awoke as if coming out from a cave. It was afternoon. She ate a bowl of cereal on the back patio.

"I'm glad you slept in, sweetie. Your father took Gogo and the boys up to Blue Hollow Ridge," her mom said.

"Isn't that a little steep?"

"I made them take the wagon trail up. Gogo seems fine. You can barely tell where her stitches were." Ella potted red geraniums in the fallow planters that lined the patio. Lily turned away from her mother's purple garden gloves that swayed as she spoke and made Lily queasy. "I'm glad you went out with Tanya. I think it's lonely for her here with so many of you kids moved away. She's been dating Charlie Graham for years. Did she say they're still an item?"

Lily nodded. Had Tanya said that? Lily didn't remember.

"Her mom still waitresses over at the Carriage House. Told me a few months ago that she was on the work-till-you-die retirement plan. She was always funny."

Ella grabbed another six-pack of bright red blooms and turned it upside down to coax the soil plugs loose.

"Could you maybe put the geraniums down?" Lily asked.

"Sure, they're loose now. Pelargonium."

"What?"

"What we call geraniums are really pelargonium."

"That Jaz woman wrote another condolence letter for Des's one-year anniversary."

"You always think of anniversaries being festive occasions. You think they would've created another name for death anniversaries. So how bad was this letter? You got it with you?" Her mother held her purple palm out to Lily.

"No. I left it home, you'll be pleased to know. Pissed me off too much to keep it with me. She recalled fun times out dancing with Des and getting her cherry popped."

Ella stood up from her haunches, stretched her back. "They still use that expression? Sounds cheery and humiliating at the same time. She said that?"

"No, said he was her first desire and fulfillment."

"She sounds like a sad person, Lil. These are what—twenty-year-old memories she's dragging up? She sounds pitiful."

"Yeah, well, I wish she'd be pitiful somewhere else."

Lily drank her orange juice. She wanted to feel ashamed for getting drunk, but she just felt far away. She didn't belong here.

"I don't know what people do here, Mom. What kind of life is it for Tanya?"

"Your dad and I made a life here, missy," Ella said.

Des had loved it here. He was fascinated that the house was so small and the land so large. That no one seemed to know where their back property ended amazed him.

"I don't mean it like that, Mom. She works at the Denso plant restocking the warehouse. She was beside herself that I was coming with her to have a beer and sing-along. She wanted to be a park ranger when we were kids, and now she's working for an auto parts factory."

"She's terribly allergic to poison ivy; within ten feet and her eyes swell up, five feet and she's covered in blisters. And you look like you had more than a beer and a sing-along last night."

"Yeah, margaritas to start. I just took two aspirin; my head's killing me. I think Christmas was the last time I had a drink, and that was a glass of white wine."

"But it was good to be out with friends, right?" She turned to face Lily using one hand to shield her eyes from the sun.

"Yes, it was good." Except that it'd been horrible. The Backstreet Boys and Marcy Playground karaoke, the too many drinks. Tanya had called as many of the so-called old gang as possible to come join them. Lily had tried too hard to show them that she wasn't too sad to enjoy herself. Hadn't been gone too long to forget her roots. No sappy "Sweet Home Alabama" for the gang at the MexBar. These were the grand-children of hardscrabble mountain folk, except they worked in offices, classrooms, insurance agencies. It'd been horrible until she lay against the earth.

Ella took off her gardening gloves. "This was a great place to raise kids. I'm not so sure about retirement, though. If your father doesn't snap out of it after this vacation cruise, I'm sending him to the doctor's. Between Des's passing and your dad's retirement, I don't wonder that there's some depression taking hold. Aunt Ruth'll come by to feed the dogs and check the house."

"You got your money back after you canceled the cruise last year?"

"Sure did. That was two years ago, honey. Everything but the deposit. It was good for your dad to be able to come and help out when Des was sick."

Her mother handed Lily the hoe. Every autumn her mother covered the raised beds of the vegetable garden with layers of wet newspaper held down by rocks. Every spring, they hoed the paper up to admire the weed-free dirt below, all fresh for new rows of seeds.

Toward the back of the garden was her father's workshop. Owen Moore Sr. had taught music at the local high school for thirty-five years: lower-level orchestra, marching band, and advanced strings. He'd planned on becoming a luthier when he retired. Dusty wood sat on his workshop shelves, unformed into the mountain banjos and dulcimers he'd envisioned. He'd always been good with his hands. When Des came along, he and his father-in-law had spent hours working on tunings and pitch, the tonal impacts of woods. From the outside, the workshop resembled a large children's playhouse with small window boxes painted green. It was all but abandoned, Ella told her daughter as she hoed.

"I dusted the workshop last weekend. Made me sad to see it like that," Ella said. "I told your father: 'You want to pass sadness on to your grandsons, or do you want to pass music to them?'"

Pass. Lily stumbled over the word, thinking of her father's mortality. This part of Tennessee, to die was to pass. Lily had never questioned it till her own widowhood. Now it seemed too silly a way to describe the loss, a Foghorn Leghorn circumvention. *Des passed, I said, he passed, I said, he passed me by.*

Behind the workshop, bright fields warmed in the afternoon light. The April rains had brought spring to bloom. White dogwoods drifted in the hills. Wild daffodils wove through the field before the woods began.

"Lily, are you suicidal?"

"Jesus, no, Mom. Why would you say that out loud?"

"How else could I ask you without saying it out loud? It's just that I've never seen you looking so down. You're wearing pajamas, and your hair is dirty. It's two in the afternoon."

She looked at her mother and smiled. "I'm hungover, I told you. Seriously. I cannot keep up with these mountain girls. I wasn't good at drinking in high school or college, and I guess I've gotten progressively worse."

Ella's delicate face smiled. "Okay, but you go in now and take a shower and get dressed. Look like your boys' mother by the time they get back. I have half a mind to write this cherry girl a letter to stop all this nonsense."

Chapter 25: Bunny

In the morning, her mother had chocolate bunnies for the boys and they had a surprise birthday breakfast for Lily. They dressed in Sunday clothes for Easter church service.

Old friends of her mom held Lily's hands in their wrinkled hands: "Hey Lily, now how are you doing since that handsome husband of yours passed?"

Old friends of her dad shook her hand with their rough, calloused hands. "Hey Lily, you and the boys are still on our prayer list since your husband passed."

"Easter," the minister preached, "Easter means that you can put love in a grave, but it won't stay there."

He passed, I say he passed, I say he passed me by.

She left early to beat the Smokies' tourist traffic. It was not quite three and the sun was bright when they arrived home. Pulling into the driveway, Lily squinted at her house and almost reversed the car back out. Her house was decorated for Easter. It hadn't been decorated when they'd left on Thursday afternoon.

Colored Easter eggs dangled like Christmas ornaments from the pink dogwood in the front yard. Origami bluebirds were nuzzled into the crooks of the branches. She noticed these details one by one. The lawn was mowed. The privet was trimmed. The boys were still in Game Boy mode in the backseat and probably hadn't realized the car was stopped. Lily got out. Gogo bounded after her. That got the boys' attention, and they followed.

Purple and white tulips had been planted by the front ironwork fence. Over the front entrance, a purple Easter flag flew on a smooth wooden pole. On the flag were three white lilies and bold script declaring, HE HAS RISEN. *Had there been a bracket there?* Lily wondered. She'd never flown a flag.

Plastic Easter eggs dotted the lawn. The boys opened them and popped jelly beans in their mouths.

"Thanks, Mom," Sam chirped between mouthfuls. Gogo sniffed the memory of strangers on the lawn.

Had this been a church project from Holy Trinity, where Des used to sometimes attend? How would they know her family would be gone for the weekend? One of her neighbors was very religious, but aside from his tattoos, she'd never seen him display religious artifacts. She hadn't told him she'd be away. Iris knew she'd be gone, but she wasn't religious. Her brother wasn't religious, either, but his wife, Anne-Claire, was.

"Finn, did you tell the Mullens we'd be away for Easter weekend?"

"Nope. I forgot. I think they were going away, too. To their cousins' or something like that."

Lily called her brother on her cell.

"Did you do this, Owen? Did Anne-Claire have a hand in this? Thank you."

"A hand in what?"

"The yard is decorated for Easter."

"Your yard? I don't know what you're talking about."

It could only have been her mother, then. They sold these seasonal house flags at Michaels, where Ella worked. But who in Nashville could she have gotten to do this if it wasn't Owen?

She used her cell to snap a photo of the front yard and messaged it to her mom's phone. She messaged Owen a few shots.

They went through the house out to the back patio off the kitchen. There were four Easter baskets on the patio table with typed names on the tags. Candy and books for the boys, including a how to draw anime for Finn and a set of plastic game pieces titled "Gogo's Crazy Bones" for Sam. In a small basket marked for Gogo was a Kong and a rawhide chew bone. In Lily's basket was artisan lavender body lotion, handmade soap, chamomile tea bags in a yellow mug, a box of Trinidads dark chocolate encased in toasted coconut.

"Why do you look sorta bummed out, Mom?" Finn asked.

"Just overwhelmed," Lily said. "This is all a nice surprise."

"Maybe there really is an Easter bunny, Mom," Sam said. He winked, the kindergartner sophisticate.

Finn answered him, "Or maybe people really care."

Her mother called her cell. "Lily, your brother and I just talked. We were not responsible for whatever helpful things happened in your yard. Maybe it was Iris or Des's church people."

Or how had the preacher put it? Easter means you can put love in a grave, but it won't stay there.

Chapter 26:
The Only One to Thank

By morning, Lily's surprise and appreciation had worn thin. She trashed all the candy from the Easter baskets. She thought of posting **No Trespassing** signs in the yard. She checked that the Hide-a-Key was still undisturbed in its faux rock beneath leaves in the tree hollow in the backyard.

She went to get the newspaper at the end of the driveway. Her neighbor Harry called to her: "Your lawn looks great, Lily! Love the 'He Has Risen' flag." Lily nodded and waved. Harry was in his late twenties, a sound engineer for a Christian recording label. He was tall, lean, and tattoo ugly. John 3:16 was penned on his neck. By Grace Alone was cursived on his right forearm. Gal 6:17 was inked where his right eyebrow was shaved off. The top of Jesus, crowned with bloody thorns, listed over his pecs at the edge of his tank shirt. *Handsome Harry*, Des used to call him.

Lily walked over to him. "Quite an Easter surprise," she said. "We were out of town. Did you see anyone here?"

"Yeah, there was a truck with lawn equipment, and I heard mowers and a chain saw. They were here Saturday afternoon and early Sunday morning."

Lily regretted walking over. She was dressed in one of the sleepwear concoctions she'd assumed since she slept by herself: one of Des's Chicago Cubs T-shirts, threadbare and oversize, and a pair of sweatpants cut off midthigh. Harry tried not to look at her spring-chilled nipples poking against the white T-shirt. She crossed her arms with the newspaper over her chest. Harry turned his face.

"Did you see a name printed on the truck?" she asked.

"Hmmm, can't say I took a good look."

An unsettling thought: "Did you see anyone go *inside* the house?"

"In the house—no. I worked Saturday night, and I was at worship late Sunday morning, so I didn't see everything. I didn't see people inside. Was it a church group?"

"Don't know who it was. I'd like to thank them if I knew."

"Sometimes the only one to thank is God."

———

She called her brother and asked him to come by before work. He got a ladder from his truck and took down the Risen flag for her.

"They did a beautiful job, whoever it was," Owen said. "A little overkill on the decorations, but the landscaping is well done. Why are you worried? Your face looks frozen."

"This is my yard. Somebody unlatched the back gate and put baskets on my back patio." She tried to unclench her jaw, unsquinch her eyes.

Owen got out his pocketknife. He asked her for a trash bag, then cut the dangling eggs from the dogwood tree. They picked up the plastic eggs still left on the lawn. They trashed the origami decorations. It took only five minutes.

"Did you call Trinity to see if they had a hand in this?" he asked.

She'd left a message but hadn't heard back yet.

"People don't know how to help, so they do something," Owen said. "Anne-Claire tries to get me on board the gratitude wagon. She says our side of the family is still stuck in the mountains, and we don't like to be beholden to anyone. She was a bit pissed off about you leaving the Wendy's gift card in the mailbox last week. Yes, sometimes we go for dinner there with the kids when you're at your grief group. We can cover the cost of Wendy's. Just allow us to do it. You don't have to leave a gift card."

"I didn't leave a Wendy's gift card, Owen. I wish I'd thought of it, but I didn't."

"Must've been Anne-Claire's mother, then. You've been falsely accused of a good deed."

Owen walked over to the dogwood, found one more origami bluebird in the crux of a limb, and crushed it in his fist. "Sam confessed to me the other day that he'd lied to you about leaving a tip for the waitress when you were at Shawnee Lodge. He said you were freaked out, and he didn't want to get anybody in trouble."

"What? Fifty dollars, Owen. Where would he get fifty dollars?"

"From my mother-in-law. The kids were going to the video game store. Finn and Teresa both had money, and he didn't. My mother-in-law slipped Sam a fifty and told him it was just between the two of them. I didn't even know about it till he confessed. Obviously he didn't buy a video game."

"Why didn't you tell me? My kid's in trouble at school, and now he's lying to me."

He jangled keys and change in his front pocket, looked her in the eye. "Your kid fought back; he's in counseling. I thought it was sweet that he tipped the waitress. Seemed very Des-like. He said she was very nice and brought them whipped cream in a can. I guess at five years old, a fifty's as good as a one. He said he'd come clean with you when you were in a good mood. Guess you haven't been in a good mood lately."

"You think you could let me know next time?"

"Yeah, sorry. My point is, just allow people to help. It helps them. Just allow." He gestured with his calloused hands. His Titans bandanna stuck out from his back pocket.

"I get the lawn, Owen. I get what Anne-Claire is saying about being grateful, but someone sent me a white honeymoon gown on my wedding anniversary last month and didn't sign the card. Why didn't they leave a note for the lawn?"

"You told me about the anniversary present. You told me you thought it was Des's mom. I'm still not sure what a honeymoon gown is. Racy?"

"Fancy. A lacy white nightgown a woman would wear on her honeymoon night. Part of a trousseau."

"Please tell me I'm not expected to know what a trousseau is." He smiled and put his arm around her shoulder. "Anne-Claire wore REI thermals on our honeymoon. We were camping at Lake Barkley."

Lily wasn't ready to let it go. "Someone is messing with me, Owen."

"The lawn? No. The gown? Maybe. Maybe your mother-in-law has some mental health issues. I'm being polite here—I liked her until Des got sick and she got strange. I was over at Vanderbilt visiting one afternoon when she was there, and Des looked exhausted. She yelled at him to sit up straight when I walked in. I mean yelled. Good God. I'd lose it, too, if my kid was terminally ill. I just can't theorize a conspiracy."

Chapter 27: Charles Ives

Owen went to work but called her forty minutes later. The boys were eating breakfast. Lily walked outside with her cell.

"I'm thinking maybe it was somebody Des knew from the opera," Owen said. "The tree trimming was a lot of money. They trimmed the deadwood off your trees."

Lily looked up. "I thought the place looked brighter, but I didn't realize. Harry next door said he heard a chain saw."

"You got three big oak trees, that's at least a grand with a licensed and bonded arborist. Plus they cleaned out all the deadwood in the clump of sweet gum trees way in the back. That's a pain to do and time consuming with that thorny fruit. Maybe it was opera people."

"I don't have a lot of contact with them." Except for Blythe Tate at Trader Joe's, but she didn't mention her to Owen. She'd gotten a few cards from the cast and choir of the opera company and an Evite to their summer picnic last year, but she'd declined; it was too soon.

"They spent so much money on the trees and then repaired the back fence with chicken wire where it was cut through," Owen said.

"Cut through? My neighbors thought the old lilac gnarled through the fence. That's where that fawn came in."

"They probably neatened the edges when they repaired it. Yeah, a fawn could've wiggled through there. And why would anybody cut through the fence to get in your backyard? You have a latch on the gate, not a lock. They'd just unlatch the gate."

"Well, I'm putting on a lock today. It bothers me that someone knew I was away for the weekend."

"Maybe they didn't know. Maybe they thought you'd be home. It wouldn't have blown your mind like this if you were home. So they thought you'd be home, but you weren't, so they cleaned up anyway. Have you asked your neighbors?"

"Just Harry next door. He saw a truck but not much else." What would she do? Go door to door to ask?

She thought about what Owen said about her being home; if she'd been home when the yard crew came, she *would* feel differently. Why had she assumed someone who knew she'd be away had done her yard decoration?

She couldn't imagine life without her brother, especially now. She and Des had almost left Nashville several times. Once for an archival data job in DC for Lily, but she was pregnant with Sam and too busy contending with morning sickness to follow through. Two years later, Des had auditioned for a small up-and-coming opera company in Berkeley, California. He'd gotten the job, but the pay offered was less than expected. So they stayed where they were. Des told her he never expected to be a star. He had a beautiful voice, but basses outnumbered bass roles, always had. Conservatories and training programs turned out far more singers than jobs available. He was lucky to have a chorus job in Nashville, and he loved singing here.

Lily wondered later, when Des was sick, if things would've been different if they'd moved, as if cancer didn't exist in DC or California or Samarra.

Lily asked Iris if she knew anything about the landscaping at her house over the weekend. Anything about leaving Easter baskets. Had she ever heard of chocolate Trinidads?

"I don't understand your question. How would I know? Trinidad is a long way from the Bahamas. If I can do more, Lily, just say so. What about those lovely Christian people Finn hangs out with? You said they planted memorial trees with Finn. Maybe they did your yard and brought baskets?"

Finn had said the Mullens had been out of town for the weekend, but Lily called Alice Mullen anyway. Alice was pleased to hear of the good deed, but it wasn't theirs. In her small, soothing voice, she spoke of Matthew and how we are cautioned not to blow a trumpet to mark our charity and to hide from our left hand what the right hand does. It took a half beat for Lily to get that it was the gospel Matthew and not a current person. Lily was again in envy of Alice's quiet faith, her sweet voice.

Holy Trinity returned her phone call. They hadn't done her yard, but they'd be happy to help in the future.

———

The gala, a week away, now required everyone's attention. Didn't matter if you were a grant writer or receptionist or music archivist, every employee was assigned tasks for the fund-raisers. Lily and Iris had completed the catalog for *Music of the Reconstruction* months ago. Iris, with her master's degree in American music history, had written the bulk of the text. Now they were at the end of coordinating old photos from the Smithsonian and the state library for the presentation to be set up in the grand hallway. A host of local talent would perform live in the small ballroom. Dinner would be served in the grand ballroom.

"Where Are the Swallows Fled?" from an old radio tape, artist unknown, played in the background. Lily and Iris checked the loop as they sat in chairs in the hallway. Iris read aloud from the catalog as Lily checked the photos against her log.

Slide 118: Freed slave in front of shanty, Memphis.

119: Girl with cart and dog, Nashville.

"I'm having a Charles Ives moment," Iris said. "Is that 'O Sacred Head Now Wounded' you're humming? No multi-music-tasking, please, Lily. This is crunch time."

120: Sheriff and mountain still.

121: *So many dead people,* Lily thought.

Chapter 28: Our Sorrow

Lily was backlogged on her grievances to share with the Circle of Compassion. The week before, she'd shared her sunrise memorial of Des's death, omitting her run-in at Trader Joe's with the feverish Blythe Tate. She thought of recounting her margarita-swigging, karaoke-singing weekend, but it felt too tawdry to share with Mrs. H., and Yvonne, the Jesus woman, was back. Then there was her yard transformation, but her anger had dissipated with her brother's lecture. With the banner down and the decorations gone, it hadn't felt so bad the last evening coming home to her tree-trimmed yard with the freshly mowed lawn. It was Finn's job to mow the lawn with the push mower, and it never looked this good.

"Fill in the blank," Miriam said this Tuesday. "I tasted sorrow, and it tastes like . . ."

"My wife's kiss," Leon said. "Now that it's gone."

"Whiskey," Carly said. "That last slug when you know you're jumping from feel-good high to no-return drunk, and you toss it back anyway."

Lily's turn: "I brought a letter from that Jasmine woman who wrote again."

"We'll get to that," Miriam said. "How about the taste of sorrow?"

Lily shrugged, and Miriam nodded to the next chair: "And you, Yvonne. What does sorrow taste like to you?" Miriam asked.

"I like your comparison of sorrow to a taste. Sorrow is temporary. We don't have to swallow it," Yvonne said.

"Sorrow tastes like honey," Mrs. Henrietta said. "As long as I hold on to grief, I hold on to my husband."

"I got Gabe's name tattooed on my right cheek," Carly said. "It's gorgeous."

Miriam's face peered from the dark outside the circle to look at Carly's face. The assistant counselor, Renée, giggled. "I think she means her butt cheek," she said.

Miriam settled back. "Is that a substitute for sorrow?" she asked. "Or a way of moving grief from your heart to another part of you?"

Before Carly answered, Mrs. H. spoke: "Do you realize that any time you get a new boyfriend, when you get married, every time you are naked or make love, he is going to have to go through Gabe's name on your behind?"

That's all there was this Tuesday evening: Mrs. H., Leon, Carly, Yvonne, Lily, and the two counselors. It was like that sometimes.

"From behind, at least," Carly said. "And anyway, I don't want anybody getting close without knowing Gabe's name."

"To me," Mrs. Henrietta said, "it would be disrespectful to my husband to put his name on my behind."

"Different generation," Carly said.

"How would your Gabe have felt if someone else's name had been tattooed to your behind?"

"If someone else had died on me before Gabe, I think Gabe would've wanted to know," Carly said.

Lily waited till the tattoo discussion wound down. She took the letter from her purse and got the nod from Miriam to read it:

. . . By honoring what is good and right, we can lift our sorrow.
Please acknowledge my deepest condolences. I feel I am crying in the wilderness.

Your servant,

Jaz Elwin

"These personal memories are more intrusive than her last letter," Miriam said, and walked behind Lily to look over her shoulder. "And her signature's even bigger. What're you going to do?"

"Write her back," Carly said. "Tell her your husband had mentioned her and said her pussy tasted bad."

"Do you have to talk like that?" Yvonne said. "Besides it being crude, it's denigrating to women."

"Wait," Miriam said. "I want to talk about past loves. Everyone in the group here tonight is mourning a dead partner, so let me say this. The past made your partner the person you loved. We are each a group project. Let's say this Jasmine was a clingy girlfriend and taught Lily's future husband that he didn't want a clingy relationship. Whatever it was, we have to respect our partners' past relationships."

"Our dead partners," Carly said.

"This letter sounds immature to me," Renée said. "Are you threatened by these letters?"

"I don't know if *threatened* is the right word."

"Do you know her? Where are they postmarked from?"

"I don't know her, and Des never mentioned her that I remember. The postmark is from Chicago."

"Good," Renée said. "So you're not likely to run into her in the neighborhood."

"My brother-in-law went to the return address for me. It was a mailbox rental place. He and his girlfriend left a note to tell her to stop writing."

"A good idea," Miriam said. "Letting her know that this isn't some sort of private correspondence between the two of you. Letting her know that there's a whole family grieving. Yes, a whole family protecting you and that she is outside this family circle. Any other suggestions from the group?"

"Don't put your return address on the envelope when you reply," Leon said.

"She already has my address, and I'm not replying," Lily said.

"Leon is right," Mrs. Henrietta said. "Even if she has your address, it sends a message not putting it on the envelope."

"You could assume she meant well," Renée said. "Write the poor woman back and thank her for her condolences in as few words as possible."

"As in tell her to get her fucking hands off your dead husband," Carly said.

Chapter 29: Start Me Up

Anne-Claire had Lily come in for a soda when she picked up the boys. Not what they normally did. Had the boys been acting up?

Anne-Claire was pale as blue willow china with navy eyes and white skin. When they stayed away from politics and religion, Lily and Anne-Claire got along fine. They'd been roomies in grad school. She asked Lily to have a seat at the kitchen table and told her she didn't think Owen had it right about the Easter surprise on Sunday. That she never let her daughter, or any child, eat food from an unknown source, which was a battle at Halloween when she let Teresa go to only a few neighbors' houses. "They left Easter baskets, right? I understand why you're uneasy. Was all the candy wrapped?"

Yes, the candy had been boxed or wrapped. Even the jelly beans in the plastic eggs on the lawn had been in little cellophane packages. Most of it had been thrown out anyway.

"Random acts of kindness aside," Anne-Claire said, "I'd be watchful, too."

Lily drove home, turned on the radio for her message from Des. There was nothing sad about The Stones' "Start Me Up" that sounded from the speakers. There was nothing personal, either; she and Des hadn't danced to it on a special date before a wild night of lovemaking. That didn't stop her from bursting into tears on Ellington Parkway with such force that she barely maneuvered the car off to the shoulder. The music stopped when she turned off the ignition. She remembered to put the hazards on, leaned her head on the steering wheel, and wept. The boys scrambled out of their seat belts and from the backseat leaned over to paw her hair, brush her wet face, pat her back.

She turned to them to see their sad puppy faces in the dim light, confused, concerned.

Sam: "Did you get stung by a wasp or something, Mom?"

Finn: "Was somebody driving crazy? Did we get run off the road?"

"No, babies," Lily said. "I just need a minute."

Several cars dopplered past.

"It's something with Dad," Sam said knowingly to his brother.

She pulled herself together, finished the drive.

"You need to see a doctor," Finn said before he got out of the car. "You know Josh Mullen's mom is training to run a half marathon. She works out with weights, too."

———

She closed the door to the den to make the phone call, getting Gina Blanton's cell phone number from her e-mail, apologizing for calling at nine o'clock at night.

"No worries, Mrs. Declan. That's why I gave you this number. Thanks for getting back to me. I scanned a donation form to your e-mail weeks ago and hadn't heard back from you. It was marked Maywood Fertility Center. I hope it didn't go to spam."

"No. I saw it. I got your cell phone number from it. I want the sperm destroyed."

"You sound rather flustered, and that's not what you said last time we spoke. Why the change of heart?"

Lily wasn't going to tell her she'd heard a song on the radio. Of course it was from Des: his radio channels; he'd programmed every button. Dead men don't come. Dead men don't get started up again. She also wasn't going to tell Gina someone had planted a "He Has Risen" flag over her door while she was away. These were just reminders; the reality was she had two beautiful boys, her husband was dead, and the sperm hadn't been left as an afterlife surprise.

"No change of heart. I hadn't formed my decision last we spoke. Do I come by and sign papers?"

"I recall that your husband wanted to be an organ donor but because of chemo and radiation, that was denied him. We, here at the clinic, have just been notified that there's a professional couple looking for somebody of Irish descent with musical talent. There may be compensation for you. I can look into it."

"Compensation? Like money? Are you offering me money?"

"I don't know what they have in mind. I'm told they sounded very dedicated."

"Did they offer you compensation, Gina? Do I need to get a lawyer to make sure this is handled properly?"

"Of course not. It's just that I work with infertile couples every day, and I hate to dash their hope when it sounded like such a good fit."

"My guess, Ms. Blanton, is that there are loads of musicians in Nashville who've donated sperm, Irish or other."

Silence. Lily waited. This felt way too Monty Python for her anger.

"Don't worry, Mrs. Declan. It'll be handled properly. The sperm will be destroyed."

Chapter 30:
Are You Dangerous?

Lily stayed at work till five on Saturday; there were endless details to check and recheck on the day of the gala. The back parking lot was already full, and the side field was cordoned off for later valet parking. The caterers had taken over the kitchen and break room. Tents, erected the day before, were being festooned with bowers and floral arrangements. The grand ballroom had been transfigured into a formal dining hall of lavenders and burnished golds. The smaller ballroom sent out jarring sound checks and speaker adjustments. "Fund-raising is a necessary evil," Mr. Linden always said. Yet he appeared to enjoy every moment.

Lily and Iris helped where needed. Lily had the boys with her. Her brother was at his in-laws' and the babysitter couldn't come till evening. Finn and Sam played outdoors with a soccer ball most of the afternoon and were hot, sweaty, and arguing over rules when Lily collected them into the car. She waited for them to buckle their seat belts. The tape loop for the gala replayed through her head. She rolled down the windows and put the AC on high to blow away the discordant soundtrack of her life.

A metallic *whamp* jerked the side of the car. Her teeth rattled. She turned to yell at the boys for whatever they could've done only to see their own shocked expressions. A woman moved by the car parked beside her.

"You guys okay?" Lily asked the boys. They nodded.

Blood shaking her heart, Lily screamed out the window: "Hey! You just hit me." She turned off the ignition, got out, walked around to the passenger side.

"I don't know what you're talking about," the woman said. She gently closed the back door of the massive Lexus SUV.

Lily could see the dent in her silver Toyota and the brown paint from the Lexus smeared across it. She pointed at it. She looked at the woman and pointed again. The woman wore yoga pants and a Nike T-shirt. Her blonde-streaked hair was pulled tight into a ponytail. "I've been parked here for an hour, I couldn't have hit you."

"Look at the dent. You just slammed your door into my car."

"No, I didn't. I opened it a smidge to adjust the child seat."

Lily saw a head of blondish curly hair in the child seat. She took her voice down a notch. "I've got kids in my car, too. My car shook. Look at the dent."

"Are you dangerous?" the woman said, nose wrinkling and eyebrows lowered.

"What? Look at the dent!" Lily ran her hand along the scar, dark-brown paint held in its groove.

"Oh, but it's just a widdle dent. Nobody needed a Band-Aid," the woman said.

Did she have a speech impediment?

"I need your insurance card, ma'am."

"It's a teeny-weeny scwatch, and you have a bad, bad attitude."

The woman hunched her shoulders and smiled a sugary smile. No, she didn't have a speech impediment: she was a woman in her forties with infantilized speech. The skin on the back of Lily's neck prickled.

"I'm calling the police," Lily said. She walked back to look at the license plate but didn't get far.

"Okeydoke. Wet me get my insurance card for the mean waidy."

The woman flung her ponytail behind her, got in her car, shut the door, and shot out in reverse so quickly that Lily had to flatten herself against her car to avoid being hit.

Breathing breathing breathing through anger, with anger, around anger, before Lily could move, take a step to the back of her car to watch the fleeing SUV peel out of the parking lot.

Lily paced as she called the front-desk receptionist. Tiffany was working today, like all the staff. Lily told her what happened and asked her to check around to see who knew the brown Lexus SUV and driver. Could be anyone—florist, decorator, caterer. There hadn't been any sort of logo or company ID on the car, and it wasn't the kind of van you stick a magnetic advertisement on. Lily calmed enough to get back in the car.

"That was really weird," Sam said. "It was a dog in the baby seat. I thought it was a kid, then it looked at me and it was a dog, like a Labradoodle puppy. Really weird."

"You need to call the police, Mom," Finn said.

"I didn't get her license plate number in time." She'd seen a three, or maybe it was an eight, before she'd jumped out of the way. "I'll call the insurance company. The babysitter comes in an hour, so we have to get home."

"Mikayla?" Finn asked.

"Yes." Drama over. Mikayla was a Kate Middleton brunette whom the boys adored. She'd babysat for them for years. Yes, drama over, and as Lily's anger subsided, she felt big-dog tired.

Lily stopped for Starbucks drive-through on West End Avenue and remembered to turn on the radio for a message. "All I Wanna Do" by Sheryl Crow. *Yeah, some fun, Des. Thanks a lot for today's musical dispatch.* She and Des had danced to this. Des would have been a good dancer except that he was so big and shouldery and he smiled so hard when he danced. They'd been in a club in Chicago where the Latino men were sharp and angular with snap motions and serious mouths. Had he and Jasmine danced there, too, she barefoot, he in high-tops? No, she needed to let that go. It was a new club. They'd gone there in a group the night after Des's cousin's wedding.

She turned off the radio, tried to remember if her car repair deductible was $300 or $500, and paid for her coffee.

Chapter 31: The Gala

"I'm sorry, Mrs. Declan. I don't know if it's food poisoning or the flu. I was fine until a half hour ago, and now I can't stop throwing up."

Lily wanted to be angry, but Mikayla had never canceled before. Owen had gone to Anne-Claire's parents' for the weekend, but Lily called Anne-Claire's cell to see if she had an idea for a babysitter. There was no answer. Charlize was babysitting elsewhere. No answer at Rhonda's. Their elderly neighbor across the street apologized that she'd already taken her sleep medication; Lily looked at the clock. It was 7:00 p.m.

She laid out her formal dresses on the bed. *Fancy-ass attire,* Des used to call it. The dresses looked so glittery, so conspicuous. Even the one widow-black dress, a vintage Ricci from a high-end consignment store, had a puffy skirt and a cut-edge neckline. She'd worn these on opening nights when Des had sung. Even if he wasn't the star, even though it was local, they were expected to attend the black-tie receptions afterward. She decided on a beige lace minidress. It was more cocktail than formal. She tried it on and felt swallowed by it. Had she lost so much weight? No, but ten pounds showed on her small frame. It was a dress meant for a happier woman with a good haircut, but it would do, with strappy sandals and a clutch.

Black tie for the boys ended up being khaki pants and button-down shirts. Finn wanted to stay home, reminded her that they stayed by themselves sometimes when Lily took the dog for a walk, when she went grocery shopping. It wasn't possible, Lily told him, the event would go on till late, she wouldn't have access to her cell.

"Just go through the kitchen entrance and nobody will even notice," Iris told her on the phone. "We'll take turns checking on them in our office. Do not *not* come. Do not leave me here by myself with all the hauterati. I love the Facebook thing, by the way, and we'll talk when you get here."

What Facebook thing? Lily wondered. The Linden Foundation did not have a Facebook page. They had an expensive, interactive website, and Henry Linden thought Facebook too common. Maybe Iris had finally talked him into it.

———

In the back of the kitchen, which was bustling with caterers and servers, she heard a man whistling "Bye Bye Blackbird." They were single file, Lily then Sam then Finn. She maneuvered carefully, following the sound. Wasn't Des's whistle; this was higher pitched, jazzier. She found the whistling man, a maître d' or perhaps the head event planner, who stood inside the door to the dining room with an air of authority and a well-cut tux.

"Why are you whistling that?" Lily said to him.

He looked at her and smiled. "A bad habit?" he said. Brown hair, short-trimmed beard and mustache, blue eyes. The kind of face that refused to have a bad day. "I do better on 'Dock of the Bay'; want to hear?"

"No," Lily said. "Thanks, but no." Of course this was the message: Sheryl *Crow* was the singer she'd heard earlier. Des wasn't telling her to have some fun in a bar with a beer and a stranger. He was telling her he was watching out for her, like the crow on Valentine's Day.

"Are you okay?" the man said.

She wiped tears from her eyes, wondered had she worn waterproof mascara. She had to stop with the radio messages. She used them like a daily horoscope. Like messages in a fortune cookie.

"Is your name on the list?" he asked. He brandished a clipboard from the table behind him.

"Yes," she replied. "I'm an employee but my babysitter has the flu and didn't show up and I called everybody and couldn't get anybody so my boys are going to my office and then I'll—"

"That's totally unnecessary. They'll sit with you."

"I'm sure there's not room at the table. They'll be fine in my office."

"I insist, madam; please follow me. I can sit you at a table with more room." He took her by the arm and pulled-pushed her out through the main ballroom.

"Sir, you don't understand," Lily said. She was angry now. Lily saw heads turn to watch them. Finn and Sam followed like frightened ducklings in a sea of swan ball gowns and tuxedos. "Sir, I work here. You don't understand."

"I work here also, so there," he said, matching her anger with mock anger.

Do these children have five-hundred-dollar tickets? Lily read thought bubbles over the heads attached to sherbet-colored silk dresses. *Is it kids-eat-free night?*

The maître d' brought them to one of the front tables, pulled out a chair for her to sit, and proceeded to sit beside her.

"I'm Gardner Linden," he said. "I've already met Iris, so you must be Lily. We all work for my father. I used to get dragged to black-tie events when I was a kid, so I don't see why your boys can't share the misery." He said it with his head cocked to the side and a joke in his voice. He held his hand out to shake hers. She shook his hand and leaned in toward his ear.

"Thank you, but this isn't necessary, and I know these seats are at a premium. They'll be fine in my office."

"I happen to know that there were two cancellations this evening, so you'd be doing us a favor. No one wants empty seats at a banquet."

Sam was delighted. He got his Star Wars coloring book from his backpack and his box of Crayola 64s. Finn looked like he'd rather be bleeding in a shark tank.

"Thanks for humoring me," Gardner Linden continued. "Smile. Enjoy the evening." He took his clipboard and left.

Iris, seating herself beside Finn, seemed to improve his mood better than Lily's sternest looks. With Iris's help, Finn and Sam chose field greens with pecans and blue cheese over the seared Moulard breast for the first course.

"What's going on here?" Henry Linden's voice appeared at her right ear.

"Your son sat us here," Lily answered.

"And? Your boys are here tonight because? Did I miss something?"

He didn't have to say anything else. She had a job she had to keep and at that moment a boss she didn't like very much. Iris tried to speak to Linden, but he'd turned to shake hands with a tuxedoed man and a satiny woman.

They herded crayons into the backpack and left. There were waiters and conversations, comings and goings, so it wasn't too horribly conspicuous. Iris fumed. Lily kept her counsel and brought the boys to her office.

Iris knocked a little later with a tray of food for them. "I guess it's not the time or place to give Linden Sr. a piece of my mind," she said.

"The least said the better, but you go back and eat out there."

"Nope. Aside from the catering staff, there're only two other black people out there. I'm tired of getting my photo snapped every two seconds like I'm the group rep for integration. Let them pick on the couple who bought tickets and actually want to be here."

It was better in the office. The boys spread out on the floor after picking at their unfamiliar food. Finn drew robots and dragons on computer paper and begrudgingly helped Sam draw his own. The night air poured through the high-arched windows. The distant sparkle of conversation, other people's happiness, felt good across the expanse.

"You're getting your picture taken 'cause you look gorgeous," Lily said.

Iris pulled up a chair to Lily's desk, and they spread their dinner out there.

"Gorgeous and black," Iris said. She was wearing an off-the-shoulder peach chiffon that grazed the tops of her platform sandals. "Sale rack at Anthro. We need to go shopping together, Lil."

"That's for sure," Lily said. Her beige minidress felt out of date and out of place.

"I don't mean it like that. I mean we need to hang out like the old days. Go shopping. Have coffee."

Iris put down her fork, pushed her plate aside, and grabbed both Lily's hands. It wasn't an easy reach over Lily's water glass and salad plate.

"Why're you grabbing my hands? I don't give a shit about my dress. I'm lucky I made it here," Lily said.

"I don't give a shit about your dress, either. But please put on lipstick before we go back out there. Maybe blush? Not why I grabbed your hands. I just wish you had more religion because once you know that you and Des are already immortal together, you can go on with your life."

How awkward, Lily thought. Maybe Mrs. Henrietta was right and the second year was worse. Lily looked over at the boys. They weren't paying attention. She'd never heard Iris talk religion before.

"What I'm saying is I like the Facebook page. It's like making an altar. I think it's healing. You've been living in a small world for a year, and this will open the window and let some air in."

"I don't know what you're talking about."

"Des's Facebook memorial page."

"I still don't know what you mean. I don't do Facebook, and he deleted his account two years ago. There's no memorial page."

"Seriously—you didn't set up a memorial page? Des's sister set it up maybe?" Iris brought her laptop over from her desk to Lily's, pushed the plates aside, and keyed in the address.

Lily watched. There he was on-screen, Lazarus raised for tribute. Des at birth, long body and closed eyes. Des at age two, chubby cheeked and round with a Transformer proudly held up to' the camera. Iris pressed the button, and the time line became a slide show.

No sound on the slide show, thank God. Lily had listened to Des sing Verdi on a CD months ago. His voice became her dead conjoined twin for days. Rest in peace was an active voice, a command.

The slide show slid on. Des with older siblings in front of a Christmas tree.

"How dare they," Lily said. Yet there was no anger in her voice. She was looking at a Rubin's chalice, a goblet illusion. Sometimes she saw the faces, sometimes the chalice; sometimes she saw dear Des and how precious his memory, sometimes she saw the intrusiveness. She couldn't see both at the same time. Someone was fucking with her; no, someone was honoring Des. The only thing certain was the illusion.

Des in a second-grade school photo with several teeth missing. Grin bigger than his face. Des in a Halloween costume. A scarecrow? Huck Finn? Hard to tell.

"Iris, couldn't they have asked me? Why would they think it's acceptable to do this? Has to be his family with all these pictures."

"You think it was his sister? Could've been his mom or one of the brothers."

"Briana took a picture of Des and Kevin together when Des was sick and tagged Des so it went to his Facebook page. When Des saw it he said it was the first time he realized how sick he was, and there were get-well comments from people he barely knew, so he deleted his account. Briana was bent out of shape about it and wanted me to post a blog so family and friends would know how he was doing. Terminal illness by blog—very big these days."

"It was a crazy time," Iris said. Her voice was gentle.

"They had no concept," Lily said. She tried to calm herself. "Yes, I vote for Briana. I don't think Kevin has a Facebook page, and I can't imagine Craig or Deidre doing this. His mother prides herself on knowing nothing about computers and technology. His father has a prehistoric refurb Mac he uses for work e-mails. It had to be someone who has access to baby pictures and recent photos, too."

Lily stopped the slides and studied the time line. She had never seen some of these photos. Sports pictures of Des in team clusters of Little League and soccer shots from childhood. Prom pics of Des in a suit or tux with different girlfriends. There were scanned newspaper clips of Des named in school musicals and later opera company programs.

"Look at this," Lily said. "There are pics of his first communion and confirmation, but they skipped his wedding. And here are several of Des with the boys on camping trips but none of me. Like Des gave birth to the kids without me."

Had these been Chicago family outings that she hadn't been on? One looked like a picture she'd taken of the boys at Shawnee Park a few years ago. Had Des sent a copy to his mother and Briana gotten it from her?

"Are there any pictures that I'm in? Here I am insulted by this whole thing, and now I'm insulted that I'm not part of the insult."

"What's going on, Mom?" Sam asked.

"Nothing that's your business," Iris answered.

"How'd you find this?" Lily asked.

"There was a 'Like' request in my Facebook messages. I was surprised you didn't tell me you were setting it up."

"No more surprised than I am to see it." Lily continued through the pictures in search of herself. Outside St. Stanislaus church for the baptism of Des's niece ten years ago. Des, the godfather, holding baby

Fiona. Lily way in the background holding Finn's toddler hand. A Fourth of July picture with Des front and center and Lily among a large group at a picnic table behind him.

"Finn," Iris said. "Do you use Facebook?"

"No," he said. "A bunch of the girls do at school. But not a lot of the boys. The girls get crazy with it."

"Those Christian friends of yours, Finn, do they have a memorial page set up for their daughter?" Iris asked.

"You mean on the computer? Don't know."

"You go to Gilda's Club. Do you use computers there?"

"Why? Mostly we talk."

"We have to go back out to the gala now," Iris said. "It's almost nine." She turned off her laptop and locked it in her desk. "This is a tribute, you see that, right? There's nothing disrespectful here. We go back to the gala and we both smile and talk to the guests."

She handed Lily a lipstick tube that Lily held like an unknown object, staring at it. Iris handed her a compact opened to a small round mirror and lifted it to Lily's face. "We'll figure it out," Iris said.

Chapter 32:
Galas, Past and Present

The grand hallway had been fitted with long benches in the middle of the thirty-foot-wide space. The somber reconstruction photos were projected directly onto the cracked walls and synched with the crackling sound loop.

Lily had been excused from the gala last year—too soon after Des's death. The one before that, "Music from the Mountains," had been a welcome break during the bleak winter of illness. She'd had times during that night when she forgot, just forgot, that Des was sick, Des was in the hospital. Until the swirly-gown night was over and she picked up her clutch from the office and found a dozen messages on her cell. She listened to only the last one from the nurse at Vanderbilt that said: "If you could call as soon as possible."

She'd called. Leaning against her car in the parking lot in a thin emerald-green silk, grateful for the cold air holding her upright. The ward clerk put her through to Nurse Harvey (Lily remembered her—a weary, lined face over Hello Kitty scrubs).

"Your husband is missing, Mrs. Declan. Do you know where he is?"

Missing. Okay. Not dead, missing. No, she didn't know where he was. *Sometimes now you still don't know where he is. You forget.*

"We have security looking through the hospital and the security tapes, and we're about to notify the police. He left a note that he'd be right back, but that was over two hours ago. He pulled out his IV and left the floor. We had a critical patient down the hall, and we didn't hear the IV alarm. He unplugged his heart monitor. He's had some fuzzy thinking, but that's not unusual with these chemo rounds. And in the hospital for weeks at a time, never getting enough sleep between med checks and IV alarms, vital signs every two hours, lights never off all the way, patients get disoriented. He's also been prescribed some antinausea medication that can induce psychosis. He seemed fine tonight before this, though—"

She was taking too long, talking too much. "What do we do now?" Lily had asked.

"Have you heard from him? I called your house when I couldn't get you on your cell. His cell goes to voice mail."

"No, I'm coming from a fund-raiser at work. Hold on, let me check my phone." She put the nurse on hold and scrolled through her calls, her texts, her e-mails. None were from Des, none were unfamiliar. She called his cell and it went to voice mail. She went back to the call.

"Is there a babysitter at home or a family member?" Nurse Harvey asked.

"No, our boys are at my brother and sister-in-law's. It'll take me less time to drive home than to have my brother drive down from Madison. I'll leave now and call you from home."

How do you lose a six-and-a-half-foot-tall man with alarms on his IV and heart monitor? She'd spoken to Des earlier. He'd seemed tired and cheerful. They'd liked this nurse, both she and Des liked her. Jo Harvey was efficient and caring. How had she lost Des?

Lily'd found him home in their bed. He was wearing scrub pants and a hospital gown half-covered in blood where he'd ripped out the IV.

"The Uber guy wouldn't take me, so I got a taxi," he said.

She called the hospital. Told them where their patient was and said she'd bring him back in the morning. The nurse didn't like it: his meds, his state of mind, hospital policy, and insurance complications from leaving the hospital against medical advice.

"I didn't lose him. You did. I found him."

Iris touched her arm, said, "Do you need to sit down, Lily? You seem a little spaced out. We'll figure the Facebook thing out. You'll have a talk with Des's sister tomorrow."

It was all she could do not to flick Iris's gentle hand from her arm. Lily'd been angry then and was still angry now. How had the hospital lost him? How had Lily lost him? Was there a treatment they hadn't tried? A clinical trial they'd missed? Had the sperm been left for a do-over? Another chance for him that she'd destroyed?

She'd gotten warm towels and soap to wipe the dried blood off Des's arm and his chest. She didn't get far. He'd started shivering and she pulled the blankets up instead.

"Why'd you do this? If you just want to come home and stop treatment for a while, I'll always come get you. This is so dramatic, Des. Escape by late-night taxi. The nurse was about to call the police."

He smiled. "I thought this might be my last chance. Your dad isn't here this week, and Kevin's not coming till next weekend. I bought a gun tonight. It's small but it packs a wallop, the guy said. It's in the safe. Here's the key." He uncurled his fingers, held out the key to her.

"Why would you buy a gun? Last chance to kill yourself?" But it didn't match. His smile. His hand holding out the key like a present. "You would fucking kill yourself in our bed?"

"No. Jesus. And have you or the kids find me? I bought it for you."

She took the key. "I don't want a gun. We don't do guns. We don't even say words like *wallop*. You're the one who wouldn't let Finn go for a sleepover until you'd checked there were no firearms in the house."

"Your brother bought one for Anne-Claire. A little one like the one I got. It's a .22 caliber, for protection. It's something you can handle."

"Owen didn't buy a gun for Anne-Claire. She bought one for herself. She grew up around guns. But back up—you left the hospital, and what? Found some guy in the parking lot and bought a gun from him?"

"No, I'd called around, and there's this twenty-four-hour pawnshop up on Trinity Lane. It's been on my mind awhile. You got all dressed to leave the hospital one night, and I felt so bad."

"I don't know what you're talking about."

"You left to pick up the boys at your brother's. Must've been near midnight. You had on that big puffy coat and a hat and a scarf and Jesus you looked so tiny and so young and you were headed out to the street by yourself."

"So you took a taxi to an all-night pawnshop. They saw you in hospital scrubs with bloodstains, and they actually sold you a gun?"

"Yep. Computer background check took about ten minutes, and they took my credit card. You still love me?"

"You know I'm getting rid of it."

"Yeah, I figured. The receipt's in there with it. Didn't ask about their return policy. Think you can turn it in at the police station, too. I'll ask Kevin to do it. You look horrified. It seemed like a good idea at the time."

"Tell me it's not loaded."

"It's not. Ammo is in the back of my underwear drawer. You're not supposed to store them together."

"Are you out of your mind, Des? Tell me. Are you drugged out?"

"We call it pain management in the oncology biz."

Lily didn't return his smile. He reached for her hand and held it. "I'm sorry. I can't bear the thought of you without me and taking care of the boys by yourself. I'm sorry I'm dying."

Iris's hand tightened on her arm. Lily looked around. Saw the men in tuxedos. Heard the swish of ball gowns. Des was dead over a year. He would not be in her bed when she drove home tonight.

She'd double-checked that the safe was locked, put the key in the toe of her winter boots on the high shelf. It was the first time, despite the prognosis, the doctors, the hospitals, the first time it hit her that he was planning their life without him.

A night. Their life. He in his bloody hospital gown. She in her green silk gown. Beside each other in their bed. Awake. Asleep. The sky traveled to morning.

Chapter 33: Outreach

The only sign of the festivities on Monday morning was a trio of men in the damp air loading tents and linens into a truck marked Forest Hills Rentals. She'd had to get the boys up early to bring her dented car in for an estimate and repair, before school, before work. She'd paid the $500 deductible.

"Boss man wants to see you," Tiffany at reception told Lily.

If Mr. Linden said one word about her having to bring the boys. One word about being told, by his son, to sit at a front patron table. One word about having to move. Just one word.

"Good mood? Bad mood?" Lily asked. "And did you ever get a line on that woman in the SUV who hit my car?"

"I asked everywhere, kitchen, caterers, flowers, even asked security setting up at the gate to keep an eye out. Nothing. Boss's mood not bad for Monday morning. Isn't his son dreamy all dressed up? Rumor has it he'll be working here with his dad soon."

"I didn't get a good look at him. So you think I have time to drop off my purse and take off my coat before heading up to the office?"

"He just said to go up when you can."

The boys' drawings of robo-aliens and sports logos littered Lily's desk, Iris's desk, the window ledge.

"Sorry about the mess," Lily said to Iris when she arrived a minute later. Iris was abruptly dressed for spring with magenta ballet flats and a turquoise dress so bright that Lily's eyes twitched. A yellow scarf completed her brilliance.

"Are you kidding? I'm going to have them framed. Did you talk to Des's people about the memorial page?"

"I slept till noon. Put out some calls and haven't heard back. Except my mother, I got her on the phone. She pulled up the page, and we both cried. She called around, just in case; nobody on my side set it up. They wouldn't have access to the Chicago pictures anyway. Linden wants to see me. I'm going upstairs. Do you know if I'm in trouble?"

"For what? Your babysitter being sick? You can handle him. Remember to call him Henry."

———

Henry Linden gestured for Lily to sit and came out from behind his desk. He pulled over a chair not far from Lily's. Lily could see the family resemblance. But Gardner was dark to his father's light hair; Gardner was designer stubble to Henry's polish.

"I was taken by surprise when I saw your children at the front table. I pride myself on a child-friendly work environment."

She was silent and folded her hands in her lap. Mr. Linden folded his hands in his lap. Lily and Iris had speculated that Mr. Linden had gone to a management seminar at one time and they'd taught him mirroring—to no good effect. She unfolded her hands and watched him do the same. It was always like this. She fought the urge to stand up and dance.

"You wouldn't have even seen my boys if your son hadn't insisted on bringing us into the dining hall and then parading them to the front. My babysitter had the flu, Mr. Linden."

"Of course childcare is difficult for you. I guess I thought you just plopped yourself down there. My son says I fall back into CEO mode too quickly. A habit I'm trying to break. I left corporate life for just that reason. It destroyed, no, *I* destroyed two marriages with my attitude."

Too much information. She didn't really care about his failed marriages at this moment. She stared out the window behind Linden's desk. Treetops and sky. The quick dart of birds. He turned to look also.

"Gardner told me afterward that you had fought him on his suggestions. The conceit of good intentions. And when I told him about your husband, he was even more upset with himself. What those boys have been through. And how you've watched over them. And I compounded the whole thing and further embarrassed you and embarrassed your sons." He paused for a breath. "Please accept my apology."

She couldn't accept it fast enough. But he wasn't finished:

"Lily, one of my friends at the dinner Saturday night reminded me, seeing your boys, that the symphony has a school outreach program. Why don't we have a school outreach program? The paucity of folkloric music among school children is alarming."

"Yes," Lily answered. "Alarming."

The phone rang. Mr. Linden answered. Lily was dismissed.

"He wants to have a school outreach program," she told Iris back in the office. "And he did apologize."

"You find out any more about that woman who hit your car?"

"No. And I'm going to put it out of my mind. And I appreciate your sanity Saturday about the memorial page. Like you said, it isn't disrespectful. It *is* a tribute."

"I've changed my mind about that. At first I had a good feeling, but that was when I thought you'd set it up. Now I don't know. The way you weren't front and center. And it has to be from Chicago with the old family memorabilia. I don't know why I thought it was Finn."

"It's fine. No worries. And there's nothing bad on the page. It's just one more thing I'm not in charge of."

"But consulted on, Lil. Asked to participate. Nixed if you didn't approve. I found a form at Facebook where you can submit a request to delete someone else's account. You tell them why it should be removed—that's all."

They filled it out together, emphasizing the posting of private family photos. Lily had no illusions that the page would be shut down. No one was pretending to be her, none of the photos were objectionable. But they sat and filled out the form and submitted it, immediately receiving the name of a "grievance officer" who would get back to them in a "timely manner."

Chapter 34: Disney World

Miriam presented her exercise for the evening: "Pick a place where your beloved liked to visit, a childhood spot, a vacation locale, perhaps a place where *you* would be comfortable knowing they were there now. Your own version of a heaven, if you will. Where would that be and how would you get them there? This is a visualization exercise, so you can be creative."

Carly rolled her eyes. Lily nodded to her. It seemed silly some nights, their artificial intimacy, like they should all have shots of whiskey to spill their guts and go on to the next morning forgetting what they'd revealed the evening before.

"Heaven," Carly said. "That kind of old-fashioned angels-singing, streets-paved-with-gold heaven that you believe in when you're a kid. I could just let him go. Like he was a bird or a spirit and he could fly up on angel wings." Her voice was balanced between sarcasm and hope; Lily couldn't read her tone.

"I'd sit him at the kitchen table with a cup of coffee and the newspaper and the kids having cereal and dishes in the sink," Mrs. Henrietta said. "And I'd tell him I'm sorry. Part of me blamed him. I always thought a positive attitude left no room for illness. And once he was sick, an optimistic approach would cure him. I would say I'm sorry, and I would just let him be, in the kitchen, in the morning, with his family."

"Disney World," Olivia said. "My partner had never been and had always wanted to go. I'd just put her in the car, maybe a convertible, and drive her. We'd both be drinking milk shakes. I fed Meghan Sustacal when she wanted shakes from Bobbie's Dairy Dip."

"Lily?" Miriam waited.

"Someone started a Facebook tribute to my husband. I don't know who it was. I've put calls out to relatives and haven't heard back. My friend asked my son if he knew anything about it, but he doesn't have a Facebook page. He says only the girls—he's in seventh grade—do Facebook." She spoke fast, as if her voice took up too much space.

"Lily, could we come back to this after the exercise? Is there a place where you can picture your husband? A place where he'd be happy?"

They waited. Miriam was silent. She scribbled notes on her clipboard. Renée, beside her, scratched at her ear, then found a ripe spot on the inside of her wrist and had at it in a noisy nails-on-flesh extravaganza.

"No," Lily said. "I can't do this cutesy stuff tonight."

Night swallowed the last of the swampy light outside.

"That's fine," Miriam said. She nodded to the woman across from Lily.

"With me," a woman said. She'd come late and hadn't introduced herself. She rocked back and forth in her seat. "With me. With me. With me." She was tall and regal with that mahogany red hair that'd been popular five years before. She had a prim mouth beneath manic eyes. She looked up from under her halo of grief and held Lily's eyes. "With me. With me. Dead. Alive. With me."

Chapter 35: Mark T'Wayne

There was shit in the mudroom when they got home. There was a storm of poly foam over the mudroom floor, white and fluffy, except where it was dipped in shit.

Gogo, lowered head and hunched dog shoulders, shimmied past Lily to the hallway.

"Get the dog!" Lily yelled. She kept Gogo in her crate at night and in the kitchen while they were gone during the day. She had a high dog gate on the door between the kitchen and the hallway. At the back of the kitchen, the door to the laundry/mudroom was open. She couldn't remember if she'd checked it before she left.

"Put her nose in it, Mom," Sam said. He pinched his nose shut with his fingers so his voice was a nasal whine. "That's what they do at Grandma's. Put her nose in it, then hit her with a newspaper."

Lily yanked plastic grocery bags from below the sink to scoop up the dog shit. "Just get the dog, Sam."

"No," Finn yelled from the bedroom. "Don't you dare hit her!"

It was the first time Lily had ever heard his voice crack. Unmistakable. They were heading into uncharted territory.

"Nobody's hitting anybody," Lily yelled back. She gagged several times and clamped her mouth shut against the rising mac-and-cheese in her throat. She put double grocery bags on both hands and managed to not breathe as she scooped the mess up. "Put her outside, damn it."

Then she saw one of Finn's new soccer cleats chewed up along with the poly foam that had been Gogo's bed. The "indestructible" dog bed was only a month old. Finn's cleats were only just broken in.

"Screw you, Mom. She was Dad's dog, and you never liked her," Finn screamed from the doorway.

She almost threw the bag of shit at him. Was this what teenhood was going to be like?

"I like Gogo," Lily said, almost whispered so she wouldn't scream. "And she rarely has accidents. I like how she plays with you boys. But she scares me a little. She's so big but still has so much puppy energy. I miss your dad. I miss him badly. Don't use that language, Finn. It hurts my heart. It's disrespectful. Fair warning: if you speak to me like that again, there will be no basketball or baseball games on TV."

Finn did his best to quell his anger. "I can give you some tips on how to handle her, Mom," he said. "And I'm sorry she ate my cleats. Coach said he could help if we can't afford them."

"Is that what he meant when he asked if we needed help? I buy you your uniforms and shin guards and shoes."

"Well, not really. The last two pairs of cleats I've taken from the discard bin in the P.E. room. I know they're expensive."

"We're not poor, Finn. We're not rich, but we can afford new shoes."

"I was trying to help."

"You do help. Thank you." She held out her arms for a hug. He grinned and walked away. She was still holding the bag of shit. Shit was still smeared on the double grocery bags on her hands.

Finn and Sam took a flashlight and walked Gogo around the block. The boys were in bed before Lily finished cleaning the mudroom. The smell of Lysol drifted through the house. She took a shower before she opened the mail. Small block print on the outside of a business envelope, typed letter folded inside:

Dearest Lillian,

I am disappointed in you. Why haven't you acknowledged my letters and the lovely memories I've shared? I'm sure you must be very busy. Or perhaps you have moved on. Remember that the boys need time and attention at their age. Also remember that Desmond's death is new to me. I don't know if I can ever move on.

Thought of other Desmond stories this week. I told him once, when we were planning to be married and I was teasing him about his Samuel Clemens proclivity, that we could name our firstborn Langhorne. He answered, no, too old-fashioned, how about T'Wayne? I laughed till I cried.

I'm crying now, Lillian. We have a lot in common. We could find solace together. My heart to you in your pain.

Jaz

The large cursive signature was in red. *Enough.* Lily thought she'd heard the last of Jaz after Kevin and Jessie had left the note on her rented mailbox. Now this stranger was giving her child-rearing tips? No. Lily went to the den and took a small white note card from the desk.

Dear Mrs. Elwin:

Thank you for taking time to write. The memory of my husband's life and death is still painful and raw. Because of this, we will not be corresponding. Enough.

Sincerely,
Mrs. Desmond Declan

Chapter 36: Life Is Short

The third day, the rental car still felt unsettling. It was a Chevy Aveo and smelled of new-car plastic. The radio's preprogrammed stations did not bring Lily messages from Des. Of course they didn't, yet she'd listened so carefully to Counting Crows sing "Mr. Jones" on the way to work and tried so hard to figure out the meaning before she remembered these weren't Des's radio stations. Remembered that she was going to stop this small madness.

Morning mist settled in on the Linden mansion. The grounds seemed more 1800s than Facebook. More "The Long Black Veil" than the cell phone in her hand and the Starbucks coffee container in the cup holder. The phone rang while she was still in the parking lot—Briana.

"Lily, what's going on?" Briana asked. Her voice held a taut line between sleep and anger. "You left four messages about setting up a Facebook tribute to my brother. Am I supposed to contribute photos? Could we not do this so close to Kevin's wedding?"

"The tribute is already set up. I was hoping you could tell me who set it up without my permission."

"I don't know what you're talking about, and I'm too tired to play games." As a charge nurse, her twelve-hour shifts could easily stretch to fourteen or fifteen hours. "The God Squad," as Briana called all things emergency room.

"There's a tribute, dedicated to Desmond Declan, on Facebook. Complete with a slide show like you wanted for Des's memorial."

"You called me up for this? This is an emergency? I just got home from work. One of your messages said to call you *immediately*. On Sunday we had a madhouse between a boating accident and pertussis. Yesterday we had a school bus go off the road—eighteen kids, three of them critical."

"Well, I'm thinking of going to the police." *Where did this come from?* Lily asked herself. She always felt the need to escalate with Briana. The way she dismissed Des: *Well, you keep singing, Baby Bro. Me, I'm out saving lives.* "I wanted to give you the opportunity to get rid of it. Before I take further action."

"You mean someone, obviously not you, and not me, by the way, put up a tribute to Des on Facebook? Maybe one of your or Des's friends? So this is an emergency and you're going to the police—do I have this correct?"

"I didn't authorize photos of my sons to be put up there. I did not give permission."

"I didn't ask permission 'cause I didn't put it up. Are these weird pics of the boys? Some kind of child porn thing?"

"No. Not at all. But they're private photos."

"As in somebody came in your house and robbed them?"

"No. I mean, I don't know."

"Lily, I don't mean to get too personal. Hold on, let me go outside for some privacy."

Lily heard movement and her brother-in-law's muffled voice. Briana *always* meant to get too personal. When Des and Lily were first dating, Briana had called her aside to ask what birth-control method she was using and went on to tell her about her IUD insertion.

Briana was back. "Are you in therapy, Lily? I personally feel I don't get the sympathy I could use from my family. You probably know all this from my mother, who is known for sharing. I took Des's death real hard. Like I should've been able to protect my baby brother. I save lives every day on the job. I talked to the priest at my parish, and he really helped. I know you're not Catholic so that's not going to help you. I also know you were upset with me for having my heart set on a slide presentation at his memorial. I wanted people to see him in context. He was a family man, a brother, your husband, a son, a father. Not just a cancer victim. That's all. I did not set up a Facebook tribute to him, with or without anyone's permission. I don't have time for social media. The last time I looked on my Facebook page was probably Christmas. But I got to say, a tribute page seems like a nice thing. So get help, Lily. For the boys' sake. If anyone knows you're hurting, it's me. You have two small kids and life is short, believe me."

Lily held the phone away from her face at arm's length, yet she could still hear Briana.

"I'm reminded of this every day on the job. Life is even short for kids, Lily."

She brought the phone back to her ear. "I'm sorry I bothered you, Briana. I really am."

"No, don't worry. I'm sorry you accused me, but at least this is good we're talking. I like it better when things are out in the open and not having my mother, whom I love deeply, as the intermediary. Let me get some sleep. I get to a point where I can't see straight until I get sleep. Then I'll look on Facebook and see if anything looks familiar. I'll call my mother, relatives. Maybe it's somebody on this side of the family. I'll take care of it if it is."

"Thanks, Briana. I appreciate your checking on this."

"You and the boys are coming up for Kevin's wedding, right? Let's keep this out of the wedding excitement, if you don't mind. Good Lord, it's getting nutty. Little Kevin and his pretty little mouse bride. You met her at Thanksgiving, right?"

"Yes. She's lovely. I've met her a few times. I don't think Kevin's on Facebook. Jessie wouldn't do something like this, would she?"

"I can't imagine. She didn't know Des. Didn't even meet Kevin until ten months ago. Look, Lily, Kevin's never really had anybody serious, and we're all happy for him. So I'd like you to keep the drama down before the wedding. No Facebook accusations, no Des's old girlfriend inquisitions, like with my mom."

"I have no intention of adding to the wedding drama. I'm happy we all have something to celebrate."

"Thank you. It's not just my brother and your husband who died. It's my mother's child. Mom's doctor has her on antianxiety meds, and she's in a fog. I want to get her through the wedding without any major scenes."

"Yes, of course." *So many with dibs on the dead,* Lily thought. She watched Iris park her BMW station wagon on the far side of the parking lot. Iris almost skipped across the lot to the employee door. Red skinny jeans with a white lace peplum top. Her hair was pushed back with a sparkly headband. She waved at Lily with an armload of bangle bracelets. *Is Iris in love?* Lily wondered.

Lily kept her headphones on most of the day, watching Iris in her spring uniform. Over baggy jeans, Lily wore a black-and-beige-striped cotton sweater, like prison wear next to her coworker. Lily envied the Victorians with their grief color coding: black to gray to mauve. She wished she had a place and time for her sorrow. That she could go away to a four-year private university of mourning. She would be a diligent student. She would graduate and come back into the spring of this world.

Chapter 37:
How Do Widows Smile?

Lily's self-consciousness bordered on adolescent. If she wore the pastel blue dress with the twirl skirt to the wedding, would it look too festive? The navy dress looked like something you'd wear to a funeral if you didn't do black. She wanted to look happy for Kevin's wedding, but Des was dead. How do widows smile?

She wore the navy dress to the rehearsal dinner. The boys were consigned to a table of cousins to eat pizza, leaving Lily with relatives that she knew she knew but couldn't remember all their names. Briana caught her in the bathroom and added a silver scarf that was big enough to be a shawl. Lily thanked her and couldn't figure a way to get rid of the large square cloth that made her feel like an Ellis Island refugee. She hadn't realized that the rehearsal dinner would be so casual with most of the women—girls, really—tossing back their heads and prancing, dressed in leggings with flowery silk tops. Jessie, the pixie bride, wore straight-leg jeans with a metallic gold T-shirt and peep-toe platforms. Lily felt far removed from their happiness, their flower prints and pastel shoes, their certainty that things turn out right in this life.

Between salad and appetizers and the excess of toasts, Lily went to the stairwell and called her mother because she thought she was losing it because she couldn't remember (*couldn't remember*) where she and

Des had had their rehearsal dinner, what she had worn, how she had smiled, who she had been when she also believed that things turn out right in this life.

"Oh baby, you didn't have a rehearsal dinner, remember? We were going to go down to Conti's for Italian, but there was that big snowstorm in Chicago and flights were canceled and we didn't know when anyone was coming in so we ended up having Chinese takeout over at Aunt Ruth and Uncle Dan's. Remember?"

Yes, now she remembered. The white boxes with the red dragons printed on them, the fortune cookies. They'd laughed over her father's fortune, whatever it'd been.

"Now, go back in there and brave it out," her mother said, and Lily tried wrapping the shimmer shawl once again.

During dessert, Jessie came and knelt beside Lily's chair. She thanked her again and again for coming. "This must be a herculean effort on your part. Any more problems from the mailbox rental girl?"

Nothing that belonged here at the wedding. Lily shook her head.

"Good. Kevin and I went back there last week—it was on my mind with you coming—and her mailbox was cleared out, open and empty. Guess she took the hint. I'm so happy you've come. It makes me feel like you're giving us your blessing and Des's blessing and giving permission to Kevin to be happy. I mean if Kevin and I have half the happiness you and Des had, well, I couldn't ask for more." And breathless with even more happiness, Jessie moved on.

Lily almost relaxed. Jaz must've gotten her note or the combination of Jessie's Post-it and Lily's note. She must have taken it seriously to shut down her whole mailbox rental.

Des's mom was on antidepressants and antianxiety medication, which seemed to do little more than paint a pink rictus on her sad face. Des's dad guarded her with quiet attention.

Kevin caught Lily in the hallway, hugged her and told her to please disregard any of his mom's calls for family silver and furniture. They already had plenty, he assured her, and were having enough trouble trying to combine their two apartments into their new condo. Kevin looked nothing like Des. He was gangly with dark-blond hair and a gold beard that gave him a young Viking look. But he smelled like Des when he hugged her.

The weekend's designated carpools were jumbled from the start. Out-of-towners had been asked to leave their cars at the hotels, since parking was limited at the venues. Lily and the boys waited in the lobby after the rehearsal dinner for forty minutes. She sat with her mother-in-law and forgave her immediately and wholly for her phone rants. Kaye was just seventy, but her age had come on quickly this past year. Her hands shook, and there was a layer of puffiness on her slender frame.

"We did it, Little Des," Kaye said. Her speech was slow. "We showed up and we smiled. We'll do it again tomorrow." Finn she called Des. Sam she called Kevin. Lily motioned gently for the boys not to correct their grandmother. Maybe Kaye had sent the white nightgown. Maybe she had called in the middle of the night and hung up; Kevin had thought it was her. She was overmedicated and confused. Maybe there were two of her now, the sane, angry one who denied sending the gown and the medicated one sitting beside "Little Des" in the lobby. Lily had Finn walk his grandmother to the door when Pops pulled up.

In the morning, there was a private buffet brunch at the hotel. It wasn't everybody from the wedding, just the friends and relatives staying there, but it was still too many. Each greeting to Lily from these almost strangers consisted of how happy they were for Kevin and Jessie and how sad they were for her and the boys. Lily said thank you and nodded. Finn tried not to roll his eyes. Sam used his five-year-old little-man voice and said "much appreciated" with a deep mumble that made him sound like an Elvis impersonator.

Chapter 38: At Last

Lily wore the pale-blue dress for the afternoon wedding. If she balanced the twirly skirt with a sad smile, it would do. She'd gotten clip-on ties for the boys because only Des knew the secret of necktie knots. The ceremony and church-hall reception were across town, and they waited in the lobby for a ride, which ended up being with Des's aunt.

"I hope you'll forgive my sister for asking for Des's family heirlooms back," the cheerful Marjory said. "Hopefully none of us will know what it's like to lose a child, and it's made her a little crazy to get back his things."

"I am Des's family," Lily said. Had the entire clan been enlisted to hound her?

"I didn't mean it like that, hon. Just the stuff you wouldn't want anyway."

"I haven't gone through everything yet."

"No time like the present. It's been over a year."

"I work full-time. I'm on my own with the boys."

"We could help, Lily. You're an independent gal, which is to be admired, but everybody needs help sometimes. My daughter-in-law has a van. Let's see about us coming down some weekend and helping you get organized. Clear things away for you. There's nothing wrong with accepting help."

It wasn't till halfway through the reception dinner that Lily realized she and the boys hadn't been put at one of the family tables. Had Des's death undone everything? What the fuck? They were at a back table with two priests in their sixties who taught at the Catholic high school that Kevin and Des had attended. There was also a singleton about her age named Nia or Nida and a friend of the bride's grandmother. The band's dinner set consisted of too-loud easy listening. Before the cake was cut, the boys wandered off to the growing ranks of cousin gangs.

"At Last," of course. "At Last" was the new couple's wedding song, just as it had been Des and hers. If there hadn't been a cup of coffee and a pre-cake fruit pastry on the table in front of her, she would've put her head down and wept. Trying to be festive had frayed her. She wondered if she could call a taxi to leave. Instead she found herself on the dance floor in a line beside Finn and Sam. "Shawty Got Low." "Brick House." The songs jumbled in her head. "Super Freak." She felt dwarfed by other people's gladness.

Craig grabbed her elbow as she went to sit down and said Nia from her table was leaving and would be happy to drive her back to the hotel if Lily wanted to leave. Had they read her mind? Craig and Deidre would watch the boys and drive them back afterward. She hugged him. He smelled like Des, too.

"Nia is a friend of Deidre's, and we knew she might not want to stay the whole time. I know Briana talked to you about sitting at a back table so it would be easier on you. It felt weird to me, and Kevin protested, but Mom thought the priests being at your table might help, too."

"Help what?" Lily said. "And no, Briana didn't discuss it with me, Craig. I know this isn't the time or place to be angry, but I'm confused. Is Briana angry with me?"

"No. Well, she's always a little pissed off at the world. She said she didn't want Mom upset."

"I'm happy to leave early with your friend."

"You know I don't agree with Briana."

"In the big scheme of things, Craig, it doesn't matter where I sit. Just felt out of place, that's all."

"I don't agree with Briana about the Facebook tribute, either. Could we go out in the hall a minute?"

They left off speaking too loud over the dance music and went to the hallway off the kitchen. Lily leaned against the wall; her strappy sandals had cut a red mark across her ankle. Craig did look like Des but an older, more *GQ* version.

"I looked at the page again this morning, and it's changed. Did you see?"

"I left my laptop at home, on purpose so I wouldn't look. I promised Briana no drama at the wedding."

"Briana thinks the Facebook tribute is just Des's old Facebook page updated. She said all somebody would have to do is submit Des's obituary with a request to change it to an open-format memorial page."

"Except Des deleted his account two years ago. He said he didn't want a sympathy site after Briana posted a picture of him following his first chemo."

"Just telling you what she told me yesterday. Deidre and I looked when you'd first called. This morning it was updated with Des's likes: films, bands, sports teams. All seems sort of what I remember him liking. And his profile picture is changed—this goofy picture from eighth grade, barely looks like him, and somebody named Dharma-69 has sixty-nine entries in the comment section, same thing each time: something about kids running in the yard and Desmond and Molly Jones."

"What—from The Beatles song? Des used to sing that to me sometimes."

"I take it you're not Dharma-69. Briana thinks you might've done it and that you're trashing something serious because you don't agree with it."

"Bullshit. This is getting way too junior high for me. And for those of you—as in Briana—not generationally Facebooked, just because it's an open forum doesn't mean anyone can change the profile pic or add likes."

"I'm also generationally handicapped. I have no idea. It's just trashy now. Weird."

"My friend Iris found a request form last week to have the page removed. Let's see what happens with that. You're good watching the boys, right? I'll go find my ride."

Yes, it would feel better to leave. Lily spied the boys on the dance floor doing the Electric Slide in a long, smooth line with the bride on one side and the groom on the other. They were safe here and maybe even joyful. She was the only one out of place.

Chapter 39:
There Are Worse Things

It was still early outside the disco-ball sparkle of the church hall. The evening sky was smeared with a yellow haze that colored the streets sepia. From the windows of Nia Summerwood's car it was still spring, still people coming and going who had nothing to do with the wedding celebration and Lily's discomfort.

Nia was content to drive without chatter, which suited Lily. Sitting quietly in the passenger seat, Lily realized how stiff she'd been holding her body all day. She uncurled little fists that were her hands. She stretched her fingers, lowered her shoulders that had gotten trapped around her ears. Unsmiling her pretend smile brought a real smile to Lily's face and a chuckle, unbidden.

"Something funny?" Nia asked.

"No, sorry. I'm widowed a year now, and coming to the wedding was a little more than I could handle. It feels good to be outside."

"I'm sorry. I know you're Desmond's wife."

"Yes. Did you know him?"

"Not well. I mean, everybody knew everybody in the parish, but I was a few years younger. This was back when a year or two younger was a different universe."

Lily nodded. The silence was easy as Nia negotiated the expressway ramp. Nia wore a sleeveless silk dress in a rich burgundy that made Lily's baby-blue dress feel Eastery and hick. Nia had short, dark hair, tousled above even features and bright-blue eyes.

"Brave of you to come," she said. "Deidre assigned me to watch out for you, but you did great."

"Gee, thanks." She'd been assigned a person? "Listen, if you didn't want to leave early, please go back. I can take a cab."

"I phrased that poorly. They were concerned for you, that's all. I was ready to leave an hour ago. My husband's not feeling well."

Car lights began to erase the evening sepia. Lily had crossed these streets a hundred times with Des driving. The shoreline, the skyline, the Chicago-ness, now seemed jagged and out of form.

"You're at the Hyatt? Do you mind if I stop off at my apartment? I want to check on my husband. I probably shouldn't have been gone so long. Won't take a minute."

Lily nodded. No drama. She'd promised no drama at the wedding.

The North Shore luxury high-rise shimmered with glass and steel and money. Rings of rosebushes encircled a wide fountain at the entrance. The doorman opened the driver's side.

Nia came around to open Lily's door. "You must run up with me. I can't very well leave you sitting in the car with tears streaming down your face."

Lily felt her sodden face with her hands. After the exertion of looking cheerful the past two days, her face had taken on a life of its own.

"I'd rather wait in the car. I'll be fine," she said.

"Of course you'll be fine. It was silly of your sister-in-law to ask me to watch over you. But I did promise I would, so as a favor to me, please come up. It'll just be a minute."

A car pulled up behind them. Nia still held Lily's door open. "Deidre and I are in a church group together," Nia said. "I'm fairly new to the group, and she's been a sweetheart to me."

Lily got out of the car. The elevator to the sixteenth floor was mirrored, which Lily used to Kleenex off the mascara fallen with her tears. Maybe they'd been right to assign her to someone.

The condo's living room was dim, but a picture light illuminated a wide painting on the distant wall. Lily recognized the landscape as something old and French. Without asking, Nia clarified, "Frédéric Bazille."

"Hmmm," Lily said. She might've known the name once.

Nia hit a switch, and a floor lamp came on. "Make yourself comfortable," she said, and gestured toward a grouping of dove-gray club chairs.

Lily sat uncomfortably in a comfortable chair for longer than she wanted. She could hear her hostess moving in another room, maybe the kitchen. Lily watched the sky through balcony doors. *Better than another three hours at the reception,* she reminded herself. A metallic jangle disturbed the sunset. Then a groan: deep, male, sudden, and close. Lily stood and wasn't sure if she groaned back in surprise. She knocked against a chest-high chinois screen cordoning off a man in a hospital bed. The bed, the man, the groan were out of place in the expanse of the plush living room. No, she realized, it was the plush living room that insulted the presence of this so human creature.

"Sir?" Lily said. Was this the husband who quote unquote wasn't feeling well? He lay on his side, unmoving, his head slightly raised on the angle of the bed. She moved so he could see her. She caught his eyes, angry and dark amid thin, folded skin. His small hairless head looked like a turtle's emerging from rounded shoulders and heavy blankets.

"Nia?" she called toward the hall.

"Oh, have you found my sweet Jude? I'm sorry you are widowed, Lily, but you see there can be worse things than death."

Jude's angry eyes grew wider. Lily followed the path of Nia's voice to the kitchen.

"Jesus, Nia. He heard you."

Low-hanging handblown glass shades lit a marble island where Nia crushed pills.

"Do you think he knows what's going on? He has brain damage. I *hope* he's only dimly aware. He was, *is*, a remarkable man. He was a real-estate broker. Smart, personable. He had this passion for matching companies to their perfect place in the universe." Nia crushed the pills harder with the mortar and pestle. "Bringing people who make things and make things happen to the spaces where they're able to create. Here, take this protein shake for him. I've got to fix his meds."

Lily took the insulated cup thrust into her hand. A plastic straw was also shoved into her hand. "Don't worry, the lid's on tight," Nia said.

The bed was freestanding. There was a small table.

"There's a lamp," Nia called. Like an obedient child, Lily turned on the bedside lamp and set the cup on the table.

"You can see the hole where the straw goes. It's a bendy straw."

She was supposed to feed him? In the lamp's glow she could see he was young. Hard to tell exactly, but closer to thirty or forty than the elder she had thought. His skin was yellowed with illness. He closed his eyes, breathed a softer groan. Lily poked the straw into the lid. Was the bed up high enough for him to sip? She held the cup over the rail. He opened his eyes and sipped small sips laden with effort. He held his mouth to the straw between sips so she wouldn't take it away.

Was this why she'd been brought here? Lily wondered. To see that there were worse things than death? For better or worse. Having Des like this might comfort her. But for him?

"Jude was only thirty when it happened," Nia said. She plopped a pudding cup on the night table and mixed in the ground pills. "Keep at it," she said. "If his mouth and throat are too dry, he can't get the medication down, even in pudding." She moved to the other side of the bed. "We're hoping to avoid a feeding tube."

The illuminated city in the windows framed Nia on the other side of the bed. She pulled on white latex gloves with a model's flair, sensual and slow. It embarrassed Lily, holding her fingers to the bendy straw at this woman's husband's mouth. Lily looked away.

"It was a car crash," Nia said. "His father was driving. It was an accident, we know that, yet Papa had been angry at Jude for having married down, as in, for having married me."

Nia made a display of moving her hands beneath the covers, intent, fiddling with something, a diaper, flesh. Lily tried to focus on the mouth, the straw.

"Of course, his papa loves me now, in more ways than one. Oh my, you love our dear Lily, don't you, Jude? I can certainly feel it."

Lily pulled the straw away, placed the cup on the table, and moved back from the bed.

"I'm sorry, was that inappropriate of me? I didn't mean it the way it came out. His father loves that Jude married someone with good nursing skills who will love his son forever."

Lily blushed, glad she'd stepped out of the light.

"I can't see his eyes," Nia said. "Do me a favor and read his eyes for me. We're not sure if he comprehends. It's one blink for yes and two for no. Jude, do you understand me?"

Lily took a step forward and saw a slow and clear blink once. Lily nodded.

"Okay. Are you hungry?"

Again the clear blink once. Lily nodded.

"Do you walk to work or carry your lunch?"

"Nia, I'm leaving."

"Please lighten up. It's like consulting a Magic 8 Ball. You start to develop a morbid sense of humor to keep going. I'll take you to your hotel."

Nia removed the latex gloves with practiced ease and threw them in a trash can. "You wear your widowhood like a crown, and while it's very attractive on you, you are not the only one with sadness in your life. I get down on my knees every night and pray for a different life. We could have children, you know. My father-in-law is always pushing me, but I don't know if he wants a grandchild or a different son."

"Holy God, I hope you're right about your husband not understanding you. I'm leaving." Lily leaned toward the bed. "I'm sorry," she whispered into Jude's ear. She took her bag from the armchair and walked out.

"Please get a cab for me," she instructed the doorman in the lobby.

"Already done, Mrs. Declan."

He escorted her outside to a waiting taxi. Opened the door. She got inside. "Tell the driver wherever you want to go," he said to her. "It's been paid for." He closed the door and went into the building.

She was almost asleep when Finn and Sam were dropped at the hotel door by Aunt Marjory at 1:00 a.m. Sam patted her hand before he crawled into bed. "I'm sorry I had such a good time, Mama. I'm sorry you didn't."

Chapter 40: Clean House

The Chicago springtime fell by the wayside as they drove the seven hours south on Sunday. By the time Lily turned off Eastland Avenue, the humidity seeped through the shut windows of the car. She turned the AC up a notch. She wished she still had the rental; the AC had been grand.

When she turned onto Ordway Street, she was relieved that her lawn hadn't been mowed in her absence. No one had decorated or erected a flag over her door. The house was as she had left it.

The boys got their bags from the trunk. She keyed the door and entered. No sound of the alarm. Had she forgotten to set it? Had she forgotten something for Gogo and her brother had come by for it? He was the only one who knew the new code she'd put in after Des died. But the house was wrong. The hallway was wrong. Like someone different lived there. She backed out of the door. She turned to the boys and told them to get back in the car.

She called Owen and asked if he had been in the house while she was gone.

"No. Why?"

"Because someone was. The alarm wasn't on. Someone moved things around in the hallway."

"Someone was inside your house? Not outside, as in mowing the grass? Inside?"

"Yes, Owen, inside."

"Call the police. Don't go in the house. I'm coming now."

———

"What is the nature of your emergency?" the 911 operator asked.

"My house was broken in to."

"Are you in the house now?"

"Right outside."

"Do you think whoever broke in is still in your house?"

"I have no idea."

"Stay on the phone and do not enter the house."

Then more questions, to which Lily stuttered answers as if she'd never recited her name and address and landline and cell phone numbers before. "Stay on the line," the operator reminded her. "Are you still there?" she asked when Lily paused to take a breath.

They sat in the car with the windows open. Lily answered the boys' questions, saying she didn't know what was going on.

"Stay on the line," the operator reminded her. "Are you still there, Ms. Declan? The police have been dispatched and will be arriving momentarily."

The first cop out of the patrol car looked as if he were still in high school. Lily walked over to meet them at the curb. How many times had she heard that one—you know you're getting old when fill-in-the-blank looks like he's right out of high school? Lily nearly choked on the sheer smooth-skinned innocence of him. And that she was noting this rather than noting her fear informed her sense of unreality: as if she were watching someone else in crisis. Officer Howe, he told her and asked her name. The other cop, who introduced himself as Officer Ennis, looked too old to be riding patrol. He had ginger hair mixed with gray, his face was pock scarred, and he chewed on a toothpick with the vehemence of someone who had given up smoking the day before. He held the lead to a well-muscled Belgian shepherd, who sat obediently.

"Tell us what happened," the boy cop asked her.

She told them in short bursts of disarray, which sounded no less ridiculous than what she'd told the 911 dispatcher:

"We were away for the weekend at a wedding. I used my key to get in the house and the alarm didn't go off and I walked in and the house is different. I didn't go all the way in but furniture is in different places and it's not the way I left it and I saw flowers everywhere and everything is cleaned up."

"Flowers?" the young cop asked. She nodded.

"I want you to stay outside, ma'am," Officer Ennis said. "You go sit with your boys. We'll come get you when we need you." He led the dog inside.

It got hotter in the car. They opened the doors. The heat seemed to come as much from the boys' nervous energy as from the afternoon sun on the car.

Her brother arrived with Gogo. When the police emerged from the house, they spoke to Owen. The Belgian shepherd was a small, darker version of Gogo. His name was Angel. He sat like a statue while Gogo pranced and sniffed and strained on her leash.

"Sit, Gogo," Lily begged. "Please sit. Sit now."

"You need dog training," Officer Ennis said.

"She's usually better than this."

"No, *you* need training. You don't repeat commands, ma'am. You don't say please. And you might try using a lower-pitched voice."

Owen took the boys and Gogo for a walk.

They went room to room, Lily and the two cops, who wore latex gloves. They told her not to touch anything. The police dog calmly sniffed. The front hallway was usually a mishmash of kids' soccer equipment, dog leashes, reusable grocery bags, rain boots. Now two large baskets, neither of which Lily had ever seen before, contained the clutter.

The overdue library books that had been sitting by the door were gone. There were several black smudges on the doorframe that hadn't been there before, as if the intruder had dirty hands. Lily pointed to them.

"That's us: we use black powder to dust for fingerprints in the likely places," Officer Howe said. "But it looks like everything was wiped down."

"Who else has a key to the house?" Officer Ennis asked.

"My parents have a key. My brother has one. He's the only one who knows the new alarm code. My friend Iris at work."

"Anyone at your church have a key?"

"No. I don't have a church. Does this look church-ish?"

"Do you have someone who comes in to clean or a cleaning service?"

"No."

"Is there a Hide-a-Key?"

"Yes, under some leaves in the tree hollow in the back. I checked it last month when somebody decorated my yard at Easter without my permission."

"Who decorated your yard?" Officer Ennis said.

"I don't know, but they weren't *in* the house. They mowed the lawn and brought Easter baskets."

The older officer nodded to the younger, and he was back in moments with the Hide-a-Key. "The safest place for a Hide-a-Key is at somebody else's house," Officer Howe said. He put the faux rock and the key in a small evidence bag.

In the living room, two chairs had been moved to face the couch as if people had come by and had a conversation. There were bouquets on every spare surface: the side tables, the mantel, the coffee table.

"Like a funeral," Officer Ennis said.

"Gee, that helped," Lily replied.

In the kitchen, the odd dish or pan perpetually drying in the rack had been put up, and the rack was gone. Lily found the rack under her sink in an undersink tableau that looked nothing like hers. The floor had been mopped. The curtains looked as if they'd been dry-cleaned.

"Are you normally a messy person?" Officer Ennis asked.

"No. Not at all. But we live in this house. This is like a show house."

A small bouquet sat in a bone-china cup and saucer on the kitchen windowsill.

She climbed a chair to make sure the silver tea set was in the upper cabinet. It was, along with the heirloom dessert plates. They had her listen to phone messages on her cell and house phone to hear if someone had left an explanation. Nothing.

They checked the bedrooms upstairs. The boys' room wasn't recognizable. Lily had never seen it so clean, and there were toy bins and a bookshelf that were new. The furniture in the guest bedroom had been rearranged. It was a more pleasing configuration, Lily noted, with the bed moved at a diagonal and a quilt she kept in the closet folded on the foot of the bed.

Her bedroom held more flowers.

"Did you make your bed before you left for the weekend?" Officer Ennis asked. Yes, she had, she always did. Making her bed was one of those few things in the universe that she had control over. But she hadn't made it like this. This looked military with tight corners and not a wrinkle beneath the spread. The books on the nightstand were straightened. In her closet, the muddle of shoes had been separated into neat pairs.

The younger officer went out to speak with her brother when Owen returned with the boys. Officer Ennis insisted Lily come with him and the dog to the dirt storm cellar.

"We've already been down there," he told her when he saw her hesitate. "I just need you to tell me if anything is missing or out of place."

"Why'd you bring the dog?" she asked.

"I'm K-9 patrol. We thought it was a burglary in progress, and we were nearby."

Lily didn't like the cellar. Cold, and earth damp, but it served its purpose. This was where they retreated during tornado sirens. The plastic bins of emergency supplies and Christmas decorations were still there, but their perpetual layer of dust was gone. The Nordstrom box was where she had left it.

Back on the main floor, the den looked the same but different. The floral armchair had been turned to face the window. Officer Ennis turned the chair away from the window and asked her to sit, and she sat. He sat across from her in the office chair.

"We looked through every flower bunch to see if there was a card tucked in somewhere to explain," he said. He put a fresh toothpick between his tight lips. "Look, someone's been in your house, and I see nothing malevolent or dangerous, but the hair on the back of my neck is standing up. If it were me and I came home to this, I would probably barricade my house, but from what? Flowers? A cleaning crew? Your brother told us about the prior tree trimming and landscaping. When exactly?"

"Easter, when we were at my parents'. I don't know who it was. They trimmed the trees and mowed the lawn. I'm widowed a year now, and neighbors have mowed the lawn before when my husband was sick. That was outside, though, not in the house. My oldest boy mows it now."

"No idea which neighbor back then?"

"Once a neighbor up the street named Max Herrera. He's since moved to Sylvan Park. Beth, she lives five houses up, her husband came after that ice storm in December and patched some shingles on the roof. Two women came twice from Holy Trinity to mow. I don't remember their names. This was more than a year ago when my husband was sick. Ken and Kendra Fleming live the next block over. They patched my fence."

"Are there any drugs in the house?"

"I don't do drugs," she said.

"Maybe your late husband had medicine left over somewhere. Or you have pain pills the doctor prescribed."

"Drug thieves leave flowers?"

"I don't get it, either," he said.

He followed her as she looked through drawers and cabinets and found nothing missing. She'd brought Des's meds to Vanderbilt pharmacy after he died. She had a third of a bottle of prescription sleep medication, which was where she'd left it in the back of her makeup drawer. She and the officer sat back down at the dining room table. There was a bouquet here, too, calla lilies and red roses.

"Is there any money missing? Any firearms or chemicals? Is there a gun in the house?"

"Chemicals?"

"Chemicals used to make methamphetamines or incendiaries? These are questions I have to ask." The toothpick had given out, and he put it in his pocket and put a fresh one in his mouth.

"No, but we had a gun."

"What happened to it?"

"I'm not sure. My husband bought a gun last year when he was still alive."

She was an idiot. Of course he'd have to be alive to buy a gun.

"Why? Was there some kind of threat?"

"No. No, he said he wanted me to have protection. I didn't want it. I think he returned it. I asked him to return it. I'm not sure." She closed her eyes to stop tears.

He waited while she gathered herself and opened her eyes. "Show me where it was kept, please."

He followed her to the back of the den closet where the safe was half-hidden behind the boys' outgrown clothes. He followed her back upstairs where she kept the safe key in an old snow boot on the top shelf of her closet. The key was still in the boot. The last time she'd been in the safe was to put in copies of Des's death certificate.

"You haven't checked on the gun in a year?"

She turned to face him. "There was only one thing back then: my husband. My husband living and my husband dying." She was surprised to hear the anger in her voice coating each word with clarity. "Afterward there was only one thing: my children."

"With kids in the house, you need to know if there's a gun. I'll take the key," he said. He still had on the latex gloves, but he handled the key and lock with dexterity. He shined his cop flashlight into the waist-high safe. He pulled out papers, college diplomas, Finn's baby book, a bottle of wine a friend had given them on their wedding that they were to drink on their twenty-year anniversary, the brown envelope with the death certificate, insurance papers, and a box of Des stuff: his wedding ring, his grandfather's gold cuff links, a silverware set wrapped in a towel (was this the monogrammed silver her mother-in-law wanted back? She didn't remember it), and more papers.

"There's no gun in here, ma'am. Could it be anywhere else? Was it a licensed gun?"

Lily got down on her knees and felt in the back of the safe, each corner of the three shelves.

"Wait, here's the approved application made out to a Desmond Declan." Ennis pulled a piece of paper from the stack. "That's good. At least we might be able to track it if it turns up at a pawnshop." He made eye contact with her, put on a gentle-cop voice; she could hear the tone change. "Now tell me again why you're not sure it was in there in the first place."

"Like I told you, my husband bought the gun for me, but I didn't want it. He was going to return it. Or ask his brother to bring it to the police station. It's all a rat's nest. They had him on a lot of medication. He got worse after that. Then I had five days of bereavement leave, then back to work, and I tried to get out of bed each day and take care of my boys. I think the only time I opened the safe was to put his death certificate in there and the box with his wedding ring."

"I'll take the registration info and see if I can track it. Did your husband die of natural causes?"

"Yes. Over at Vanderbilt. Here's his death certificate if you need it."

He shook his head. She got the certificate from the envelope and handed it to him anyway. He was rough to glance at, but once Lily looked she saw a well-arranged face, an easy face if it hadn't been scarred. He handed it back. "Sorry for your loss," he said. He had clear green eyes. "I don't see any ammo for the pistol."

"My husband had a box of bullets in his underwear drawer. I threw them away when I threw away his underwear."

"We need to track down the gun. I'll need your brother-in-law's number. We'll take care of calling him."

Lily wrote Kevin's name, his number. The cop walked outside to the patrol car and talked with the other cop. He came back to the house.

"Anything else unusual since your husband died? Aside from the Easter decorations?"

"Sir, everything feels unusual since he died. My mother-in-law sent me a white nightgown and didn't sign the card. Not what you meant, right?" She sniffed back tears and straightened her shoulders. "I got some strange condolence letters from a college friend of my husband. And someone started a Facebook memorial page to him without my permission."

"May I see the letters? Will you pull up the page for me on your computer, please. Was your husband a known community figure? Entertainer? Politician? What's your occupation?"

"My husband sang bass in the Nashville Opera Chorus."

"Did that make him well known in the community?"

"No."

"Your work?"

"I'm a music archivist for a private foundation. I mostly work with computer databases."

"Professional rivals or enemies at either of your jobs?"

"Not hardly." She got the letters from the kitchen drawer, explaining that the moderator at her grief group had one of them. He stood reading.

"Presumptuous," he said. "Some people like to rubberneck other people's pain. No manners. No threats, though. The letter you don't have—same or worse?"

"It was the first one. Surprising, uncomfortable, but not worse."

Lily called up the tribute page on her laptop. He scrolled quickly through it at the kitchen table.

"Who is Dharma-69?"

"I have no idea."

"A troll maybe. The pictures—your husband's side of the family, right?"

"Yes," Lily said.

"No threats? No mention of cleaning your house or delivering flowers?"

"No."

"Please come with me," he said. They walked slowly around the house. He'd stop at windows, letting the police dog sniff.

"Ma'am, there's no sign of forced entry. No indication of an alarm going off, and we called the alarm company. Officer Howe has already interviewed several neighbors. Yes, someone was in your house. There was a cleaning company van here. We're trying to get a line on that. So it doesn't seem like people were sneaking around or trying to hide. One of your neighbors said they saw a pretty African American woman in a maid's uniform go in your front door on Saturday. Any African American friends or acquaintances?"

"Iris Malone is my friend from work. She's Bahamian, doesn't work for a cleaning company, and wouldn't go into my house without permission." Lily's voice rose with her anxiety.

"I'm not accusing her of anything. Has anyone ever volunteered to send their housekeeper or cleaning company to help you out?"

"No, and cleaning companies don't bring flowers. There are dish towels in my kitchen that I've never seen before." Lily didn't know why she'd zoned in on the dish towels. Such an ordinary consolation, drying the pots from the rack after dinner with her sweet, familiar blue cotton dish towels, and now there were dish towels she'd never seen before hanging on the towel rack.

"Did you touch them?"

"No," Lily said.

"Go back in the kitchen and don't touch them."

Officer Ennis came into the kitchen with Angel a few minutes later. He took off his latex gloves with guy awkwardness and put on another pair. He took the new dish towels Lily pointed out to him and held them under Angel's nose and waited. They were ivory-colored linen with a pattern of tumbling yellow roses. The cop whispered in Angel's ear, and the dog got squirrelly and excited. "Wait here," Ennis said to Lily.

They were gone a good ten minutes. The cop held Angel's lead in front of him like a diviner in search of water. They went out through the front and back in through the patio and the mudroom, they went down the creaky stairs to the storm cellar, then through the rooms to upstairs and back to the kitchen where Lily sat. She wondered if she should tell him about Des's coworker wearing winter gloves on a warm evening at Trader Joe's.

He sat at the kitchen table with the dog at his side. "I've worked K-9 twenty-three years. This is speculation as Angel can't talk, but following his lead I think the person who came in your house came through the back using your Hide-a-Key. They didn't know the code. The breaker was tripped. I missed it on my first go-round. When is the last time your alarm went off?"

"I don't know. I mean, I really have no idea. I set it when we go out and put the code in when we come home. We reset the code last year."

"We?"

"My brother and I. So many people had a key and the code when my husband was sick. We even had a few home health-care aides toward the end before he went back in the hospital."

"It's a dedicated breaker. A squirrel could've gnawed through the wire months ago. Or somebody could've tripped the breaker purposely when they came in. My advice, Ms. Declan, is to have your brother stay here a few days till you get this sorted. Get all your locks changed and do not use a Hide-a-Key. Call the alarm company and have a new system put in. This is a twenty-year-old system, maybe older. Come with the house?"

She nodded.

"You want a system not on a breaker and with battery backup. Here's my card and say a prayer that this was something well intentioned, disturbing as it is. Officer Howe has spoken to your brother-in-law, and he knows nothing about the gun. We'll put some extra patrols on the house for now. Maybe whoever did this will come forward either to be thanked or with the realization that they should've ID'd themselves. Let us know. You should stay on alert until they do."

Chapter 41: Smiley Face

Owen and Lily downplayed the incident with the boys. They told them somebody thought they were helping, but it was wrong because they didn't have permission. Always easier to play down, calm down, with her brother's solid presence. Owen refused the guest bedroom upstairs and slept on the couch downstairs with Gogo by his side.

It was after 2:00 a.m. when Lily found the photo. She'd spent the night riffling through her dresser drawers, the closet, the wardrobe, looking for evidence of the invasion.

There on the top of the high wardrobe was a dusty snow globe of Chicago that Des had had since he was a child. Beside it was a framed photo of the four of them. It'd been there for years. Des was smiling with a squirming baby Sam in his arms. Finn held Lily's hand. Everything was the same except covering Lily's face was a small yellow smiley-face sticker. That's all. One face erased with a smile sticker.

She went downstairs and sat in the kitchen till Owen awoke. She started coffee. Showed him the picture when he came in.

"When's the last time you looked at this picture?" Owen said.

"I don't know. It's been on top of the wardrobe for years."

"It's pretty dusty. Even the sticker looks dusty."

Yes, it did. Except for her own finger smudges where she'd just touched it.

Owen and Lily tossed every bouquet into the outside garbage bin. Owen made no attempt to assuage Lily. He spat in the garbage after the last rose was tossed. Lily took seventeen vases, large and small, over to the Gallatin Road Goodwill. She was too shaky to make phone calls, so Owen took numbers from Lily to call places he thought might've done this. He called the church where Des used to go. He called the Chicago Declans. He called Des's friends in the opera company. No one had information on the house cleaning or the previous Easter decorations.

The locksmith drilled and bored and changed locks. They added inside bolts on the doors and windows. Owen said he'd seen a police car cruise by a few times. The electrician installed motion-detector lights over the doors and on the corners of the house. Owen got a security latch for the back patio door. The alarm company took another day to dismantle the old system and install a new one.

Lily reassured her brother that she was fine with him going home on the third night, but he said no, he wanted to be sure everything that'd been installed was working properly. After the alarm crew left, they picked up the boys from aftercare and went to Owen's for dinner. While Owen was at Lily's, Anne-Claire's mother had been staying there. Shelby had made homemade lasagna. Dinner was fun in this small chaos. Anne-Claire was three months pregnant and had that Alabama girl chatter thing always going on. Their eight-year-old daughter, Teresa, had the same gift for small talk. Finn and Sam loved being with their uncle Owen. He did things with them, hockey games, camping at the zoo. He was solid and safe and near. Sam sat close by his side.

Chapter 42:
Ob-La-Di Ob-La-Da

They were to write letters of gratitude to the dead. Renée passed around small yellow lined pads at the Circle of Compassion and held a fistful of pens in her eczemic hand.

Lily was aware. She was aware the way you wake in the morning from sleep. She hadn't been holding on to grief, she'd been letting it do what it needed to do. There was no longer a black veil tinting her vision. There was no longer a fog closing her in. Her sorrow didn't need to be fed or be sent away hungry—it was there, would always be there, would walk side by side with her and whatever her future.

She was aware.

With the plastic ballpoint pen, she wrote three paragraphs on her pad of yellow paper. Miriam asked her to read aloud when the ten-minute timer went off, and Lily said she'd prefer to read last. She listened attentively to the gratitude lists. Even the hollow-eyed burgundy-haired woman named Stevie had sweet things to say about her dead twin—how he'd always held the water fountain button for her when they were kids. How he'd shoved a boy who'd called her a dork in third grade. How he didn't care if his socks matched. It made her less caustic, less my-pain-is-worse-than-yours.

Lily's turn: "I think I'm in danger."

"Does this have to do with your gratitude letter to your husband?" Mrs. Henrietta said. Peeved, she liked the rules followed.

"It has to do with what I want to say." Lily took her laptop from her carryall. She'd bookmarked the Facebook page.

"Why do you think you're in danger?" Yvonne asked. She tucked her hair behind her ear, and Lily was aware that it wasn't hair grooming. Yvonne had tiny pavé cross earrings. She was touching a crucifix, a talisman, a prayer.

Lily read from the yellow-lined notes she'd just written:

"Someone was in my house without my permission while I was away last weekend. They cleaned, moved furniture, and left enough flowers for a funeral. They didn't identify themselves. Didn't leave a note. The police are treating it as a break-in and think they may have tripped the breaker on the alarm system." "Where were you when this happened? Who knew you'd be away?" Miriam asked.

"At my brother-in-law's wedding in Chicago. I had to take a day off, so they knew at work. My family knew I'd be away. All my in-laws were there, so that takes them off the list."

"What about your parents?" Mrs. H. said. "You've always said how much they helped you out."

"They're on a Disney cruise ship in the Caribbean."

"Are you accusing us?" Stevie said.

"I never mentioned here that I was going away. No, I'm not accusing you. I'm asking for help." Lily looked down at her pad to her second note and opened the Facebook memorial page. She turned the screen so it faced out. "I told you someone started a Facebook tribute to my husband. It pissed me off, but I don't own the Internet. It changed over the weekend. The profile picture changed, and somebody named Dharma-69 left sixty-nine messages repeating the same lyric."

The circle leaned in, bobbed heads to get a better look. Stevie started humming "Ob-La-Di Ob-La-Da" and sat back, arms folded across her chest, rocking.

"Please stop," Lily said.

"What? It's cute. I didn't realize your last name was Jones. Lily and Desmond Jones. It's Molly in the song, right? Is that a picture of your son?"

"My last name isn't Jones."

"Well, that's a tribute page to Desmond Jones," Carly said.

Lily turned the computer around to look. It'd been changed from the morning. Same picture, different name, no more likes, no friends. Just Des's young picture and Dharma-69's messages. She shut it down. Typed "Desmond Declan memorial facebook" into Google and nothing came up. Went to her bookmarks and hit the entry she'd marked as "Des FB Mem" and up came this new page. Stevie giggled as she hummed.

"Stop!" Lily said.

Miriam fiddled with pages on her clipboard. "Do you think it was that Jaz person? The one who wrote the letters?"

"Don't know. But as you said, she likes signing her work. No one has taken credit for this."

"Buy a gun," Yvonne said, fingering both her ears.

"No," Leon said. "Having a gun in the house is not a good statistic. Let's not bring violence into this."

Lily didn't want to get into the stolen gun. "And here's the other thing I found after this weekend's break-in." She shut the laptop, dug into her bag for the family picture, and held it up. "This photo has been on top of my wardrobe for years. After the break-in, someone got rid of my head with a smiley face."

Holding it up like a show-and-tell in a classroom gave Lily the same reaction of dread that she saw in the others' faces.

Miriam was standing inside the circle now. She wore a dress of faded pink flowers. She handed each of them a typed sheet marked "Private Therapy" with names and addresses and phone numbers. "Group therapy is not for everyone," she said. "And even for those who benefit, private therapy can be a good addition. Not just for you, Lily."

"You think I'm paranoid?" Lily asked. "You think I've gaslighted myself crazy?" She watched the framed photo in her hand shake with indignation and lowered it to her lap.

"I'm glad you turned this over to the police. A break-in is outside the purview of this group. I presume you were told to have your locks and security redone. And even if it was meant well, even if it was some cleanup by friends or family, it was an intrusion into your space. I bring up private therapy because the cold fact is mortality rates for the bereaved are anywhere from forty to sixty percent higher than the general population for up to two years after the death. This isn't just for suicide. It's accidents, illness, not paying attention."

"I am paying attention," Lily said. *The purview of the group—is that a legal term?* she wondered. She took a sheet along with the rest.

"There's help available," Miriam said. "This list contains counselors and therapists who I know do fine work in grief counseling. Some may be booked or not take new patients and some may not take insurance, so ask when you call and mention my name as a referral. Lily, please stay after and talk to me."

Lily didn't stay after. She was aware that she'd crossed some sort of line with Miriam and the group. The line between being a person who elicits sympathy to a person who needs more help. Leon and Miriam discussed names on the private practice list as the group broke up. Yvonne told Lily that she'd pray for her. Owen had driven Lily and would be waiting outside. It was Renée who trotted after Lily in the hall. Walking with her, Renée said, "This is Miriam's card. She asked me to give it to you, and she wants you to call her. But allow me to speak with you?"

Lily took the card and nodded.

"How sure are you that the new picture on Facebook is your husband? It's the picture of a thirteen- or fourteen-year-old, and it seems pixelated."

"It's him."

"Police or no police, you need to respect your feelings. Apprehension, fear, they can be constructive emotions," Renée said. Her scratched hands moved lightly with her words. "Wait, let's call fear a survival response, not an emotion."

Lily stopped walking. "My brother is waiting. I'm not sure I understand what you're saying. What do you mean?"

"I mean that in modern life, we're constantly on alert. There's so much auditory and visual noise. We have to constantly talk ourselves out of alert." Renée kept her head down and focused her fierce eyes upward. Her eyes were dark brown, almost black; Lily hadn't noticed their intensity in Miriam's shadow. They started walking. "We're studying vestigial fears in one of my courses this semester. Here's an example: an elephant comes charging at us in the wild, we run and jump to the side into some bushes. When a huge truck comes careening at us in a city, the same flight response is released. But we don't run or jump or scream, because we look to see that the light at the intersection is turning red, so the truck will stop. We are so used to talking ourselves out of impending—but not really—danger that when real danger comes, we just go right on calming ourselves. Miriam knows you better than I do, but I have to disagree. I don't think all this boils down to needing private therapy. I found the Facebook tribute to your husband intrusive even before that Beatles thing. Maybe it was a church group who brought flowers and cleaned your house, but that sticker over your face feels malevolent."

"Do you think I'm in danger?" Lily said.

"I don't know. I'm only saying that maybe feeling danger *is* the appropriate response at this time."

Chapter 43: Vaudeville

Sleep didn't come easy. The scent of flowers lingered, funereal and stale. Lily could still smell one monstrosity of yellow and lavender roses that'd been on the upstairs hall table. The house was now fortified against invaders. Owen slept on the downstairs couch again with Gogo by his side. Yet a subtle release of sweetness decomposed into her dreams to wake her. Maybe it was a poison, something released gradually inside the house. She wanted to open the window but didn't. Past midnight, she got up to wander the second floor, checking the window locks, checking that the boys were still asleep. The outdoor motion lights went off three times. The third time, from the upstairs hall window, she saw a group of raccoons crossing the backyard like a troupe of vaudeville performers.

She went back to bed. If she hadn't dreamed, she wouldn't have believed she finally slept. She followed Des in her dream. He walked through dark streets to downtown. He slipped into the ink-black river fully clothed and struggled against the Cumberland's current. She dove after him; the icy cold of the water stunned her, not at all dreamlike. She swam after him, finding pieces of his clothing like Hansel and Gretel crumbs floating on the cold. The faster she swam, the harder she kicked, the farther away he disappeared. Then she came. Wave after wave of convulsing orgasm. There was no comfort in it. It felt like a Kinsey experiment gone wrong. She sat up and turned on the light. She noted dispassionately, like an archivist, that she hadn't had an orgasm in almost two years. She noted that she'd never come in her sleep before. She noted that she never had caught up to Des. She argued in the light of her bedside lamp that she'd been trying to catch him, to save him, but knew in the reality of the dream that she'd been following him into death.

She rose and pushed back the curtain. Outside it was early morning, the milky color of a faded movie.

Not a bad thing, she thought, *to follow love into the dark water.* Every day, every hour of every day since Des had died, had been a small war against following him. Against reaching through the fragile curtain of life to hold him again. To be held by him.

She stood under the hot shower for a long time before the river cold melted from her veins.

She let Gogo out the back door to the yard. Already hot and muggy. She ate a bowl of cereal. Fed the dog. Drank hot coffee. Went over her date book and the remaining brochures for summer day camps for the boys. She'd plugged most of the holes in their vacation schedule. There were three and a half weeks of school left, and whatever madness her life had become would be done by then. It was with this assertion of future normalcy that she read the colorful leaflets. YMCA, St. Bernard's, Science Quest, Parks and Recreation, Summer Soccer League. Her parents always filled in the weeks they could when the boys were on vacation. Summer was an expensive landscape with kids.

Lily made eggs and toast for Owen. They talked about Lily and the kids coming to his house for a few days. Having Mom and Dad come to Lily's when they got back. Finn, always up before Sam, made himself cereal and poured a glass of OJ. He pointed to the counter with a smile and a mouth full of cornflakes, said: "Sorry about that, Mom."

On the counter by the microwave was the framed family photo with the smiley-face sticker over her face.

"Sorry for what?" Lily said.

"Will the sticker come off? I was going to put one on each face."

"You did this? Why? Why would you do this?"

"Jeez—I thought it was funny. I was, like, five or six years old. It was up behind Dad's snow globe."

"Told you it was dusty," Owen said.

Chapter 44:

The Comfort of Place

Owen drove the boys to school on the way to his jobsite, and Lily was early for work. The long plank hallway creaked lightly with her steps. Alone in the office, she sat at her computer, the music on her headphones low, her coffee warm. Even when Des was sick, this place had offered comfort, out of time with the real world.

She continued archiving the Dust Bowl radio shows. She listened to a recording of a live broadcast of *Holbar's Grocers Variety Morning*. The female voice singing "Hold Me Up to Jesus" crossed over from crackly to plaintive. The catalog listed it as Cora Mays, sister of the famous Texas troubadour Vernon Mays. She hit "Play" again. It was a clean recording remastered by a digimix company from San Jose: "They broke out whiskey broke out gin / They broke out whiskey broke out gin / Come sweet mother from your weeping / I'm knocking on heaven's door come let me in."

She'd heard this voice before, and it wasn't Cora Mays. There wasn't a vocal frill in this song, no jumped octaves, a southern accent but no twang.

She moved the tape forward and back and checked the transcriptions. The announcer said to please welcome our own Texas troubadour's sister, but he hadn't said a name and never said what Texas troubadour, and there were plenty before Vernon Mays and Ernest Tubb had picked up the moniker.

Sadie Wexler, yes, that's who sang. Lily searched archives and found several other Wexler recordings, much later, with much better recording microphones. It was Wexler.

She put the notation down and sent it along as an attachment to her boss, as she did after every ten or so recording hours.

Lily saw the message light on her cell. She took off her headphones. Officer Ennis had left the message fifteen minutes earlier. They had not found any record in a database search of the gun from her house after its having been purchased by Desmond Declan. No record of it being returned or resold or reregistered, so they were going to treat it as stolen during the break-in.

Surely Des had gotten rid of it. The safe hadn't been forced open, and the one key had still been in the toe of her boot.

Lily went back to her headphones. Outside the window, the dogwood leaves trembled in the breeze like so many lost hearts. Two mockingbirds performed an elaborate fan dance on the lawn.

Iris was in her face when she looked up. Angry eyes inches from Lily's forehead. Lily ripped off her headphones and rolled her desk chair back away from her.

"What the fuck?"

"Masser wants to see you, Missus," Iris said. She shoved her angry hands into her trench coat pockets. "Now should I curtsy to you, Missus? Or should I wear my maid uniform?"

"Get out of my face. Stop with the routine!"

"I said Mr. Linden wants you in his office, my *old* friend."

"Why're you mad at me?"

"The po-po came and interviewed me, here at work. Asked me if I had a maid's uniform."

"So sorry if your feelings got hurt. My house was broken in to. I had to give them the name of every person who had a key, including my brother and my brother-in-law. A fucking break, please."

"Bet they didn't ask them if they had a maid's uniform. Think you could've called me? Think you could've let me know your house was broken in to? Think you could've let me know they were going to come to work to interview me? Linden wants to see you *now*."

Lily's heart was still crazy beating when she got to Mr. Linden's office. Was she in trouble for the police questioning Iris, for the police coming to work?

Mr. Linden—she reminded herself to call him Henry—swept his arm to the chair facing his desk.

"Do you know what this means that this is Sadie Wexler? I read your e-mail."

"I know it's her," Lily said.

"I think you're right. I listened and agreed. I sent it on to a friend who's a professor at Austin. He's running sound checks right now. Wexler was a transitional figure in folk recording. We thought she was in Chicago in 1934, not in Texas."

Lily didn't know these histories. Her job was a narrow niche. She was glad her boss was happy after she'd been absent four days. She tried to smile. Tried to remember how to smile. It came out as a grimace.

"I'm sorry about the break-in. The police were by here on Monday," Mr. Linden said.

"It was very unnerving, Henry. I've had to put in a new security system and motion lights. I had to change the locks, too. I was sorry to take off."

"Do you truly think Iris had anything to do with it?"

"No. Of course not."

"The police questioned her for a long time. She had a key. A neighbor had seen someone matching her description enter your house in a uniform."

"I had to give the police the names of everyone with a key. She had a key from when my husband was sick and she picked up the kids for me and brought groceries. I never told the cops I thought it was her. Never."

"She was also upset that you never called her to say you had given her name to the police."

"I didn't *give* her name. The police said one of the neighbors had seen an African American woman in a maid's uniform. They'd already asked me who had a key. I told them it wasn't Iris and that she was Bahamian not African American. I can't even imagine her in a maid's uniform. I also gave my brother's name and my parents'."

Lily stopped for a minute. Had she given them Kevin's name? She couldn't remember. He had a key also from when he'd come down on weekends when Des was in the hospital.

"You know the Bahamas are part of the Americas? Which is neither here nor there, but we people from the United States seem to think we're the real Americans, the only Americans."

"I've had a rough few days here, Mr. Linden. I can't deal with Iris's personal resentment right now."

Lily's mind scattered across Iris's anger and Mr. Linden's questions. She stared at her boss and considered what his suit cost. She'd just put $1,200 on her credit cards for the electrician and the security system revamp and the locksmith. The suit had to be custom tailored. It was a pale-cream linen or maybe silk, lightweight for summer. He was always dressed for the next PR moment, the next guest contributor.

"The police said someone broke in to your house and cleaned it? Is that right? Maybe it wasn't a break-in the way one normally thinks of a break-in."

"I don't think Iris came to my house to clean it if that's what you're asking."

"Do you need a leave of absence, Lily?"

"No."

"I think it would be a good thing in light of all this."

"Sir? Am I being punished for cooperating with the police? I can't afford a leave of absence."

"Wrong expression. My son suggested a different work arrangement. You would work from home. I'm very impressed by your discovery of the Wexler recording. Your work has always been solid. I think it'll be a good way for you to guard your house and still get paid. You can come for meetings. Your boys will be out of school for summer soon. You'll keep a log. You can understand why Iris feels put out. She'll just need time to settle down. Let's walk back to your office now."

Henry Linden buttoned his jacket when they stood. His pale-blue tie matched his eyes. "I was in the corporate world for thirty years. Almost destroyed me."

"My boys will be at camps for the summer or with my parents. I don't need to work from home."

"This kind of infighting was one of the reasons I left the corporate world."

"I'm not fighting with anyone."

"It'll be good for your boys to have you home. I'll miss seeing you every day. You have a landscape around you, a sort of floral sadness about you that is very touching."

"Floral sadness?" Lily asked. "Why isn't Iris getting a work-from-home order? She's the one who's upset." Lily could hear the whine in her voice as she spoke, a life-isn't-fair timbre. She wished she had Iris's in-your-face, fuck-you tone.

Take care of your boys. Hold on to your home. Hold on to your job. Go with the fucking flow. Take your fucking floral sadness and work from home.

"Have you met Brooks Maslin, Lily?" Henry Linden said. A well-made frosted blonde in a red sheath and high heels rose from a chair in the sitting room outside his office. She held her hand out to Lily.

Lily ignored the hand. She remembered this woman well, only she'd been in a yoga outfit the afternoon of the gala.

"Yes, we met," Lily said. "You have a brown SUV and a dog, right?"

"I have a dog, as do many people, and I have an SUV, but it's maroon agate, not brown." Her hair was free flowing and out of its ponytail.

"We'll call it brownish, then. You hit my car the afternoon of the gala in the parking lot. You were talking baby talk. I guess you forgot to leave your insurance info when you left so fast."

"I think you are mistaken." She enunciated each word, taking the time to smooth her dress over her hips.

"I think it's called leaving the scene of the crime. I think it's called almost fucking hitting me when you left the scene of the crime. I think I'm tired of being fucked over. I think I'm not mistaken. I think you're a liar."

"I do not know you," Ms. Maslin said. She pushed her hands in front of her and walked by Lily into Henry Linden's office.

Chapter 45: Insubordination

It only took ten minutes to be dismissed from her job of eight years. It wasn't even Mr. Linden but Camille Padgett, who did payroll and accounting, and Tiffany, the front-desk receptionist, who told her she was dismissed and handed her forms to sign and an application for COBRA insurance continuation.

Lily said to Camille, "*Dismissed*, as in fired? Don't you have to receive warnings?"

"Not from a private institution," Camille said. "And not for insubordination."

"Insubordination? That woman in Mr. Linden's office was the person who hit my car and drove off the afternoon of the gala. I had a five-hundred-dollar deductible. I had to drive a rental for three days while it got fixed."

"She's also a donor and may soon be on the board. Not that it matters—you've gone over your sick time and your vacation days, and a lot of times, like most of the time, you don't even call in when you take off," Camille said.

"You were way over your sick time and vacation time when you took off from work Thursday and Friday for that wedding," Tiffany said. "Then you didn't even call in on Monday or Tuesday, and if the police hadn't come, we wouldn't have known what happened to you."

Had the wedding only been last weekend? Why had she even gone? To be put at a back table with two priests and that horrid Nia woman? To have someone break in to her house while she was away?

It took one cardboard box from the copy room for Lily to pack her belongings. Iris wasn't in the office.

Chapter 46:
The Changing Landscape

Lily took byroads home, not trusting herself at any speed over forty. She'd never noticed before that the streets weren't the simple black trail she'd thought them. They were a pasty gray. The rising heat miraged into pale liquid in the distance. She turned on the radio to hear Des's message and heard the sweet, dead Buddy Holly sing "Not Fade Away." "Thanks, Des," she whispered. But the song didn't feel right. It gave rise to a vision of Grateful Dead roses crowning a skull. She didn't know how she'd made this jump. She turned off the radio.

She recited goals. *Take care of the boys.* Where were they now? At school among strangers. Anyone could snatch them off the playground. *Where's Little Man Sam?* Ms. Greene would ask. Had he stopped at the water fountain on the way back from the playground and not returned to class? A horn growled behind her, and she realized she was driving too slowly. She sped up to the speed limit. Where was Finn? He was growing tall, too big to be lifted into a kidnapper's car, but old enough to wander off into the world by himself. How old was Mark Twain when he left home for work? *Young,* Lily thought, *maybe younger than Finn.*

Keep your job—ah, the second priority. She stopped there. *Keep the house* was on her list, too. But why? It smelled of funeral flowers. She could keep the windows open for years and that still wouldn't erase that someone had been in her home. Poisoned the air. Left furniture dents in the carpet where her real life had been. She'd had a niche job at the Linden Foundation; it wouldn't be easy to replace. She'd paid off the hospital and had the last of Des's life-insurance policy, enough that she could keep up with house payments and health insurance for a few months. Then she'd have to sell, move to her parents' where her degree could get her a job filing in an office, and on Saturday nights she could sing karaoke.

She stopped at a red light. Rose red. The horrible quiet of being stopped again. She turned on the radio; surely Des would have a better message than fading away.

"I awoke in the wrong city," sang the radio. "Paradise empty as a joke. Only touched by dust and smoke."

No, not the wrong city. No, not fade away. She turned off the radio.

There was a woman sitting on the front steps of her house. Lily could see her when she turned the corner to her street. A half block away and she could hear the scratchy voices of a police scanner. The police cruiser was parked in front of her house. Had they caught this woman breaking in?

It was Iris—Lily could see the tilt of her head. Had it been Iris all along? Then it could only have been a good deed gone bad. The flowers had been superfluous, not maleficent. It'd been Finn who'd put the sticker on the family photo so many years before. Iris—a flower name. Surely a coincidence.

It was the baby cop, Officer Howe. Lily felt old beside him when she got out of her car. Iris waved to her as if she were simply a friend sitting on the front steps. She wore a pattern of scarlet and orange flowers on a silky sundress that looked like a nosegay.

Lily stood beside Officer Howe.

"You'll please tell this eager young officer that I'm your friend," Iris called over.

"Your *old* friend?" Lily said.

Officer Howe walked to his car and motioned Lily to follow. They moved to the driver's side, with Lily's back to Iris.

"This is the woman we interviewed. She had a solid alibi for the weekend. We made sure it checked out. She says she's been waiting here for you for ten minutes. Are you comfortable with this? You know we've been running extra patrols by."

He was even younger up close, yet there was an outline of hard lines forming around his mouth.

"Yes, she's my friend," Lily said, thoroughly relieved that Iris's alibi had been checked. Thoroughly ashamed that she'd thought Iris needed an alibi. Hearing the automaton in her voice, she continued with more cheer: "I had to leave early from my job today, but yes, she's my friend from work. If you need to, you can check back later. I'd appreciate that. Not because I'm afraid of her, just that I've been on edge since the break-in."

"I understand, ma'am. This is my regular patrol, so barring an emergency, I'll check back. Here's my card. You can call the number I circled unless it's a 911 call."

Officer Howe walked by Lily and over to Iris. "Thank you for your cooperation, Ms. Malone. When we think a house has been targeted, we do extra patrols. Routine procedure."

"No racial profiling?" Iris said.

Howe went to his car, put in a call on his radio, drove off.

Lily made a point of carrying her box from work out in front of her chest, a cardboard shield against the future.

"Tiffany told me you were let go, but I didn't believe her. Tell me I didn't get you fired."

"No, I did that all on my own. I accused some hotshot donor of a hit-and-run."

"Tiffany told me that, too, but I didn't believe it. Ms. Maslin is more than just another donor."

"Ms. Maslin, the woman who was in Linden's waiting room, is the bitch who hit my car the afternoon of the gala. I didn't know her name then, as she was not kind enough to leave it. This isn't speculation on my part. It's truth."

"Was it worth your job? Why didn't you walk away? Like you taught Sam to do with bullies. Walk away and talk to Linden privately."

Lily couldn't move for fear of throwing the box she held at Iris. Gogo whined from inside the house. She knew Iris, so she wouldn't bark.

"You don't need a lecture from me right now, do you?" Iris said. She took the box from Lily's arms and placed it by the door. She patted the step for Lily to sit. "Too nice to be inside anyway. We should enjoy this last bit of sweetness till real summer sets in." Everything Iris said in that lively accent made the world seem doable. Less dangerous.

"I also didn't call in to work for a few days after the burglary. Who knows, maybe Linden was still pissed that I brought the boys to the gala. Or maybe I was fired for being a general nuisance."

"Yeah, for a little girl, you do create big fuss," Iris said. "I think you need to get out of here for a bit. Go to your brother's or come to my house?"

"No need. My brother's been staying here. We've changed the locks and have a new security system. You understand that I gave your name to the police because they asked me who had a key. I told you this. I don't know why you're bent out of shape."

"Okay, I get it. It would've been nice if you had told me before they came to interview me, and it was a little rough when they asked if I had a maid's uniform. Bet they didn't ask your brother or your parents that."

"Okay, *I* get it."

"Maybe you can call those grief group people and see if they know where you can get help."

"I'll figure it out."

"Don't be too sure your job is gone."

"I'm gone, Iris."

"What does that mean? You're taking all your toys and going home even if Linden apologizes and reinstates you? He was all atwitter that you discovered the Wexler recording in Texas."

"Concentrating at work is a huge enterprise right now."

"Bullshit. You wouldn't have made that discovery this morning if you couldn't concentrate."

"More like anxiety hyperalert."

"So let that work for you until things calm down."

"Sure, except I don't have a job."

An unfamiliar black car pulled up where the cop car had been. Its high-end sleekness couldn't be mistaken for an unmarked patrol.

A man got out and bounded toward them. He was scraggly and unshaven, in a T-shirt and jeans. It was Mr. Linden's son.

"Sorry about your job, Lily," he said in a rush.

Iris smiled at him. Rumor still had it that Gardner was joining the Linden Foundation, but it was more like he dropped by some afternoons.

"We'll get it back," he said. "You don't know what it's like having stepmothers my age. And younger. Oh, but Brooks Maslin was the worst. Whenever she got distressed, she lapsed into this odd baby talk. She was still in my dad's office looking wounded when I left, so we'll have to wait to prod him back to sanity."

"She's your stepmother?"

"I was avoiding telling you that part," Iris said.

"Past tense. They've been divorced nine or ten years now, but she still holds a peculiar sway over my dad. I think they're dating again. She's also moneyed and has recently contributed to the foundation."

Lily's anxiety hadn't faded with Gardner's explanation. Why would he just show up at her house?

"Iris gave me your address," he said, as if reading her mind. He leaned over and planted a kiss on Iris's cheek. They smiled at each other. "We thought we could take you out for lunch while we plan our strategy. We're here for you. We'll get this sorted."

We: Iris and Gardner. They were friends. Good friends.

"'We'? Why didn't you tell me?" Lily said. She faced Iris.

"Tell you what, Lily? That Gardner and I are friends? And that I'm dating a close friend of his? One of his ex-girlfriends, in fact. You're so miserable you barely look up from your computer some days. What would I have said? 'Oh, please share my happiness'?"

"I just didn't know you and Gardner were such good pals. That he was fixing you up with his friends."

"So maybe just the two of you would like to have lunch?" Gardner said. "I can meet up later. Or wait for another day?" Lily ignored him. Iris nodded to him, and he walked away. They watched till they heard the ignition.

"I'm not allowed to make friends? I'm not allowed to date? You have your right to be sad," Iris said. "I have my right to be happy. I spend my days tiptoeing around you, and it's more than a year now."

"It's not something with an expiration date. Des is still dead. More than a year and he's still dead."

"I'm sorry, Lily. Please let me pull those words back into my mouth. I can't believe I said them. I've let you pull words back."

"It's what I thought, too. That there was an end date. And if there wasn't, I thought at least I'd be, I don't know, a better person by now. More wounded-healer type. Every time I think I'm getting better, something else comes along."

"Like the condolence letters? Facebook page? Kids bullying little Sam? Like a break-in? You've had a lot on your plate. I know that."

"Sorry you've had to tiptoe around me. I don't begrudge you your happiness. Don't blame you for not sharing, either. Anything with a smile on it makes me nervous nowadays. Your spring dress blinded me when I drove up the street."

"What do we do now, Lily?"

"You go back to work and beat the shit out of Ms. Maslin. Get my five-hundred-dollar deductible from her while you're at it."

"Better the two of us go to lunch, I think."

"No. Later in the week maybe. I've never been fired before. I need to regroup," Lily said. "Draw up a new plan."

"A plan and a prayer," Iris said, and smiled. "We'll get your job back."

Chapter 47:
You May Find Yourself

The house was always cold when she first entered, even now, with the end of spring giving way to the humid Nashville summer. Two locks now to enter the house. A beeping alarm that Lily shut off with a new code. The eye of her heart went to the emptiness, wondered maybe if Des'd escaped again. Left death a note that he'd be right back. Held a key in his hand to tell her he was still watching out for them.

Lily went to the kitchen to unlatch the dog gate. Gogo wasn't there. She'd heard her whining a minute before, so she knew she was nearby. Lily heard the slow tap dance of Gogo slinking down the hall. Gogo kept her eyes averted and her head low.

"Please, Gogo, I don't want to have to crate you again," she said. But Lily didn't have a job to go to and would be home now for a while. She took a breath of courage and went into the den. It was filled with what looked like a child's diorama of misshapen clouds. There were white clouds and dark clouds. Clouds formed of white cotton and clouds formed of brown horsehair. Gogo had gutted the floral armchair down to the wood frame.

Lily got black garbage bags from under the kitchen sink and filled two of them with the fluff and horsehair. The bare bones of the chair were too heavy to move by herself, so she'd have Finn help her bring it out to the trash tonight. She sat on the floor and remembered it. She thought to cry because it was Des's chair and now it was gone. The loss of the chair was more real than the loss of her job. She had to remind herself that she'd never liked the chair to begin with. It was too big, too floral, but Des had grown up with it and loved its comfort. *It should've been cremated with him,* she thought.

Gogo came and nestled her nose against Lily's neck. Gogo yawned and smiled. Even when Gogo was affectionate, those jaws were huge.

Lily got the broom for the small tufts remaining and put the garbage bags out front in the bins.

Gogo whined to be let out, and Lily opened the back door to the patio. Gogo rushed outside, barking and growling.

There was someone in the yard. Someone too tall, too ghostly in a white fancy dress. Someone dangling from the sweet gum tree in the back corner of the yard. Faceless. Headless. Armless.

"Heel! Come! Shit! Stay!" Lily yelled, stepping into the yard. She didn't know the command for *save me.*

Gogo barked and sat right below it, below where feet should've been but weren't. Lily staggered back. It wasn't alive. It wasn't a body. A human form devoid of human. It was the back of a white dress, on a white satin hanger, hung on a leafy branch of the tree.

Relief descended in the seconds it took for her heart rate to return to a range compatible with life. It was a dress. Only a dress. Something someone would post on a Pinterest board. The white chiffon ruffled in the breeze, its fairy sway delicate among the green leaves.

It didn't belong in her yard.

She dipped to grab Gogo's collar and moved around to look at the front of the dress. The layers of chiffon were hiked up in the center, and sewn up or pinned where the crotch would've been was a thick patch of black pubic hair. She was so close she could have touched it.

Lily backed away. Her hand came to her mouth as she bent forward to retch. A dry retch that brought nothing but dry air. No breath in, no breath out.

———

Officer Howe took too much time. He took too many pictures. He asked too many questions:

Had this ever happened before?

Was Lily sure the gown hadn't been there in the morning before she left for work?

The woman—Ms. Malone—who had been on the steps earlier today, was she angry with Lily?

Did Lily know how long Ms. Malone had been here before Lily got home? Lily told him Iris hadn't done this. That Iris and Gardner Linden had only come to take her to lunch. Wouldn't do this. There was simply no reason for either of them to do this.

Had her boys been acting out in any way since her husband died?

No. For God's sake, no.

He stopped and turned to her but spoke to himself: "This is weird. Malicious trespassing, maybe."

He resumed his walk around the gown, the tree, checking the intact lock on the back gate.

Had Lily ever seen the dress before?

Yes, it looked like the same gown someone had sent her from Nordstrom for her wedding anniversary in March, except that she was widowed.

He put on latex gloves to touch the crotch of black hair. His hands were cautious, intimate; he explained he wanted to be sure it wasn't an animal.

"The hair looks like yours." He turned to Lily. She saw that now. It wasn't pubic hair. Knew what it was.

"It's my dead husband's hair. We had the same kind of hair. Almost the same color."

"Ma'am, how would someone get your dead husband's hair?" His look at her. His I-got-this-figured-out look. *You did this. You're the Munchausen who demands attention.*

"I didn't do this, if that's what you're asking. Tell me you don't think I did this."

She explained Des shaving his head after that first chemo, shaving his hair before it fell out. That whoever had broken in to her house last weekend must've taken the bag of hair that she'd put in the den drawer, below the tax returns and the boxes of old checks. Officer Howe called the security company to have them verify there'd been no security breaches in the past few hours. Just to make sure there hadn't been anyone inside the house while she'd been at work.

He walked her through the house. Lily showed him where the bag of hair had been.

When had the bag been there last? he asked.

She didn't know when she'd put it there; she explained that she'd found it before Easter and hadn't checked on it since. She showed him where the gown had been in the cellar among the containers of Christmas decorations. The empty dress box was still there.

He called in for Officer Ennis, but he and his dog were elsewhere at an active crime site.

Howe took more pictures. He dusted the desk drawer for fingerprints. Lily was asked to explain the gutted chair, the bits of fluff she'd missed in cleanup.

What'd they call that kind of gown? he asked her back outside in the yard. A peignoir? A negligee? Looked kind of like a skimpy wedding gown, he commented.

None of this would help, Lily knew. The police force couldn't come and live at her house. She answered Officer Howe with clear, direct answers, but her mind was elsewhere, working on what was now imperative: to get her family away from here. Lily composed a checklist in her head. Cancel newspaper and mail. Assuming that someone was watching the house, she'd have to leave so they wouldn't know she was leaving. She'd sneak clothes into the car in garbage bags.

Another patrol car arrived. The new cop introduced herself as Rita Flores, and she had a slight Hispanic lean on her southern accent. The two police conferred out of Lily's earshot. Officer Flores took more pictures, bagged the gown and hanger in a large plastic bag, and labeled it.

Lily would of course tell her brother she was leaving and maybe that older K-9 cop she had a number for, but she wouldn't tell anyone else. She couldn't go to stay at Owen's. He had his own family. He'd just spent three days at her house. She'd need to cancel the summer camps for the boys. There were three and a half weeks left of school. She wouldn't tell the schools, only call them in sick every day with pink eye or strep throat. Surely Miriam would know the name of a safe house, but Lily couldn't tell them at grief group, not with that new mahogany-haired woman named Stevie. What did she really know of the others except what they said? Carly kept her dead boyfriend's Facebook page going. She'd looked Des up online, had said he was good looking. Leon didn't *seem* like a sociopath. And that horrible Stevie.

At least Lily didn't have to call in to work. Oh God, if she hadn't been fired it might've been the boys taking the dog out to the yard when they got home, to find the gown, the dark thatch of Des's hair on the ghost crotch.

"Do you think my boys are in danger? Should I get them? They're at school," Lily said.

"I have no way of knowing that, ma'am," Officer Howe said. "Your brother—maybe your brother could help you out with some of these decisions. Aside from the break-in, have there been any threats against your person or your family?"

"*This* threatens me. What is this? What if one of my boys found this?"

"Any beefs with the neighbors?" Officer Flores said.

"No."

"The back gate had the lock on when you left for work?"

"Yes. I unlocked it when the police came."

"Do you have someplace you can go, Mrs. Declan? That you can bring your family to till you find out what this is about?" Flores said.

Lily nodded.

"Share that information with me, please. A name, address."

"Out of town," Lily said. "With family. You can reach me by cell."

She'd call her parents on the cruise and let them know she'd stay at their house in Maryville. Aunt Ruth always watched her parents' house. It'd be less suspicious at school if she picked the boys up as usual at aftercare. Lily remembered how early it was, not even one. She wouldn't wait till five or six to leave.

"Please make sure your house alarm is on, whether you're home or not," Flores said.

Lily nodded. "I'll have lights set on the timer also. If you come by and see lights."

"We will have to interview your friend again, ma'am," Howe said. "She may have seen something before you arrived. We'd appreciate you not forewarning her. Let us do our job."

Maybe Des had been right about needing a gun for protection. Now it was gone.

She worked with haste after the police left. She packed crackers and water bottles for the car. She put clothes in duffel bags and put the duffels in large black garbage bags and into the trunk of the car. She checked off lists: toothbrushes, phone charger, laptop. All the while she pretended she was bringing clothes to Goodwill, as if someone was watching her and could read her intentions, inside her house, inside her mind. She called the newspaper to cancel. She left a message on Aunt Ruth's landline. Lily plugged several house lamps into timers. She set the house alarm, grabbed Gogo, started the car, and kept pretending. She went to the Goodwill on Gallatin Road, backed her car in, opened the trunk, and talked to the attendant about donations without actually giving him anything. She went to the post office, casually walking inside with an unopened bill in her hand and putting it in an inside mail slot along with the yellow stop-mail order.

She went to Sam's school first and pretended he had a doctor's appointment and pretended she'd already told his teacher. At Finn's school, she simply signed him out.

She told the boys she had several days off and that Nana and Granddad needed help house-sitting. She'd deal with her firing when they were safe. They didn't question her. She was unquestionable by then, and they picked up on it without words. They played with their Game Boys and took care of Gogo. On the long I-40 corridor from Nashville to Maryville, she watched to make sure her car wasn't being followed. She took several exits to towns she didn't know and watched in her rearview before getting back on the interstate. There wasn't much traffic, and she made good time even with the detours.

PART III

Come on, my enemy; we have yet to wrestle for our lives.

—*Mary Shelley*

PART III

Chapter 48: Summer Radio

They arrived in Maryville midafternoon. The soft bondage of summer had entangled the countryside. Vines crept up the foothills to the mountains. Kudzu embraced trees and encircled fences.

Lily didn't hear back from the message she'd left on Aunt Ruth's phone, nor from the message she'd left on her parents' house phone, so she drove north of town to her uncle and aunt's house. She didn't want Ruth coming to walk the dogs or get the mail and not know somebody was in the house. Ruth, retired from the phone company, was her mom's older sister. Uncle Dan still worked for the county utility board, still thought The Beatles were the best band in the world.

Uncle Dan opened the door accompanied by the clamor of their three Yorkies. The boys waited with Gogo in the car. Dan smiled, hugged his niece, and closed the door on the dogs so he could go see the boys and Gogo.

Dan was a young seventy who looked unendingly uncomfortable in his work dress shirt and chinos; he preferred jeans and Tevas.

"Good Lord, you boys have grown since last month. Bet you have to fight the girls off. I'll put the dogs in the back bedroom, you all come in for colas and a snack."

"Thanks, Uncle Dan. We're headed for Mom's, and I just wanted to tell Aunt Ruth. I left a message on the phone earlier."

"I'm home from work five minutes so I haven't listened to the messages yet. Everything all right?"

"Yep. Boys are out of school for a few days, and I got permission to work from my computer, so we're headed over to the house. I didn't want to startle Ruth if she was there."

Dan put a hand to his heart. "My ninety-three-year-old mom had hip replacement surgery over in Asheville, and Ruth is up taking care of her for a week or two. I might drive over after work tomorrow and spend a few days. Your mother got a gal from church to mind the house. Don't know if you've met her. Think she works for the parks department."

"Glad I didn't go right over. I didn't call Mom. I have an emergency number for the cruise line but didn't think it was an emergency."

"You come in and we'll get this sorted. Ruth's got the number for the gal from church."

Such comfort. The boys had cheese sandwiches and soda. Gogo sat impatiently. The dogs yapped from the back bedroom where Uncle Dan made phone calls. Lily drank sweet tea and inhaled the familial smell of kitchen. There were magnetic ABCs on the bottom of the fridge for their grandkids to arrange. Lily felt sleepy and good.

"Here, I got your mom on the phone," Uncle Dan said. "They got one of those out-of-the country disposables for emergencies."

Her mother's voice on the phone was distorted by echo. "Baby, it's about a million dollars a minute, so be quick. We're having a great time. Are you all right, Lily?"

"Yes, the boys are out of school and I have permission to work from home, so I wanted to spend time at the house if that's okay?"

"Sure it is. Honey Summers is the gal from church house-sitting. She works during the day, so I don't know what time she gets over there. Things got a little hectic when Ruth had to back out. I just gave Dan Honey's cell number. Let her know we'll pay her for the whole time. Give her a call so you won't scare the bejesus out of her. She's got the instructions for the dogs' meds. We stop at Martinique tomorrow. Your father actually danced last night."

Honey Summers's voice mail told Lily to leave a message and have a blessed day. They stopped for takeout pizza on the way over to the house. Nobody delivered as far out as her parents', and she wasn't in the mood to grocery shop. She'd heat it up later, grocery shop tomorrow.

Lily turned on the radio. "And I said, run from that river it'll steal your soul." These weren't Des's channels so far from Nashville. This was local radio, the Americana she grew up with. Three women harmonizing souls and rivers and fire and sorrows. "The river steals and the river takes." She was home now, hadn't turned the radio on the whole way from Nashville. Her attention on the rearview mirror and being certain she wasn't followed took up her focus. But now, the familiar roads and the familiar music—maybe being fired would turn out to be a good thing. She grew up fine here. Her boys could, too, if it came to that.

Chapter 49: Hello the House

Late shadows drifted over the fields. When she stopped at the end of the driveway to check the mailbox, she saw a text from the house sitter saying she'd wait at the house to give Lily the instructions for the dogs.

Gogo and the boys hauled out of the car the moment she stopped. There was something to be said for this kind of running space. Something to be said for space that allowed children to play, to explore. Time away from overly organized sports. Time away from Gilda's Club and the endless circle of grief. They headed toward the back open fields and the trails through the hills.

"You come back before dark," she called after them. "We'll bring in the bags after."

The white clapboard seemed larger now. The stark homesteader feel the house carried through winter and early spring was gone. It looked friendlier draped in the lush greenery. The hand of nature had connected the dots between the roof and the maples and the rose bushes and the window boxes. The door was locked, so she rang the bell. With no answer, she used her key.

Lily put the pizza box on the hall table. "Hello the house," she called out. It took only seconds to walk from the open hallway, the kitchen on the left, to the living room TV straight ahead. Honey Summers sat in the living room watching *Ellen* with the sound loud. She had a head of frizzy blonde hair and thin shoulders. Only seconds for Lily to scare herself silly when Honey Summers didn't turn. Lily had the horrid feeling that she was dead. The way the woman sat so straight. Only death could hold someone so still.

"Hello!" Lily called.

"Sorry, it's the end of the segment. Be with you in a sec." She had a thick accent, the kind Lily grew up with.

Miss Summers cut the television off with the remote and turned.

"You must be the daughter. Lily, your mom said."

The frizzy head turned, and there was that odd feeling of meeting someone out of place. Of knowing someone from one place and the impossibility of knowing the same person in another place. In a place where they didn't belong. And a voice that sounded vaguely familiar but didn't belong here.

Lily froze on the name. The hair was different. It was the woman from the Circle of Compassion. Not the mahogany-haired woman. No, not one of the sad women. It was the counselor from TSU. The itchy one whose hair was softly waved. Her hair must be like this when she didn't blow it dry.

"Renée?" Lily said.

"Where are those sweet boys?" she said.

"Are you Renée?"

Renée wasn't a young gal from church.

"Honey Summers?" Lily said. This didn't make sense. Things seemed to stand still—a game of freeze tag with children who were almost frozen but not quite. There was no sound of yapping from her mom's dogs. The house was too clean. The pillows were plumped on the couch. Books were arranged and neatened. Lily looked to her left where the usual clumpings of spices and omega-3s and One A Days had been cleared from the kitchen counter.

The gal from church stood. She was wearing an oversize plaid shirt and a long denim skirt. She fumbled, dropping something on the chair, knitting or a handcraft, Lily thought. But when she turned to pick it up, Lily saw it was a gun. Why would she have a gun? Had she been expecting a burglar?

"What're you doing here?" Lily said.

"House-sitting."

"What do you want?"

"Desmond," she said.

"He's dead." Lily knew this. Now. Irrevocably. Was this part of her grief counseling, to finally understand that Des was really dead? He wouldn't have left her here otherwise, with this woman with a gun and her childhood house frozen before her eyes.

"I don't believe in death," Renée said. Smiled.

Chapter 50: Dress-Up

"I don't know why people think that wide-eyed anime look is so attractive. You look terrible," Renée said. "Heroin-chic, we called it back in college, remember?"

Lily formed a "what?" with her mouth, but the sound never issued.

"Oh, do close your mouth," Renée said. "Though it's gratifying to see you look so stupid."

Lily closed her bloodless lips.

"Don't worry about the gun. I only have it because I'm in charge of guarding the homestead."

"Is that Des's gun?"

"Yes, he left it for me."

"Left it for you? How would he even know you? Why are you here and not in Nashville? How'd you get here?"

"Let's see—by car?"

It couldn't be Renée. Renée was scratchy. Lily didn't remember Renée having a Tennessee accent, but then how much attention had she paid to her except at the end, when Renée had validated her apprehension? Had Lily ever really looked at her, or had she been more interested in seeing her own pain reflected in the other members of the grief group?

Lily wasn't sure that she'd locked the door behind her. When she walked into her house in Nashville, she always locked the door behind her. City habit. She needed to lock the door so the boys couldn't come in. She needed to get rid of Renée before the boys came back. They had car energy to burn, but it wouldn't last long. They'd be hungry; they'd only had cheese on white bread at Dan's. They wouldn't want her to worry if they were gone too long and too far.

"My uncle said you were from church."

"Oh, you mean how'd I get into your parents' house as caretaker? Caretaker—I like the word so much better than caregiver, don't you? Wasn't hard. I didn't knock off Honey Summers from church if that's what you mean. I just made up a name and went a few times to Sunday services. Stayed behind to do the dishes once or twice after potluck, or hospitality, or whatever that snack thing is called after the service." The southern accent fell away as she spoke. "I didn't make friends with your mom straight off. I thought it best to make friends with your aunt Ruth. Then Ruth introduced me to your mom and to your mom's friends and hey, we all love Jesus. Then when your uncle's mom had to have the hip replacement—talk about manifesting intention. Almost made me believe in God the way things fell into place. But if it wasn't this time, there would've been another."

"This is wrong that you've ingratiated yourself with my family, Renée. I'm going to call my uncle Dan and make sure you're supposed to be here."

"Seriously, Lillian, I'd have to kill you if you did. There's no reason this has to be difficult."

She said "I'd have to kill you" so lightly and with a small, witty smile. Lily's clarity, instant and absolute, was to live. For her boys. For herself. It bypassed her confusion, bypassed her fright.

The woman put her left hand, the hand not holding the gun, over her mouth and pulled on her teeth.

The mouth guard slid out, changing the shape of her mouth, narrowing her cheeks, changing how she spoke. "Sit down," she said, using the gun to point to the settee in the living room. "I don't want you dead, though it might make things easier. Just sit."

Lily stumbled backward toward the settee and caught herself from falling. She didn't take her eyes from Renée.

"Sit down. You have two boys outside. They're what's important. No sudden movement. Do you hear me?"

Yes, she heard; the woman was calm and articulate. Lily sat. She was glad Renée's voice wasn't so loud as to bring the boys. Maybe they wouldn't come. They'd get lost on a trail. Or Gogo would sense the danger, Lassie-like, and not let them enter the house.

The room was no longer frozen. Lily could see that it had been rearranged, depersonalized as if for a real-estate showing. Her father's book of psalms that he kept by his TV chair was gone. The family pictures on the back of the upright piano were gone. She could see their absence with a clarity that she'd never seen in the real photos: her brother's formal wedding photo with Anne-Claire. An outdoor pic of Lily and Des. The grandchildren in handmade frames. Her mother with a host of small dogs in her lap. All were gone.

"Where are my mother's dogs?"

"I'm having them groomed. They smelled like dogs and were shedding everywhere."

Lily turned back to Renée. As she watched, Renée switched the gun to her left hand, then reached up. She took out the two pins that held her wig and jerked it off.

The skull she'd expected beneath the wig was instead short, dark curly hair. This was a beautiful woman who Lily knew from somewhere. No overbite now. No scratchy skin.

Still holding the gun in her hand, Renée undid her oversize plaid shirt and, transferring the gun, disrobed to her camisole beneath. "Desmond was never good at improv," she said. "His gestures were too big. His thought process too big, too methodical. No sense of spontaneity. He could find the grand concept but never the small hooks that an actor needs to inhabit a character."

She stripped with a flirty smile. The wide denim skirt had an elasticized waist, and she wiggled it slowly to her butt, past her thighs, to the floor, exposing black leggings.

"It was only his good nature that got him through, and I think there was a collective sigh from the faculty when he transferred out of the theater arts department and over to music."

She grinned and fluffed out her short, tousled cut. Recognition hit Lily like a landslide. Perception catching up to reality.

"You might *think* he left opera's echelon to stay in Nashville and spend more time with his boys, but he never would've advanced to the next level. He was too wooden onstage, even for opera. It was never his voice. His voice was golden, huge."

Chapter 51: Theater Arts

Nia stood before her—Nia, Deidre's strange friend from Chicago who had given Lily a ride from the wedding. The facade disappeared with her striptease: Tennessee church gal to counselor-in-training to a well-educated Chicagoan. She sat with a sigh in the chair behind her, continued as if she hadn't just transformed herself into another person:

"It was hard on us when he transferred schools. We were so in love, you can't imagine. There was a breakup, as I explained in my letter."

"Your letter?" Lily said.

Nia tucked one leg under the other, yoga style, and leaned forward in Lily's father's chair. "Hello? You bitched and moaned about the letters in Circle."

"Who are you? Who's taking care of your husband?"

"I had fun writing them. All that young love. All those memories. They wrote themselves, a mystical experience, right from my soul."

The calmer Nia got, the louder Lily's heart beat. She'd grown extra arteries and veins, new pathways for fear to move through her body. Her heartbeat became a din that filled the room and threatened to drown out Nia's voice.

"I wrote those letters with love and a simple request for friendship from you. Damn it, Lillian. Jasmine is just a name I gave to those emotions. I thought you'd relate to the flower thing. Technically, what you see is what you get." She stood up to demonstrate this—this Nia—and did a little twirl, ballet-style, with her eyes fixed on Lily for all but a split-second head jerk. The gun twirled with her.

"Do you think Finn will like this? Or should I dress up as a fairy princess? Kids are more sophisticated than that nowadays, but that might be fun for him."

"What're you talking about?" Lily said. *Take care of your boys. Forget everything else in the universe. No fairy princesses.*

"It didn't have to be like this, Lillian. We could've been friends." Nia sat.

"So you are Jasmine and Renée and Nia and all this because I didn't answer your letter?"

"Plural. Letter*sss*. I was so worried about the boys, and you never even let me know how they were doing. You think there's nothing I can alter about Desmond's dying, but this is not true. You're such a cop-out. Oh God, I'm sounding like Jasmine again. I have to stop that."

"Are you a multiple personality?"

"No. Jesus—why the pathology? Was Shakespeare a so-called multiple personality or a playwright? It's called theater arts. At worst I'm a theater arts major, at best I'm an actor. A good one, methinks. I didn't have to impersonate Jasmine, she wasn't a person, just a name signed on some letters. Honey Summers was a cameo. Renée was my only role. My creation, truly. I'm just Nia, plain and simple."

The sun waned in the window behind Nia. The boys would come soon. The outline of trees against the sky was lazy and indistinct.

"Why did you hang the gown in the tree?" Lily asked.

"You're here, aren't you? Duh. Was it Finn who found it? Provocative yet tasteful. Beautiful, wasn't it? How do you want to heat the pizza you brought? The microwave destroys the crust. Why don't you stick it in the oven on low; it's probably not cold-cold."

"If you put it in the tree this morning, how'd you get here?"

"I drove here. Not rocket science. I just had to arrive before you did, whether at the Circle of Compassion or Maryville or wherever else. That's all."

"What do you want from me?"

"Put it in the oven," Nia commanded. "You have two young boys who will need to eat. Be responsible!"

The authority was unexpected. It stopped the sound of Lily's heartbeat, her fear, as if Nia had turned a switch. Knives in the kitchen, requisite knives in the kitchen. Lily would put the pizza in the oven, take a knife from the drawer, and stab this woman.

Nia followed her, her bare feet dainty on the transition from living room carpet to kitchen linoleum. She took Lily's shoulder bag from the hall table. One hand taking Lily's cell phone from the bag's side pocket, the other holding the gun on Lily. Nia put the cell phone in the waistband of her pants and tucked the purse on a shelf by the front door.

Lily opened the knife drawer, casually, as if looking for a pot holder. It was empty.

"We have a slight resemblance, don't you think, Lillian? I'm taller and prettier. You're shorter and cuter. I guess I set Desmond up for a certain type. He could only search for me after I left. He could only love what reminded him of me. Don't take offense. He did love you, too, Lily. I understood from the Circle of Compassion that you loved him the best you could."

"Pizza is in the oven. What do you want, Nia?"

"Desmond, first of all. I told you that, but since I can't have him, I'll need his kids."

"Shoot me now, then. You will not have my boys."

"Jesus, relax. I don't want *your* boys. I want mine. Desmond's and mine. I don't understand why you had Desmond's sperm destroyed. I stopped *trying* to understand you once you had the sperm destroyed. It was tough enough finding out where it was to begin with. I wasn't even sure you'd had the foresight to freeze some, though it's usually offered pre-chemo in his age group. It sooo slowed me down. Phone call after phone call. Form after form after form: Irish descent, college educated, hair texture, body build. If I hadn't said I had a keen interest in classical music and opera it might've gone on forever. Then *you* pulled the plug. *You* killed them for everybody, even for the rich patron who would've made major financial contributions helping loads of people, not just me, but people who can't afford fertility treatments at the clinic. I would've paid well. It would've helped Gina, who was the manager there. Her oldest son will be applying to college soon. I could've helped out with his tuition and her pension. But you only think about yourself, Lily. It's all about you. You had your little Desmonds and there was no thought about other people. We could've all gone our separate ways. Except now we have to be a little family, at least for a while. By the way, don't tell me ever again to 'shoot me now' because I will."

Chapter 52:
Her Furious Angels

A little family? Lily watched her hard, as if this would help it all make sense. Nia's calm frightened Lily as much as the gun in her hand.

Nia walked around the kitchen table. With a flick of the gun barrel, she pulled the rings of the window curtains shut. There was a small black fanny pack slung over the kitchen chair. Nia walked to the wall and switched the kitchen light on. Lily noticed how delicate her hands were. Her feet were tiny, too. For a tall woman with long arms and long legs, her body had forgotten to grow the little-girl hands and feet.

"What time did you tell the boys to come home? It's getting late," Nia said.

"They're not coming back here. They walked to my cousin's."

"Dear Lillian, you're as bad at improv as Desmond was." Nia lowered herself into a chair at the kitchen table. She leaned forward. "He was missing finesse. It was endearing in real life but not good onstage. It's the small things that make a difference, like making my face wider and a smidge of overbite with the mouthpiece. If I'd painted a port wine birthmark, you'd think people would turn away, but they think they're being politically correct by looking you directly in the disfigurement. Being plain is a better disguise. And the scratching does make people turn away—some primitive fear of parasites perhaps, or burrowing lice.

You never looked me in the face at the grief group. I forgot my brown contacts one night and no one noticed. All of you were just so sad, so self-absorbed."

Nia gesticulated with her hands, and one of them held the gun. "When Miriam sent me after you in the hall Tuesday night, you kept walking, kept me by your side rather than face-to-face. That was the only night I was nervous. You'd just been with me at the wedding."

Lily leaned against the counter and tried for the same level of nonchalance. "Exactly what do you want?"

"I don't admire you, you know. You aren't a good widow. Fucking around would have been more understandable than your indifference. One of your Chicago sisters-in-law told me how you didn't want a slide presentation at the memorial. No Celebration of Life, just a funeral. No Facebook page. All in the name of good taste. Look around, Lillian, it's not like you were raised in any sort of elegance."

Nia pointed her gun at the cross-stitch samplers framed on the walls. Lily's mom was an avid cross-stitcher. I READ BANNED BOOKS! was framed over the living room bookshelf. DANCE LIKE NOBODY'S WATCHING; LOVE LIKE YOU'VE NEVER BEEN HURT. SING LIKE NOBODY'S LISTENING; LIVE LIKE IT'S HEAVEN ON EARTH hung over the couch. In the hallway, a colorful LIVE! LOVE! LAUGH!

"The one that annoys me the most is the dance-like-nobody's-watching one. Really, to attribute that to Mark Twain is ludicrous."

"Even if you get rid of me, my family would hunt—"

"Just stop there." Nia held up her little talk-to-the-hand gesture. "I told you I don't want your children. I don't even like you. Nothing personal. When Desmond couldn't have me, he just wandered for a while and then drifted into you. Sit down, Lillian."

There were four chairs arranged around the table, just like always.

"No. I wouldn't know where to sit with you flashing that gun every time you talk."

"I can shoot you just as easily when you're standing as I can with you sitting. So sit." Nia used her foot to scoot a chair out from beneath the table. "Sweet of Des to leave me this gun. Makes it more personal. I found the key first, looking through your closet. I didn't know what it unlocked, but then I saw the safe in the den closet."

Lily sat. Nia rose and went to her right, giving Lily a wide berth. Nia got two plastic tumblers down from the cupboard and filled one with water from the tap. "Care for some water?" she asked.

Lily saw how things had been rearranged in the kitchen. The table and chairs had been moved closer to the long window. The plastic tumblers, too—her mother kept glass glasses in the cabinet, not plastic. Nia had paced this out. If Lily lunged at her from where she sat she'd end up on the floor and not on Nia. And there would be no sharps from broken glass to use as a weapon. Nia brought one water back to the table via the wide berth; the other tumbler she left on the counter.

Nia sat and gestured to Lily to get her own. Lily didn't move.

"Suit yourself," Nia said. She lifted her tumbler toward the framed cross-stitch on the kitchen wall behind her: HOLDING ON TO ANGER IS LIKE DRINKING POISON AND HOPING THE OTHER PERSON DIES.

"Well, here's to hope!" Nia said, and drank her water.

Chapter 53: Ohio Players

Lily heard Gogo from far away, a happy playing-with-the-boys bark. She was sure that if she went for Nia, she'd be shot. That wouldn't help the boys. Was Nia going to kidnap them and Stockholm syndrome everyone into a cohesive family? Lily focused on keeping Nia talking, keeping her attention.

"So you want to have Des's children, but not Des's and my children. I don't get it, but why now? Why didn't you have Des's baby back when you were together?"

"That's rather a personal question and I'd rather not say. Jesus, Lillian!" Nia rose from the chair. "This could've been so easy. You write me a nice letter back, which makes me happy. We share some memories. We walk into the rest of our lives with something shared. Our loss binds us together, and our shared love of Des lifts our loss above the abyss."

Lily could hear the seams in her acting, between what was rehearsed and what was improvised. The binding of loss and shared love above the abyss had been rehearsed, verse trying to pass as chitchat.

"Well, I shall answer your question. I didn't want to hurt your feelings, and I didn't want to denigrate Desmond's memory. Desmond had so little finesse onstage but—we do not live onstage. In the real world, there was something else missing in our Desmond. He was filled with sunshine from his smiling eyes to his great big feet, but he lacked fire. Do you understand the difference between sunshine and fire? My husband had fire, before his father gave him his whack in the head, so to speak, courtesy of the car accident. Desmond needed fire; he needed someone to push him. You weren't very supportive. I found some of his old voice tapes in your kitchen whatnot drawer along with grocery receipts, a screwdriver, a package of lightbulbs, birthday candles. So disorganized. I've got the tapes now, thank you very much. I have a museum-trained technician restoring them, and then I'll have them properly stored."

Lily listened but listened harder for the boys. She was careful not to angle her ear toward the door, not to stare at the closed kitchen curtains in search of a crack. There'd only been that one distant bark. Nothing closer since. "So this is why you and Des didn't have a baby?" It came out sarcastic; she added in a neutral tone: "I'm still not sure I understand."

"What I didn't know then, Lillian, because I was a child almost, is that it didn't matter that Desmond didn't have that fire because *I* have it. I could have used *my* fire for him. I could have *made* something out of his sunshine. We were crazy for each other. It wasn't like you, where he was settling down—the key word here being *settling*. We were, Ohio Players aside, 'too hot.' We were"—Nia lifted her un-gunned hand upward as if holding Yorick's skull—"in bondage to each other. Unless you've had that kind of love, of souls fusing, you couldn't be made to understand. 'Too hot' was an understatement. Desmond used to sing that 'too hot' song to me."

He used to sing it to Lily, too. Except it was a Kool & The Gang song, not the Ohio Players. And somehow because Nia got the group wrong, it didn't matter quite as much.

"We were destined, Desmond and me. There's no way I can explain this to you, Lillian. Lily—eek, your name is so cute, and I'm sure what you and Desmond had was lively and *cute*. What we had was nearer Icarus and the sun. Leda and the swan."

Lily heard the boys. Not at the door, but close, around the side of the house.

227

"Do we have to pick up the dogs from the groomers?" Lily asked. There was never this kind of quiet in her parents' house.

"All taken care of. And calling the police after your house was cleaned. Really? The words are 'Thank you.' Not 'Call the police.'"

Lily went cold to hear the boys so close. They were in the front yard. She heard Sam say: "That's not how we set up the rules. You just change them when you feel like it." She heard Finn reply, "You don't have a clue." Then she heard "I'm hungry" and "Me, too" and didn't know which voice was which.

"What do you want, Nia? What can we do for you? I can hear you are in a lot of pain over Des."

"I thought of suicide. Jude in the hospital bed and then Desmond's obituary. But there was a whole life he had that I had to find out about."

"And going into my house was part of that? As an African American woman? And why did you clean?"

"To help. And to leave flowers, of course. It was where Desmond lived. But dear God, do you think I actually cleaned your house? Your toilets? You think I was up in your trees trimming branches? I hired a company. The maid was from the cleaning service. From Kentucky. I didn't want any local firms. I supervised, of course. Sometime I'll show you my timetable spreadsheets; I'm extremely proud of them. None of this was easy. Getting info on when you'd be away and coordinating my schedule and my husband's nurses' schedules and Renée's schedule. The wedding was really tough. I had to skip the rehearsal dinner to go to Nashville and drive back for the wedding. Then I drove all night to finish things up in Nashville after you so rudely left my apartment that night. It was exhilarating. Coming here for church was another pain in the butt. Sometimes I had to fly, but I prefer to drive; it offers so much time for reflection, songs on the radio."

"You know that Mom won't let us back out if we go in." Finn's voice, a little closer now.

Chapter 54: Cubs Logo

No. The boys hadn't run off. They were still in the front yard. "There *are* no ghosts on the road," Sam whined. "There wasn't one in the tree, either, and I'm telling Mom how you try to scare me."

"So now you're going to run in to tell Mom?"

She didn't know why Nia didn't pause at the sound of the boys' voices. Didn't turn her head. "I named Desmond; did you know that? I can't stand when I hear you call him Des; it's disrespectful. His family did that Desi thing sometimes, à la Cuban bandleader. I called him Desmond, and other people started to, and then he started using it professionally."

Lily didn't interrupt. Didn't tell her Des had introduced himself as Des, had preferred it. Through the narrow lintel over the curtained windows, Lily watched the sky turn dark, solid. Wondered what defense there was against this woman waving her hands as she spoke. Waving the gun. If it went off, would the boys come running toward the sound or away from it?

"I've had this fantasy—no, not a fantasy, an ambition—where we all live in Chicago together and I send the boys to good schools. I mean good schools, maybe in Switzerland, not that parochial garbage Desmond went to or public schools like they're doing now. I wanted to help out with their education. But you have connected me to reality, and this is not going to happen. You've given me every indication that you act against the best interests of our family. So plan B—no pun intended. You know your kids, the whiney ones outside, shouldn't have happened."

"They did happen."

"*Shouldn't* have, I said, not *didn't* happen."

Lily shifted her attention from trying to track the boys to looking for an object to throw. The iron trivet that sat in the middle of the table with the napkin holder was gone. There'd been a heavy crystal bowl her father kept keys in on the kitchen counter. It was gone.

"In your twenties you think of love only. Then you approach thirty and find out the star quarterback you adored is teaching high school gym. Or like Desmond, Mister Opera Star is now singing in the chorus, and in Nashville. Not Paris. Not Vienna. And you think, God I was right: he didn't have that fire. Then when I saw Desmond at his nephew's first communion two years ago, I realized none of that mattered. You all looked so happy. So uncomplicated. My father-in-law arranged for us to go to Europe for yet another new treatment for Jude. When we got home, I read the alumni obits and I remembered how much I loved Desmond. I shouldn't have let him go. I shouldn't have allowed it. He should've been saved. That makes me angry. Did you just run out of energy? Did you just give up? I could have found a cure."

Lily had no memory of Nia from Ryan's first communion, but there'd been a catechism class of fifty children and their relatives at the church, the girls giggly in their white confections, the boys serious in gray and blue jackets. Des had been in the manageable part of his illness then; you wouldn't have known he was sick to look at him. They probably had looked uncomplicated.

"I try to think you did your best," Nia said.

Lily sensed the boys nearing more than heard them. She kept her head very still. She felt very cold. She'd felt cold like this when Des was dying.

"Desmond wasn't technically a University of Chicago alumnus. Do you know that? He left halfway through junior year to transfer to the music conservatory. Yet they published his obituary because so many knew and loved him there. That was a sign to me. If they hadn't published the obit, I might not have remembered how much we'd meant to each other. It might've been months before I ran into someone from his family."

"Did you and Des see each other at the first communion?" Lily said.

"I hope you're not thinking what I think you're thinking. Desmond was an honorable man. No matter how much he loved me, he would never ask me to renege on my wedding vows."

Gogo barked outside, a gentle remember-me bark. Lily's mother kept the knife block behind the dish towels on the upper shelf of the broom closet. Part of her childproofing operation years ago when the grandchildren had arrived. It'd never been moved back to the counter. Lily squeezed her eyes shut and made a show of wiping her forehead. "Maybe you're right," Lily said. "Why didn't you reach out to him? You could've saved him. I need a towel. Where are the dish towels?"

Lily got up and opened the long cabinet to the side of the refrigerator. She could hurl the wooden knife block at Nia. Throw her off guard so she could stab her. She felt behind the towels.

"Do you actually think I left the knives or the block there, Lillian? Not dealing with a full deck, as Desmond's mom said about you. Stay there. Do not turn around or I'll shoot your legs."

Lily did not turn around. The side of the refrigerator within her field of vision was oddly white, devoid of the clutter of family photos and William Wegman magnets, church schedules and kid art.

"You decide in this moment whether this gets handled with the gun or without. I've worked with a professional and I've been practicing. Takes me less than three seconds to take the gun out, but I don't even have to. It'll shoot right through the canvas. Here are your boys. You can turn now. Try to act natural, would you try that?"

Lily turned and saw that Nia now wore the black fanny pack loosely below her waist.

"It's really a custom holster I had specially made for me, and it's open on the side," Nia said. "You like the Cubs logo? I added that.

"I don't need you, Lillian. Just to be clear. I took your birth certificates from the desk in the den. I've already gotten a Tennessee driver's license in your name with my picture. The passports will be easy if I have to. I made a vow not to destroy anything Desmond loved, and your cooperation could be useful with the boys. Though I will remove obstacles if I need to."

Chapter 55: Dirty Boys

The boys came through the dark evening to the bright kitchen. They were tired jumpy, tired hungry. Gogo trailed them and headed straight for the water bowl. Just like all the other times at her parents' house. The boys pulled up short at the sight of a stranger in the kitchen.

"Hello, Gogo! How good to see you!" Nia said. Gogo left the water bowl and galloped to Nia. She bent to pet the dog. "Hey guys, I'm an old friend of your dad's. We met at your cousin Ryan's first communion a while ago and just last weekend at your uncle Kevin's wedding. Great to see you again!"

"I'm ready for that pizza," Sam announced in his little-man voice.

"Cubs fan?" Finn asked.

Nia rose from the chair. "Oh yes! Thanks for noticing." She'd practiced, she'd told Lily, could shoot right through the canvas. She'd practiced the cheery voice for the boys, too.

"Hey, I know you," Sam said. "You're the lady who handed out the flyers for that judo after-school program, except you had long hair then."

"Not me," Nia said. "You're a very observant boy, though. That was my sister; we're all old friends of the family. I'm Nia. You may call me Aunt Nia."

Finn shrugged. Sam got a juice box from the fridge and tossed one to his brother.

"Mom, can we eat now?" Sam said.

"No," Nia said. "Your mom and I discussed this, and you should get out of those dirty clothes and wash up immediately."

"Let them get a slice or two of pizza first."

Sam stuck a straw in his juice box.

"No," Nia said. "No pizza now, they need to clean up."

"What're you doing here?" Finn said.

"Boys have to be fed at this age and often," Lily said.

"Thanks for the advice," Nia said. She pulled a kitchen chair away from the table, angled it toward the hallway, and sat, resting her hand by the Cubs logo on the fanny pack. "After they clean up, we'll sit down and eat together like a civilized family. I have ice cream in the freezer for dessert."

Finn watched them, didn't know yet knew—Lily could see it in his face. It was his mom who gave orders, not this stranger.

"You remembered dog food, Lillian?" Nia asked.

"I just feed her whatever my mom has here for the dogs."

"Hey, where are Nana's dogs? She take them on vacation with her and Granddad?" Sam asked.

"No. They're having a spa treatment. I'm watching the house for your grandparents while they're away."

"What's a spa treatment?" Sam said.

"Shampoo, blow-dry, nails clipped. Sleeping on satin pillows."

Sam shrugged. The boys stood slurping their juice. Sam had no other care but his thirst. Lily trained her eyes on Finn and tried to drill daggers into his soul. *Run away. Go out the window in the back room. Take your brother and run.*

Finn frowned. "What? Am I doing something wrong?" he said.

"Don't speak to your mother in that tone," Nia said.

"No, darling," Lily said. "You aren't doing anything wrong. Your hands are just dirty."

"Okay, that's enough. Stinky boys into the shower," Nia said.

"Your bags are in *Aunt Amanda's* room. Put on clean clothes after," Lily said.

"Are you Aunt Amanda?" Sam asked.

"No, I'm Aunt Nia. Who's Amanda?"

"The guest bedroom. Before it was my brother's room it was my mother's aunt Amanda's room," Lily said.

"Amanda—she's the old one in the nursing home. We should go visit her while we're here," Finn said. Lily almost smiled, feeling the first shard of hope since they'd walked in the door.

Sam followed Finn down the hall. Gogo followed them.

"No, the dog stays here," Nia said. "Come, Gogo."

The dog came to her. Tail wagging, she let Nia sink her hand into her thick fur. Iago. Betrayer.

"Leave your clothes by the washer," Nia said. The stacked washer and dryer were in the first hall door to the left in what had been a closet. "Do *not* track all that dirt through the house. I had to vacuum before I unpacked my bag."

The boys looked to Lily. "They can drop them on the bathroom floor. It's cold in the hall," Lily said.

"No. Take off your filthy clothes!" Nia screamed. Screamed loud.

Sam balled up his face and screamed back. "Maybe you are a friend of my dad's, but you aren't allowed to yell like that. My dad doesn't like it!"

Nia slipped her hand into the fanny pack and waved it toward Sam.

"Just do as she says, boys," Lily said. "Get clean clothes from your bags and shower up. Go on, Aunt Amanda's room. Make sure to shampoo your hair."

They stripped to their underpants. "All of it off," Nia said.

Sam stepped out of his underpants and trotted naked down the hall.

"No," Finn said, and glared at Nia. He turned and walked down the hall in his jockey shorts.

Even if Finn remembered the code, they wouldn't go now, Lily knew. They wouldn't leave the house naked or in underpants. Sam had recently found a sense of modesty to the outside world, and Finn was almost a teenager. Their clothes weren't in the back bedroom; the bags were still in the car. But there might be something in the dressers or the closet, towels or a bag of clothes for the jumble sale at church.

"I have to get the rest of the bags from the car," Lily said.

"Really? You think I'll just hand you the keys? I'll deal with it later," Nia answered.

Finn went into the bathroom, and Lily heard the shower run. He came out and went back to the bedroom and shut the door.

"They shouldn't waste water like that," Nia said.

"Well water takes a while to get hot," Lily said.

She pulled a chair from the kitchen table and leaned toward this woman who had a gun and was crazy. Lily spoke softly: "You need to leave now. Nothing's happened yet, just go before it does. They're kids, leave them be. Your husband needs you. We can come visit in Chicago and get to know each other. Thanks for helping us out. Sorry I wasn't more grateful at the time. I didn't understand, and like you said, I wasn't playing with a full deck. I think it's a tribute to Des that you want to help out with my sons' education."

"*Your* sons? Sam may be your son, but Finn is Desmond's. You only have to look at him. His height. His walk. If ever a woman was a vessel, it was you. My husband's seed passed straight through you into handsome Finn."

"Your husband is in a bed in your apartment in Chicago. Please go now."

"You don't seem to understand that I will have Desmond's child. That's the nice thing about boys that age, their bodies act without any help from their minds. Conception may take time because of his age, but the mechanics are there. I want to show Finn how I loved his father. Please don't worry; I won't abandon him after I have my own children."

Chapter 56: Family

"You will not rape my son," Lily said.

"Oh please, cut the drama. It's not like he's a girl. This is simply an initiation for him; he'll be thirteen in a few weeks. Sooner or later you'll have to let go. I brought sedation for him, if necessary. And as far as his being underage, I'm sure you wouldn't want to drag your son through the court system. Not with my money.

"Get me a juice box and push your chair in at the table when you get up. I don't like things out of order. Even in this quaint little shithole."

Lily got a juice box from the fridge and tossed it to Nia. It landed with a thunk by her feet.

"Good try. Let's see, I was going to reach for it with my right hand, and you were going to rush me, unhook the holster, and take the gun?"

"No. I thought you'd catch it."

Nia picked it up from the floor. "These ones in the red containers are organic."

The fridge had been cleaned out. No gallon of milk that Lily could throw, no large jars of Bubbies pickles that her father loved.

"You're right about the sperm at the fertility clinic being destroyed," Lily said. "But there's still sperm at Vanderbilt Oncology. We were in a program for genetic testing and cancer. It was only destroyed for private use at the fertility clinic. I'll give permission for it to be released to you. Just promise you'll leave us alone afterward."

Nia looked hopeful for a moment, looked sane. "Everybody assumes if you're a theater major that you're not smart. I checked every possibility. Every hope. Every kindness you didn't give me. Lillian the Destroyer. I checked out cloning, too. There are places that are experimenting. For the right money, I might've had a shot. I thought hard about that. It would be a privilege to give birth to Desmond. A true rebirth, a renaissance. That's how I came up with Renée's name. Then I thought it might be messy. That if I gave birth to him, he might not want to have a child with me."

Lily felt vomit rising in her throat. She swallowed. She rose and casually picked up her chair to throw. It would be easy to throw.

"Put the chair down. Once you're gone, it'll be much easier, at least in the short term."

Lily put the chair down. She sat. She tried to cry. She tried to cry to keep Nia's attention focused on her and not the boys.

"It doesn't have to be this way, Lillian. We could be friends. You could share your boys. If Finn knew it was okay with you, this could all go nicely. I know you weren't brought up Catholic with a sense of purpose like Desmond and me, but you need to tell your son it's a gift for his dad, that he could be a hero for his dad's friend."

From the corner of her eye, Lily saw Finn's face in the crack of the back bedroom door. She heard the door click shut. She went to the fridge and opened it again. "What happened to the Brita pitcher of water?"

"I had to clean everything here. Everything. Did Desmond actually come here, actually meet your parents before you got married? Close the refrigerator unless you're getting something out. You're wasting electricity."

"This is well water. It needs to be filtered."

"Speaking of—the water must be hot in the shower by now."

"Sam's already in there," Lily said, and hoped he wasn't. She hadn't seen him. "Wasting electricity? What, were you poor growing up?"

"No, we weren't poor growing up. We weren't wasteful, either. What're you looking for?"

"Where did you say you put the Brita pitcher?"

"Get tap water from the sink or take a juice box and close the refrigerator. This isn't a restaurant."

Gogo, who'd been content by Nia's feet, whined and trotted to the hall. Lily prayed that the small rustling noises in the back were the boys going out a window.

"How long are you going to keep us? Until you're pregnant? My parents—"

"Your parents will be back in ten days. I know that. Just because I'm a big-picture person doesn't mean I've ignored any details. If we can all get along, this could be a time of celebration. I haven't given up on that. There's dog food in that gray container by the dog bowls on the place mat. There's a plastic cup in there to measure it out, since you didn't bring your own."

Nia called Gogo, and she came with tail wagging. Lily fed the dog. She thought she heard noise again. Over the sound of her heart beating in her ears she wasn't sure. Nia didn't seem to hear it.

"You see how Gogo and I are friends? I could have killed her so many times. She takes raw meat from my palm. Poison is easy. You see I don't want to kill her. Desmond picked her out. Like he picked you out after I left. I don't want to kill you if I don't have to. This is a mark of respect to Desmond; you don't quite get that. You could come to Chicago in summer. I could send them to good day camps. Not the Y, prep-school day camps. They would love their little brother. It might be more than one. I'm on fertility drugs. The time is right. I told you, my father-in-law is crazy for a grandchild. He wants a boy, sort of like a do-over for him."

"What if you have a girl?" Lily went back to the fridge and took out a juice box.

"I'm not feeling that. Fate can be culled if necessary. Do sit down, you're so clunky."

Lily sat. "What if one of the neighbors drops by? What if Uncle Dan comes by? This is the country, people come by."

"Then I'll have your sweet Sam in back with the gun to his head or a knife to his heart and tape over his mouth when you go to the door. Let's not make it come to that, shall we? By the way, your uncle is headed over to North Carolina tomorrow." Nia stopped and tilted her head up. "Did you hear that?"

This time, Lily didn't hear anything. "No." She slurped the bottom of her juice box. "Did you get me fired at work?"

"You were fired?"

"Yes. I was fired this morning."

"No. How wonderful. I just thought you took sick time after the bride effigy. Wasn't she beautiful! Of course I knew you'd come here. Don't worry about money until you find another job. I like how you kept a lot of Desmond's clothes in your closet. Thank you. I could smell him in the tuxedo. We need to check on the boys now. Do they shower together? I'm all keyed up. This is so much better than the proverbial turkey baster. Do you know that *that* actually is the preferred way, after good old-fashioned sex, that is. I've learned a lot in the fertility program. I thought the whole thing would be very clinical. That they'd harvest my current husband's sperm through a needle and harvest my eggs, give them a night of dancing in the petri dish, and then inject the fertilized eggs into me. Jude, he's got viable sperm, so we didn't have to do that. It didn't need to be frozen, since it had already been tested. I get rid of the help for the evening, put the lights low, and put on something lacy, like the nightgown I sent you for your anniversary. I didn't expect to find it abandoned in the basement! I play music, too, opera. Then I play with him into this sterile cup that goes into a type of needleless syringe, a little more high-tech than a baster but not much, and then I'm supposed to lie down, which I do, and put it in me, which I don't. I never finish it. There's just no fire.

"Let's get the boys, okay? You're right, they need to eat. I have a freezing medium to store Finn's ejaculate just in case this doesn't work the way it should. But fresh and natural is best."

Lily heard steps in the hall.

Chapter 57: Sweet Amanda

Finn knew the code. You hear Amanda's name when it doesn't belong, you run.

He didn't like the lady in the kitchen. She was making his mother angry—that kind of underskin anger like when she was really pissed at him or Sam but they were in public and she couldn't say anything. Telling him to take off all his clothes in the hall was creepy. It was one thing for a kindergartner like Sam, but he was older.

In the room, which had been his uncle Owen's room, there were no clothes. Their bags were still in the car, but it didn't seem like a good time to remind her. Finn knew the code, but nobody mentioned not having a pair of pants on and a naked brother. He went through the drawers hoping some of his uncle's old clothes were in them. All there was was a bunch of Nana's projects, crochet stuff and needlework. He peeked out in the hall and saw no one. He went to get their clothes.

"Young man!" the lady said. She was standing in the kitchen by his seated mother. "You were told to take a shower. Is your brother finished in there yet?"

He didn't tell her Sam wasn't in the shower. "I have to get gum out of my pocket."

"This is no time for gum. I don't like gum chewing. It's not a nice habit."

He watched her, embarrassed by the intense way she was looking at him, and managed a bored voice: "Mom says I have to take the gum out of my pockets before they go in the wash 'cause it screws up the washer and dryer. She says we have to—"

"Just go ahead, then, and get moving!" The lady put her hand on his mother's shoulder. It wasn't friendly, though.

He slipped Sam's jeans next to his own and spread the shirts out on the floor so it looked like a lot of messy clothes still there. His mom, still in the chair, moved her hand in a fist to her heart and stared dagger eyes into his. He didn't want to leave her by herself, but he knew his job. One time she'd told them she was an old-fashioned mountain girl and could take care of herself, but he couldn't remember the context and their dad had been alive then. Dad had smiled when she'd said it.

Down the hall in the kitchen, his mom got up from her chair, turned her back to him, and opened the oven door. "We had this on way too low, it's not even warm," she said.

Finn struggled not to look back at his mom as he returned down the hall.

In the room, he tried to lock the door behind him. It was a push lock on the knob that just popped back out when he pressed it. He took the chair by the desk and jammed its back under the knob.

Sam was sitting on the floor reading a picture book. Finn leaned down. "Look, Sam. Mom has given us permission to have a secret adventure, but we have to go now, and we have to be quiet."

"She packed us sandwiches or something?"

"No. That would be like cheating. Put on your pants and be real quiet."

"I'm not putting on my jeans without underpants. Are you crazy?"

"It's an adventure thing. All topsy-turvy-like. Hurry."

"I'm checking with Mom first." He opened his mouth but didn't get a sound out before Finn had his hand over Sam's mouth.

"Mom said the code, Sam. She said *Amanda*. She said the code for running away."

———

"If the pizza isn't hot, how about turning the oven higher? Ya think!" Nia said.

"You'll have to do it," Lily said. Her voice was flimsy. Her knees were tired. She sat back down at the table.

The light above the kitchen table hummed. The yellow kitchen hummed. It wasn't just the color that was bright and cheerful. It was where Lily had grown up. She and her brother did homework on the kitchen table. Her mother did cross-stitch while she waited for dinner to cook. Her brother, destined for construction from childhood, built a Native American village for a history assignment on this table. The village had turned out so extraordinary, so perfect in detail, that it garnered criticism for parental interference. Once the accusation had been dismissed, it was assigned to permanent display at Blue Hills Elementary School. This kitchen had been a safe place long before Des came along. Maybe Owen would bring the boys over to the school one day and show them his project. Maybe she should call him. Her heart settled. The comfort of family. The kitchen table.

"How the fuck did you drug me?" Lily asked.

"The juice boxes. It's easy to do, just a syringe with a needle next to that little straw opening. You got one of the strong doses in the red container. You didn't really think that I expected cooperation from you?"

Lily watched Nia's clever face unform.

"I guess you didn't notice I didn't drink mine. You never truly think about me, Lillian. You don't think about what I do, how I feel, do you?"

Chapter 58:
Gertie's Milk Shakes

Lily's bedroom blurred with shadows. The audio was mostly static; voices faded in and out, dust radio.

"Little shits never took a shower, either. They're god-awful stinky."

It wasn't just the screen of sight and sound that was unfocused. Her thoughts moved like cigarette-smoke ghosts that formed and unformed.

"I'll have to titrate their dosage way down. They're full-out asleep. They're breathing fine, but I can't move them."

Lily tried to think without saying her thoughts aloud, but she heard herself moaning. She tried to make her thoughts into tiptoes: *Don't let her know you are awake. Don't let her know what you are thinking.*

"I'd prefer Finn mobile, unlike my husband. Yes, I can jerk him off, but the only reaction, aside from the sperm jumping, is those sad eyes. You can move, Lillian, just not much."

Nia's petite hands lifted some type of sweet milky substance up to Lily's mouth. "Don't worry, no drugs here. You've already had plenty. Take a sip. Desmond's mouth always tasted like Gertie's vanilla milk shakes. Did you know that? You didn't know that, did you? You didn't know him then. You were so much later. We were young and pure and sweet."

———

Lily slept. She dreamed someone came into the room and placed stones atop her. Their weight woke her. Every muscle, every piece of skin was dull and a thousand pounds heavy. A thick chemical taste rested in her mouth. She cleared her head to remember she'd been drugged, to remember her boys had been drugged and hadn't made an escape. She knew she had to placate the woman sitting at her childhood desk. She knew she had to kill her.

She watched Nia's back sitting at the desk. She remembered Nia pulling on the latex gloves to touch her husband beneath the sheets and remembered his angry eyes. Maybe her husband wasn't quadriplegic; maybe Nia kept him drugged. Lily took hold of her pain and hurled it out in one long scream: "Finn! Sam!" She could hear it, but it came out as two long grunts that sounded like *Hinnn* and *Hannn*.

Nia startled and laughed. "They're fine, Lillian. I told you I gave them too much to begin with, so I've adjusted the dosage. Not too much for Finn. I want him up and ready tonight. At least twice a day for the next four to five days should do the trick. I have the best fertility doctors in Chicago—my father-in-law desperately wants that new son since we got back from Europe. I'm very lucky to have this all coincide. It's almost a done deal with the fertility meds. Are you thirsty?"

Lily scrunched her mouth as tight as she could against the straw Nia poked at her face. "There's no medication in this, Lillian. It's just the milk shake in honor of Desmond. How he smelled. What he could do with his mouth."

"I have to pee," Lily said. Her words came out fine, just slow. "I don't think I can walk."

"See if you can crawl, then. I have hospital pads under you if you can't crawl."

Lily pushed her hair back off her forehead. It was gone. Only an inch or two left in small tufts.

"You cut my hair?" Lily said.

"I was bored. All of you slept through a day. So yes, I did. Snip snip. Desmond always liked my hair long, so I wasn't going to let you be the one with the long, pretty hair."

Nia left the room. Lily tested moving her arms and her legs. Leaning back on her elbows, she edged her head and torso to a sitting position. She swung her feet over the side of the bed and stood. She was wobbly, but it was possible. She didn't have to pee; she'd dried up on the drugs. If she could make it to the bathroom, she could find something to hit Nia over the head with, a bottle of mouthwash, a wastepaper basket. She hadn't seen the gun, and Nia hadn't been wearing the Cubs fanny pack.

Walking turned out to be more difficult than standing. She eased back down to the bed. Maybe her arms and fingers would be stronger. She would get Nia to walk her to the bathroom and she would strangle her. Lily wrapped her hands around her pillow and squeezed until the pillow died.

She shook herself awake every time she drug-nodded off. She lay still, transformed by the practice of killing, disappeared into the waiting: listening, assembling escape routes.

Chapter 59: Long Way Around

Nia took the pillow Lily had her arms around and arranged it behind her head, then leaned over and kissed Lily's mouth with great tenderness. "You can help, Lillian. I am only too aware that your mouth was the last mouth Desmond kissed. Your body was the last he touched. If I had known he was sick, if you had called on an old friend, I could've helped, emotionally and financially. Because of my other husband's illness, I know where alternative treatments are researched. It wasn't even a cancer that's usually fatal at Desmond's age. I could have brought him to Europe. I could've kept him alive. At least until I had our baby. We'd get him a bed next to Jude if he wasn't feeling well. Nursing care already in place. We'd be at the park right now, you and I. The boys would be admiring their new baby brother. You'd be giving me advice. How long to nurse. The best brand of organic baby food. Should we use those sweet little buckskin shoes when baby first starts to walk or do you think a more structured shoe is preferable? You know, the things I thought would be difficult, like breaking in to Desmond's house, the constant travel, forging a résumé and the interview for that self-pity circle you're in, were easy. Even getting you to come here was relatively straightforward. The boys, however, haven't been as cooperative as I'd imagined."

Nia rose from the edge of the bed. She paced: "Through my fault. Through my fault. Through my most grievous fault." She pounded her chest with the words, a light pound at the end of a dramatic arm.

"I can't just blame you. I share some of this responsibility. What if two years ago when I saw you all at the first communion, I had been honest with myself? If I had just allowed myself an honest thought that yours was the life I wanted to lead? I didn't expect to be married to a paralyzed man. I could've gotten a divorce, taken my share, and come for Desmond. My poor other husband probably wouldn't know the difference between some nurse and me. We would travel, Desmond and me and our children. He would sing at the great opera houses."

The blue walls and low light cast a glow over Nia's face. Lily tried to center Nia in her vision, to listen, to keep Nia here with her and away from the boys.

A phone rang, an old-fashioned landline ring. Her parents' phone, as distant as childhood.

"I did your voice on the answering machine," Nia said. "It came out good. Can you hear it?"

Lily couldn't hear it.

Nia came and sat on the edge of the bed beside her. "Listen how I made your voice—a sad person trying to be chipper. Listen how I am your voice. We are still one, Lillian. Even if your life wasn't what Desmond's and my life was. What we share binds us. Holds us together in his love." Nia stroked Lily's shoulder without intent, the way one strokes the dog beside you on the couch. Lily lifted her hand and stroked Nia's cheek. Nia's neck was so close, but Lily's arms were still heavy, her drugged fingers dusty tree branches. Nia caressed Lily's hand against her cheek.

"You are very beautiful, Nia. I can't understand why you let him go."

"I took a wrong turn, that's all."

"Well, you were so generous to share him with me, even if I was second best."

"Don't put words in my mouth," Nia said. Yet her words were playful. "How dare you think I would've shared him with someone like you. You clipped his wings. You—"

"He didn't know you would've come. He didn't know then. Now he knows. Now he's spirit and knows all."

Nia lifted her cami and moved Lily's hand to her breast, kneading Lily's fingers against herself. Nia whispered, "He loved me."

She dropped Lily's hand and stood. She paced the small room. Lily wanted to test her limbs again, see how far the drugs had worn off. Her arms and legs still seemed more part of the bed than part of her will. Nia stopped at the foot of the bed and jerked the bedspread off. She attacked Lily's clothes. She pulled her out of her jeans, jerked her arms and head out of her T-shirt, unhooked her bra and tugged it from Lily's leaden arms. "Can't you help at all?"

"I don't know. Let me try. Give me a minute."

"Too late. I see you. Now you can look at me."

Nia disrobed, continuing the striptease she'd started when she'd been Renée. Well rehearsed, perhaps for her unmoving husband. Perhaps for a mirror. *Dance like you hope somebody's watching.*

Nia crossed her arms to pull her cami up over her head. She paused with her head hidden as if she were stuck and shimmied her naked torso as if this would disentangle her. She freed herself from the shirt and used it like a towel to wipe her cheek, her long neck, each breast, a long midline swipe from her belly to her crotch, where it lingered, in slow seduction. She wiggled slowly from her tight yoga pants as if the fabric clung to her sweat. Lily saw that they did have the same body. The high, tight breasts pointed upward. The same small hips. Nia paused at her thong, slipping her fingers into herself, and turned her back. Lily could see the same little bump ass as her own. Nia was longer and leaner. She threw her head over her shoulder toward Lily. Nia's glance was seductive, but there was no eye contact. Its purpose was to see how she fared in the mirror. No stretch marks at the top of Nia's thighs. She turned back around, licking her fingers. Nia's breasts were firmer. No striation on her nonmaternal belly. Nia took off her thong with one leg up on the bottom of the bed, then the other leg. The same dark patch between rounded thighs.

"Let me feel you," Lily said. "You were Des's Salome, the first, the best."

Every moment, Lily felt more alive. Adrenaline and time countered the drugs in her system. She felt a warmth in her breasts, a sweet tightness in her crotch. She could barely wait for Nia to lie atop her. To feel her body on her body. To wrap her arms around her. To take her mouth in her mouth and place her hands around her neck and kill her. The hate Lily held in her heart would give her strength. The hate she held for Des that he could've ever in his lifetime loved this creature who would hurt their children, take their unformed sperm, their innocence. What had he been thinking at nineteen or twenty? All time past walks with the future.

"You're beautiful," Lily said. "Your face is exquisite. Your body— you look like a twenty-year-old."

"I'm much taller than you."

"Yes, like a model."

"My feet," Nia said. She held her leg up, her foot en pointe. "I take a size five. Desmond loved my tiny feet." She lowered her leg to fifth position. "He loved my feminine hands." She waved her hands to Lily, who held her own hands out. Nia put her hands, palm to palm, to Lily. They were dwarfed against Lily's hands. Lily was glad to see how her arms were working. Her hands and her fingers had come back to life. Nia closed her eyes. "Desmond loved to hold his hands against mine. My hand was half his. Little-girl hands, he said."

Gogo whined. Gogo barked. "Damn. Let me take care of her first. I locked her in my room so she wouldn't bother the kids." Nia put her yoga pants and shirt on. She shut the door behind her.

Lily sat up slowly. She could move. Brain fog cleared to a pounding headache, but her limbs worked. She stood, walked in place, shook her arms and hands out. She listened hard so she could flop back down when Nia came. A parade of sounds began. Doors slammed. Gogo barked. Nia cursed. Nia yelled. Lily sat back on the bed. The door opened.

"They're gone," Nia screamed. "Get some clothes on. We've got to find them. I checked all through the workshop out back, too, and they're not there. Why would they do this? Good Lord, have they ever run away before?"

Lily didn't move. Seconds could give them an edge.

"At least they couldn't have gone anywhere fast. They're drugged and tired and it's dark out," Nia said, back to her controlled self. "And the dog isn't with them. Get up and put clothes on."

Nia threw Lily's jeans at her, her sneakers, one bouncing off her arm and the other hitting her square in the face. The plaid shirt that Renée had worn landed in Lily's lap. Lily untangled the shirt. Nia ran at her and shoved her off the bed. Lily moved herself up to all fours, naked, tucked her head to her chin, and waited for Nia's kick—she didn't know why she knew it would come. Every second's delay was another footstep for Finn and Sam.

Lily felt something cold and hard between her legs. The gun.

"I need you to help. I need you to show me where they like to go. I need you to come with me because it's easier to get rid of you out in the woods than in a house. But it's not that vital, Lillian."

Nia moved, taking the gun muzzle with her, holding it loosely. Lily rolled over, struggled with her jeans. The shoes were difficult. Navy-blue Keds. She couldn't get the laces tied.

"I'm drugged-out here, remember?" She tugged the shirt on. "I want to help you. I know the trails."

Chapter 60: Cool, Dark Night

The night was half-moon dark. Nia guided Lily out the back door. A damp chill floated through the air like ground cover. The cool coaxed Lily just enough to remember fear, her heart drum, her cold fingers, the woman holding Des's gun beside her.

Nia held Finn's shirt under Gogo's nose. It was a pale-blue button-down that he'd worn to school the day they'd left Nashville. Lily didn't know what day it was, but the sight of the shirt now being used by Nia to track her son woke her all the way. The dog inhaled the smell like an old friend. Nia snapped open the lead on the retractable leash. "Follow!" she said. Instead Gogo rubbed against Nia's legs with grand affection. Nia directed Gogo's nose back to Finn's shirt. "Fetch!" Nia commanded. Gogo sat.

"Didn't you teach her anything?" Nia said.

"Do you have dog treats?" Lily asked. Her words sounded distant from herself. No, she hadn't taught Gogo anything, and that might be good.

"Forget it. We're not wasting time going back to the house."

"I want them found, too. Do you have treats for the dog?" This time her voice was closer, more recognizable as her own.

"No, I don't have treats." They were only a few yards from the house. "Okay, we go back. I'll find an undershirt; there will be more stinky smell on Finn's undershirt."

Nia jogged back with the dog, and Lily thought to scream but didn't want the boys to come back. She walked to the patio and felt around the barbecue for a weapon: a lighter to burn the house down, a shish kebab skewer or a screwdriver. Her father was organized; he put tools in the toolshed and skewers and lighters in the kitchen drawer. She found a rock, a flat-edged shale, probably one the boys would have found and saved. It fit nicely in her hand.

"Drop it, Lillian," Nia said. So close. Lily hadn't heard her approach. "You've had muscle relaxants in your milk shake, and you'll hurt yourself with your girlie fight hands. I can shoot your hand if you'd prefer." Lily dropped the rock.

Nia held Finn's undershirt to Gogo's nose. She wagged her tail.

"They probably went to Mrs. Yarnell's. They've gone there before. She's the closest neighbor," Lily said. "They'd take the road in front."

"No, Gogo came around back by herself, and I hope they have enough sense not to take the road at night. By the way, Mrs. Yarnell is out of town; she left a message on the landline. Think, Lillian! You've got two kids out there at eleven o'clock at night. They're not comatose like yesterday, but they're still drugged. Sam is small enough to be attacked by a coyote or a bobcat." Nia's energetic voice got the dog up and alert. She held a treat in her fist and used the high-pitched tone Lily had used. "Go get Finn. Go, girl!"

Off trotted Gogo, almost dragging Nia on the lead. She called back over her shoulder, "Keep up or I'll use the gun."

Lily struggled in the half moonlight to keep Nia in her sight. Lily knew the trail Gogo led them to and knew it was the likely one the boys would take. The wider lane to the west was the family stroll on what had been a wagon road a generation back. It was much easier, much longer. They'd be too easy to follow on that trail. Gogo padded up the path they'd hiked with Des. It led up to the ridge that ran above Eagle's Nest and the precipitous drop to Blue Hollow, where the ancient river bed had dried. It wasn't a trail for small boys in the large night, but there were places to hide along the way, and on the ridge there was a lean-to against the side of the mountain, hidden in the trees, that Lily and Owen had built when they were children. She'd shown Des and the boys where it'd been. Three years before, Des and the boys had rebuilt it with branches and leaves and old curtains from her mom. It was a Mother's Day surprise with a picnic lunch. Sam was only three then; Des had carried him most of the way. So long ago, three years, when they had been, simply, arrogantly, alive.

That's where they'd go, Lily knew this.

The gnarled surface of the earth threw up stones and roots. Hands of low-hanging branches grabbed at Lily's face, but this was a trail traveled over a lifetime. She knew this path, this mountain. At fifty yards, the trail narrowed, and Lily was able to get closer. Gogo lost traction, and her paws scampered downward with dislodged pebbles.

A half mile in, the trail curved upward to a flat ledge. Lily caught up with Nia there, where she sat on a rock calming her breath with Gogo beside her. It was colder moving up. There were microclimates all around, small countries that had nothing to do with the rest of the world.

"Some asthma as a child," Nia said with shallow breath. "Nothing to worry about." She shined an LED flashlight in Lily's eyes. "The boys were here. Gogo went right over to this." She shined a light over a discarded apple juice box. "Wish they hadn't packed a lunch—all the apple juices are spiked."

Lily walked closer to see. Nia cut off the light and pulled the gun from her waistband. No fanny pack.

"I want to find them, too. Could you not wave the gun around every time I move?" Lily said.

Lily's eyes readjusted to the pale moonlight. In the black-and-white dimness, Nia's lipstick glowed coral red. Her dark curls were plastered to her sweaty brow like a Kewpie doll.

Lily took Gogo's leash. It was easy. Nia just handed the leash over to her. The gun still in her other hand. Maybe farther on Lily could push Gogo off the side of the cliff before she led them to the boys. "We've got drugged children out here, you coming?" Lily asked.

They continued up the trail. This time Lily led.

"Thanks, Lillian. Thanks for saying 'we.' Not that I want your kids, but they'll be half brothers to Desmond's and my children. They'll be blood, all of them. They're more important than our little disagreements."

No, Finn would be the father. Lily kept walking, did not correct her. She felt stronger with movement. She'd never forgive Des. Not for buying the gun. Not for this woman. The anger helped.

The cold seemed to aggravate Nia's breathing. She fell a dozen steps behind. Lily clicked shut the retractable lead and tried to keep Gogo under control. Maybe Gogo wouldn't die when Lily nudged her off the mountain. She could come back later and have her rescued, have her broken legs set.

Lily felt the bullet through her shoulder before she heard the sound of the gun. She felt the bullet go through, back to front, before the noise imploded between her ears. Then she felt the searing path, more like fire than blood. She screamed, dropped down. Over the buzzing in her head she heard giggling. A little girl giggling. If it weren't for the pain, it would've been a dream.

"See, I'm not kidding, Lillian. My asthma is bothering me. How about you call the boys and we can go back to the house. Fucking call the boys. Now."

"I can't yell. I can barely breathe. I think you got a lung," Lily whispered.

"No I didn't. Look, it's just the top of your arm. I wasn't even aiming at you. I thought it would whiz by and scare you. Probably only nicked the bone. Buck up." She shined the flashlight on Lily's shoulder. Blood stained the shirt.

"Finn! Sam!" Nia yelled. Her voice tore through the night and the rocks. "Come quick. Your mom is hurt. We need your help."

Lily smelled Des. It was his shirt, she realized. Why hadn't she seen that? One of those horrible plaid shirts he wore when he cleaned the gutters or raked leaves. She tried to get up but couldn't find her legs. "Amanda!" Lily yelled. "Amanda! Amanda!" She pulled in everything to give her voice strength, the sky and the night and the smell of Des from the shirt.

She felt the gun brush against her cheek. Nia leaned in toward her ear: "The shoulder was to remind you who's in charge. But if I shoot you in the head you'll be dead dead. Who's Amanda? Why would you shout Aunt Amanda?"

"It's the safe word," Lily said. "If there's an emergency and a stranger needs to pick them up at school, they have to have a safe word so they know it's not a trick. Finn was close to Aunt Amanda when he was little."

"Then yell it again." She moved the gun away.

"You'll have to do it. I can't catch my breath." Gogo nuzzled her shoulder, licked the blood. Lily sat back and kicked her away.

"Amanda," Nia yelled. "Amanda! Finn and Sam, come and help your mom."

Nia held the gun like a rock and smashed Lily's face. Her nose broke. "Don't ever kick the dog. That's Desmond's dog."

Nia called Gogo, took the leash firmly, and walked past Lily. She heard Nia scream the name Amanda farther and farther up the trail.

Lily bunched the bottom of Des's shirt and held it to the blood. The smell of him closed around her.

She heard a little girl call out: "I don't like being out here in the dark by myself."

Lily lost consciousness.

Chapter 61: Dink's Song

She woke to darkness faded, a pale existence that lacked demarcation between day and night, life and death. *It hardly matters,* Lily thought, *in the grand scheme of mountain.* Some people, like Des, lived grand operatic songs and died young. Others just stumbled. She'd stumbled through the night, waking and struggling to her feet, walking, falling, crawling when the trail got steep, passing out, waking again. She heard death call like a mother wolf and felt very small. Her sons smaller.

"I can hear you, sweet boys. Come out, come out, wherever you are." Lily heard a high-pitched voice.

"I don't like being out here by myself," Nia said. She sat like Little Sally Saucer in the middle of the clearing with her knees pulled up to her chin. Nia turned to see Lily walking, holding her useless left arm with her tired right arm.

"I thought you were dead," Nia said. "But this is better. I thought I was alone, but now you're here. You can call the boys out for me. Gogo is gone, too. Here, kitty kitty. She won't come when she's called even though I've got treats. Kitty—that's what Desmond called me. His mom still calls me that. Maybe the boys would like to call me Kitty, too. It's very youthful, don't you think?" The bright smear of lipstick looked muddy across her face. "Everyone else called me Pet. My mother was English, a ballet dancer. She had no idea Petunia was the name of a pig here in this country. Or a cow, someone told me once, a cow's name."

Her right hand held the gun. She looked down at it like a forgotten hand.

Crazy Kitty. Yes, Des had mentioned her, but always with *Crazy* before her name and only in passing, not as love lost. He said she'd been a glorious six-month mistake who'd just pretended they'd never broken up. Months and months of pretending till he'd switched majors.

The lean-to Des and the boys had rebuilt was thirty yards away, against a copse of birch to the east. To the west was the edge of the ridge and the eighty-foot plunge into Blue Hollow.

"So Mother and I changed it to Pet. She told people she'd heard an old Pet Clark song when she was pregnant. Desmond changed it to Kitty. He thought it was cute. Don't dare start with pussy jokes, I've had enough of those. He wouldn't allow it, do you understand?"

A dirty tennis ball rolled out just inches from Lily's feet. Her feet were bare now, having lost the sneakers on the climb. Lily held still, did not stumble, did not look at the ball, did not direct Nia's eyes to it.

"I changed it to Nia when I left Desmond. I cut my hair short." It was hard for Lily to keep her eyes from the ball and not to look where it'd rolled out from.

"You look so indifferent, Lillian. I bet you wouldn't look that way if I shot you again."

So still. Afraid to sit, to kneel, to draw attention to the dirty tennis ball. Nothing to hold on to, so much open sky around her. She was a giant target to Nia's gun, held so casually. Lily could no longer recall the run word. *Amanda*, maybe—but what if that was the safe word, you could go with someone if they knew about Halley's Comet? Maybe you should run from a comet. The space around her tumbled and swirled. She fell. Her bones rattled when gravity struck. She tried to sit, swallowing the pain from her shoulder and forcing it into her words:

"Stay hidden, boys! Do not come out no matter what happens to me! She is not a friend of your dad's."

She kept her eyes on Nia. She pulled the tennis ball behind her. Her stealth movement not necessary as Nia didn't even turn when she yelled.

Nia said, "Well, Lillian, I'm actually glad this happened because now everybody has this out of their system."

Nia took a packet from her waistband and took a hand wipe from the packet. Lily sat straighter and started to laugh. This woman was going to wipe her hands clean out in the middle of the dirt, the rocks, the sky?

"So everybody has this out of their system and we can concentrate on the matter at hand." Nia took something else from her waistband, a pair of latex gloves, and Lily stopped laughing. Nia put them on, one at a time, while still holding the gun, and once the gloves were on, she used the wipe to wipe the gun.

"I need a clean surface for your fingerprints. Look what you've done now. I merely wanted to be your friend and now this is so horrible for you to do this and I hope your boys are watching. It's bad enough that their dad is dead, now they'll have the trauma of you choosing to leave them by swallowing your husband's gun."

She got up and came to Lily. She bent beside her and picked up Lily's useless arm. It was beyond pain. Lily swung her right arm and batted Nia's face. She swung her knees around to kick and swiped at air. Nia pushed her flat to the ground and backed away.

"Thank you for stopping me; I almost used your left hand, and you're right-handed like me, not a mirror image. 'Incorrigible in her grief,' it'll say in your obituary. I'll need your good hand."

If I had wings. Like Nora's dove or Noah's dove? She couldn't remember. They'd heard the soprano singing it when they first met. A big voice. A little song.

Nia stomped on Lily's shoulder and ground her foot in. How could there be so much pain left in her body?

"It'll barely hurt," Nia said. "It's not like cancer, not like lingering. I'll do it for you. I can get your fingerprints after."

He'd told Lily she sounded like a scratchy 45 record. Mouth, Lily remembered—she still had her scratchy 45 mouth.

Nia leaned down. "Turn to look at me." She grabbed Lily's shorn hair and pulled her head up. Lily used the momentum to jerk her face to Nia's calf. She bit hard, clamping her jaws together and pulling. She tore flesh into her mouth. The blood was blinding, was everywhere.

The rest was quick confusion: the boys with sticks, the screaming like something out of *Lord of the Flies*, the dog barking. A wolf biting her so hard she thought Gogo was Nia for a moment and that she, who had been Lily, turned into the flash of teeth. And there was falling.

Chapter 62: Free Fall

They found the body at the bottom of Blue Hollow. Her tight-cropped curls caught the rays of sunrise to form a dark halo around her bloodied face.

"Fucking gravity," Sheriff Coffman said, as if gravity were the cause of death, all deaths for that matter.

A red hawk screamed from blue sky. The sheriff looked up the side of the mountain. One of those lovely spring mornings where shadow was as brilliant as light.

He did as little messing with the body as possible but got his hand into a back pocket where there was a grocery list—dog food, bread, lemonade—along with her driver's license reading Lillian Declan.

"Know her parents, damn," the sheriff said to Deputy Hart. "Her dad is Owen Moore, taught music over at the high school."

They took a statement and identification from the couple who found the body. They were townies who had planned an early hike to the falls and had nothing to do with the dead woman that the sheriff could figure out. He dismissed them and waited for reinforcements to secure the area for the coroner.

Sheriff Coffman and Deputy Hart drove around to the Moores' after the coroner's crew came. Informing the family was never easy. Coffman knew the Moore girl had been widowed recently because his mom went to the same church as the Moores, but he didn't mention it to Hart so as not to predispose their thinking to suicide before they had more facts. They'd need statements and they'd need to look for a suicide note. Hart was four months on the job, and this was only his second body. The first one had been what was left behind from a knife fight at the Moonshiner Bar off Highway 33.

It was a ten-minute drive around to the Moore house. Coffman didn't remember Lily too well but remembered Mr. Moore and that painful year of marching band trombone. He was a good man, Owen Moore Sr., but seemed to have no comprehension of how difficult it was for some people to march and play an instrument at the same time. Some people were just not born with the ability, the sheriff supposed.

Two cars in the driveway. Hart called in the Davidson County tags. Both cars were locked. Too many lights on in the house for close to 8:00 a.m. The front door was locked but the door to the back was wide open. Cute little house, clean and cozy, no Mr. and Mrs. Moore at home.

A cross-stitch over a Barcalounger read: MUSIC IS THE SPEECH OF ANGELS. There were suitcases with women's clothing in the big bedroom. The other two small bedrooms were empty, but people had been in the unmade beds. Back outside, two visible trails ran up past the back acre. The field hadn't been mowed in weeks, and there was a straightforward track of freshly tramped grass toward the steeper path to the ridgetop. Sheriff Coffman considered himself in good shape, but it was still a nasty climb. He was relieved to see Hart, twenty years his junior, out of breath, too, when they reached the ledge.

They walked thirty yards and stopped. Without a word, Hart handed the sheriff a pair of latex gloves and put on his own pair. He also handed over a pair of Tyvek shoe covers, and they both put them on. There had been a struggle. Looked like what would be left if a high school wrestling match were held outdoors. They couldn't tell by sight that it was blood that made the dirt clump, but they could smell it, a rusty sweetness that was morning fresh.

Deputy Hart took out his cell, but the sheriff held up his hand and gestured his head over to a bit of shade next to a bower lean-to. He'd never seen a German shepherd that big. Next to the dog were two boys, shivering and shirtless, and a bloody woman, eyes closed. Neither Coffman nor Hart spoke; they needed the silence to focus, to comprehend. It wasn't as if the woods were without humans, but like a fox crossing the road, it was unexpected.

"We mighta killed her," the little boy said, holding a stick up. "We're sorry."

"Who's that lady with you?" Sheriff Coffman said.

"She's our mom," the bigger boy said.

"Who went off the ledge?"

"That lady said she was our aunt," the bigger boy said.

"We think we killed her, too," the little boy said.

"You got a leash on that dog?" Sheriff asked.

"Yes, sir," the bigger boy said.

The paramedics arrived by helicopter. The adult female with the boys didn't look like she'd make it. Her pulse was thready and the responders had trouble intubating with her face smashed. Her left arm hung lifeless. Her left thigh was dog chewed, and the older boy's forearm was dog bitten.

The account from the boys was disjointed, but they were exhausted and frightened and if he were asked, the sheriff would've said they'd been drugged.

The driver's license in a purse back at the Moore house was for a Renée Hollis, and the address put her on Carter Street in Murfreesboro, but the number didn't match with any house.

There was a small-caliber handgun found not far from the dead woman's body in the hollow, registered to the boys' father, a Desmond Declan, who was deceased, the records indicated. The gun had been reported stolen. They found a cell phone in a drawer at the Moores' house registered under Desmond Declan's family phone plan. There was an ICE number for Owen Moore Jr. Hours later, Owen was unable to ID the dead body, and he was insistent the dead woman's license and picture weren't his sister's, although the date of birth and address matched.

"The picture looks a little like her but not quite. And her name isn't Lillian. It's Lily. She was born on Easter." He didn't know a Renée Hollis.

The hurt woman received eight units of blood and was in surgery for four hours before she was stabilized. Owen Moore Jr. ID'd her in post-op. He was certain it was his sister, Lily Declan, the boys' mom. He was sure, he said, even with her disfigured nose and swollen face.

It wasn't till the boys were assured that Gogo wasn't in trouble and wouldn't be taken away that the story flew from their little mouths like uncaged birds. Mrs. Declan confirmed some of the account when she woke in the ICU, but it was days before she was alert enough for the particulars. The Nashville police verified further details.

After the emergency room and the police report, Owen took the boys and the dog to their uncle Dan's.

Lily Declan was transferred to the county trauma center in Knoxville. The surgical team went back in the next day to pin her arm together and repair her thigh.

Owen and Ella Moore flew home from their Disney cruise. Mrs. Yarnell, the closest neighbor, was feared dead but turned up a few days later. She'd won a seven-day vacation in Blowing Rock, which was traced to the credit card of a Nia Summerwood in Chicago. The Summerwood woman's family was not asked to ID her body, but dental records confirmed her identity, and her father-in-law claimed the body. He cooperated fully with the police and handed over a second cell phone and his daughter-in-law's laptop. Spreadsheet pages of Nia Summerwood's schedule were found on her computer and aligned with her time in Nashville and Maryville.

———

Lily faded into the illuminated world of the intensive care unit. It was jarring out-of-season Christmas-tree bright for days on end. Then there would come the kind darkness of morphine when she would fold herself into the crisp sheets that smelled like Des at his end. There were several operations. The .45-caliber had sliced the triceps muscle and chipped the bone. The head of the bone at the shoulder was also eggshell fractured where it had been stomped. Her cheekbone and nose required another surgery. Sometimes she'd come out to the light, agitated and scared for her husband and her children. Sometimes she woke nauseated with blood in her mouth and the sweet softness of flesh in her teeth.

There was an investigation. "I don't quite understand what you went through," Sheriff Coffman said to Lily outside the courthouse two months later. "For your part everything says justifiable homicide, as in self-defense. Be that as it may, it's not too late for me to change that to an accidental fall on Mrs. Summerwood's sorry-ass part. That way you won't even have to get up on the stand."

After all, Sheriff Coffman knew her father, and Lily's mom went to church with his mom. Nobody should have to retell what she went through.

"No," Lily said. "I want it on the record that I killed her and that I was right to kill her."

"Well, the least we can do, then, is try to keep it out of the papers. With minors involved, we should be able to have the names sealed."

They found the Moores' dogs that Honey Summers had been called on to house-sit in a supermarket parking lot in nearby Alcoa. The janitor had been feeding them.

Chapter 63: Time

How much of grief sits perfectly still until time passes? How much of grief must arm itself against the undiscovered country? Some nights Lily dreamed of climbing the mountainside and baying at the moon. Other nights she screamed falling from the cliff.

She never did remember all of it, and there was no Miriam, no Circle of Compassion that she was willing to let probe all the places she hurt. The Circle of Compassion disbanded, but Miriam retained her license; Renée's forged résumé and documents had been impeccable.

It troubled Lily that the boys remembered more than she did, as if she had absented herself from their struggle. But it was common, she was told, that trauma blocked memory. The boys recounted a melee that sometimes lit up their eyes.

"We were very brave," Sam said in his little-man voice. "I hit the lady's hand with a stick and Finn kicked the gun off the cliff like you told us to." She didn't remember telling them.

Gogo had bitten Lily during the fight, and Finn, and Nia. Finn and Sam had fought Nia with fists and sticks.

"I'm not sure how, but after you bit the lady, Gogo kinda turned into a wolf," Finn said, "and you and Gogo pushed her off the cliff."

"You were really a good fighter, Mom," Sam said. But she didn't remember. Once she thought she could hear her voice telling Finn to kick the gun away because she didn't want her boy to have that on him, a shooting, a death. He was too young; she would need to do it herself. Yet she knew it must've happened too fast for her to have thought of that then.

"What did that lady want, Mom?" Sam asked.

"We'll never know for certain, but we think she wanted to steal you. Your dad didn't want her years ago, so she wanted his children. We were strong and we fought." She had to tell them many times. Whenever they asked. She had to listen to them tell what they remembered. Whenever they needed.

Lily and the boys never went back to their house except in the autumn to pack and put it on the market. Even with all the lights on and her family and Iris helping her pack up the house, Lily would still turn a corner, walk a hallway, and feel the presence of the ghost in the white gown. As much as it scared her, the dry rustle of gossamer gave her solace that Nia was still searching for what she couldn't have. She hadn't found it on this earth and wouldn't find it in eternity. *An apt hell,* Lily judged.

Rehab took time: relearning how to use her arm, cognitive therapy for memory problems from her head injury. They stayed at her brother's and celebrated the gurgly new baby girl Anne-Claire gave birth to. Most of Des's family grew distant. They'd liked Nia Summerwood. Kaye still called her Kitty. She'd been a scrawny neighborhood kid who had made good and then gone through so much with her husband's car accident. It wasn't as if there'd been betrayals; she'd just been an old girlfriend who'd dated Des in college, who'd known the family when they were kids. Months after Des had died, Nia'd come to the house and sat with Des's mom. Brought her flowers. Remembered stories about him. Helped her with a photo album and scrapbook entries. She must've snapped if the whole strange story was true. Only Kevin and his new wife visited Lily in the hospital and came to Owen's with flowers. They took the boys to Six Flags Kentucky Kingdom in the summer.

Iris brought books and sent get-well cards during Lily's recuperation. Iris and the boys took turns reading to her when she couldn't do much else. Sam read from his first-grade readers. Iris and Finn took turns with Robert Louis Stevenson. When she was better, sometimes Gardner Linden came with Iris when they went for lunch. He was flirty and fun, but Lily had no inclination toward him past his cheery banter, despite Iris's push.

Lily's dismissal from the Linden Foundation had never been processed. Her COBRA forms never filled out. The foundation kept her on sick leave with paid insurance until disability kicked in. It was six months before Lily ventured out to work. Henry Linden helped her get a part-time job at the Country Music Hall of Fame in downtown Nashville. Her ears were still good, and she sat in a back booth on the second floor and transcribed old radio tapes.

There was comfort in the passing of voices, laughter from the dead. Nothing disappears. Is that religion? But time passed. Some of the old tapes were too old for remaster or interpretation. She closed her eyes, stretched her hand to adjust the sound. "Fare thee well, O honey, fare thee well."

There was no going back. Never is. Yet years later when she'd wake in the dull zone of night, she'd still taste flesh in her mouth. The meat primal and ungovernable. Pray the rage into breath.

Epilogue

In the spring a year gone by, Lily and the boys took Gogo to obedience school. It was in an open field beside the Primitive Baptist Church in Ashland City. Behind them, a hundred-year-old graveyard lay peaceful and unattended, its headstones rising from the ground like earth's crooked teeth. The three of them had a good time each Saturday morning getting Gogo to sit and stay and lie down—all the basic commands Gogo already knew from Des so long ago. Still it took three turns before Gogo passed the basic course.

The intermediate instructor was an Officer Ennis who used his given name of Will.

He didn't remember her name, but he remembered the dog and the break-in, and the boys, and most of all, her. Sheriff Coffman had talked to Ennis when they were tracing the gun they found in Blue Hollow, and Will Ennis was the officer who had signed off on the report from the year before.

"You still widowed?" he asked.

Do you grow out of being widowed? she wondered, and nodded. He told her he was long divorced but didn't ask her to coffee till months later.

He had patience Lily didn't know was possible. There were months of quiet walks with one dog or another beside them. The rocky path of his face was not handsome, but his eyes were true. He was good to the boys. He had two dogs, a grown daughter in Memphis, and an ex-wife who lived in Orlando.

Will was unexpectedly graceful and taught Lily and the boys the basics for contra dance, which they went to on Sunday afternoons. They were married a year later and moved to Sumner County. The boys liked their new schools, and Lily was glad for the fresh start.

Yet some summer nights, fear would roll in like a hard rain and in the small room of her heart, the fear would pulse to anger. She would quiet herself from the bedroom and go out back to confront the darkness. She would walk through the night until her tears cleared and she could see to stare down the moon. Will would be awake when she returned to the bedroom.

He smelled of pine and wind when he held her. If we forgive the dead for dying, will they forgive us for living?

She loves again; this is absolution. The fox runs across the field; this is absolution. The crow caws, flies off.

Acknowledgments and Commendations

With special thanks to Caitlin Alexander, Rhea Borzak, Jane DeHart, Matthew Freedman, Jane Heller, Jill Marr, Lisa McGovern, Kevin Ottem, Meryl Peters, Paul Skenazy, Rebecca Thornton, Jodi Warshaw, and the continued inspiration of Dorna May. Thank you, Louise Connor, for so much encouragement over so many readings. Thank you, J.F. Freedman, for everything.

Graditude to Sherman Alexie for quotes from his poem "Grief Calls Us to the Things of This World," with permission from Hanging Loose Press and Editor Robert Hershon.

Gratitude to Bea Troxel of Nashville's Bea, Rita, & Maeve for lyrics from "The River," used with permission.

Gratitude to Maeve Thorne of Maeve Thorne Music for permission to use lyrics from "Silence, Silence" and "California."

Mary Shelley's words from the still-lively *Frankenstein* provide section headings.

Dink's lyrics from the public domain and private brilliance of "Dink's Song (Fare Thee Well)" are used with admiration.

About the Author

Christine Bell's first novel, *Saint*, was optioned for a feature film and praised by the *Philadelphia Inquirer* as "a brilliant first novel, an extraordinary book." *The Seven-Year Atomic Make-Over Guide*, a short-story collection, was described by the *New York Times* as "accessible, entertaining, and infused with the improvisation energies of a writer who refuses to play it safe." Bell's next novel, *The Perez Family*, was made into a film directed by Mira Nair and named Notable Adult Fiction of the Year by both the American Library Association and the New York Public Library. It was also named Notable Book of the Year by the *Philadelphia Inquirer* and the *New York Times*, which hailed it as "a loud, gaudy, sentimental heartbreaker of a book, a triumph."

Bell lives in the Central California Coast area with her husband, writer J.F. Freedman, and their family.